A VILLAIN FOR CHRISTMAS

VEXING VILLAINS
BOOK 1

ALICE WINTERS

Copyright © 2019 by Alice Winters

All rights reserved.

Edited by: Lori Parks

Proofreading by: Courtney Bassett

Cover: Cate Ashwood Designs

No part of this book may be reproduced in any form or by any electronic or mechanical means, including information storage and retrieval systems, without written permission from the author, except for the use of brief quotations in a book review.

CHAPTER ONE

"Landon, I want you to help me rob a bank."

I try to ignore my brother, since I clearly didn't hear him right.

"Won't you do me a favor?" he asks after letting himself into my house without bothering to knock. Not that knocking would have done him any good since I wasn't planning on letting him into my house at all anyway.

"No," I say without bothering to look up from the book I'm reading.

"Just hear me out!" he exclaims.

I lower the book and look up at my older brother Brandon. Thankfully, I don't take much after him. Not that he's ugly or anything like that, he's not, but just because he's an idiot. And the one thing I don't want to be is an idiot. "What, Brandon?"

"I want you to help me rob a bank."

"No! You asked me last week, and I already told you I have better things to do. Like..." I look around as I try to think of something. It's hard when my life consists of trying to avoid my family and reading every book I can get my hands on. Oh, and did I mention avoiding my family? Honestly, that's a full-time career when they all have powers that allow them to better annoy the shit out of me. "Work."

"Mom told me you got fired," Brandon says as he sits down on the couch next to me.

"I got fired because Mom came in and told the boss that she needed me. When he said I was working and couldn't just leave, she told him he looks like an overripe nut sac."

Brandon starts laughing. "That's so cool."

"I hate all of you," I decide as I lift my book back up.

"About the bank. Come on, you borrowed money from me last week."

I stare at my brother in disbelief. "Five dollars. You honestly think the equivalent of you lending me five dollars is me helping you rob a bank? I'm not going to help you rob a bank again!"

———

Why am I robbing a bank again?

I'd like to blame it on my family. See, we're supervillains—at least, that's what my family claims we are. I think they're basically a group of lunatics with barely any superpowers who ache to be villains. There *are* superheroes and supervillains, but it's not like in the movies where they're flying around and morphing into giant green humanoids.

There are a lot of people who have what we call powers, that are able to do little things. Super strength, excellent vision, those kinds of things. But powers are judged by strength and deadliness on a scale of D to A. So ninety percent of people with powers fall into the rank of D. It means they're basically harmless. Almost all of the rest fall into rank C with barely any in B or A. While my powers are in line with individuals who have rank A abilities, I managed to mess with the test so they think I'm only a rank C. My parents are rank D, but my oldest brother, Nolan, is a B.

As for Brandon? His superpower is being a dumbass.

And maybe invincibility. Which puts him into a ranking of C.

Ranks are also how they determine things. Like the main superheroes who protect each city generally have powers that fall into rank A. If they were any lower they wouldn't be powerful enough to take down the villains who insist on pestering them.

"I don't have all day," I say as I wait outside the bathroom for my brother to come out.

"I have to get my suit on!" Brandon says.

"Don't bother. Your face is ugly enough no one's going to look at it anyway."

"Mom says we look almost identical."

I scoff. "In no way do we even look kinda alike. She screwed the mailman in order to conceive you, and I'm adopted."

"You're not adopted."

I glance over at the mirror that sits in the corner of my bedroom. And there I stand, a grown man of twenty-eight in my supervillain outfit. My parents bought me a real one with spandex and a black cape, but I refused to wear it and donated it to Goodwill. That resulted in Mom *making* me another one that I grudgingly kept but refuse to wear for this.

Instead, I'm in baggy black sweats over a pair of jeans, a black hoodie over a t-shirt, and a mask that covers all of my face. I look like a burglar out of a children's TV show. The only visible part of my body is my brown eyes that are currently judging me. Just in case there's a fuck up, I grab my spare mask and stuff it into my pocket. One can never have too many masks when they don't want their face broadcast all over the world.

The door behind me swings open and Brandon emerges wearing his new "super outfit."

It looks like he went to some adult store and bought a latex suit. Immediately, I start laughing because my brother *really* can't pull off a latex sex suit. "Ah, finally embracing your fetishes, I see."

"What are you talking about? Isn't this sexy? The ladies can see *all* of me," he says as he waves to his groin area, which is showing a bulge that he couldn't even dream of possessing.

"Do you have a sock rolled up in there?" I ask in disbelief.

"Two socks."

"Oh my god. I hope we get caught and you go to jail," I say as I head for the door.

"We can't get caught with you helping," he says as he heads out the door to an old beat-up pickup truck he's had since he was sixteen. It's the only thing reliable in his life.

3

"And you promise that if I do this, you'll keep Mom off my ass?" I ask.

"Yep. I'll cover for you."

"Good. We're only taking what's in the registers, nothing else."

"Got it."

Even though it's not yet Thanksgiving, the city is filled with holiday and Christmas décor. There are lights and wreaths hanging from the lamp posts. The huge Christmas tree sits in the city square where they open up ice skating and other festivities. The moment Halloween is over, Christmas begins.

As Brandon drives through the city streets adorned with holiday decorations, I contemplate my life and my decisions. It's really not my fault I was raised by supervillains. Honestly, robbing a bank is like second nature to me. Hell, I was robbing banks by the age of five once my parents figured out what my power was. I used to love it back then because I thought it was a normal family tradition. At school, when the teacher asked us to do show and tell, I brought in a bag of jewels I'd stolen from a safe and told the enthralled classroom all about how I was a supervillain and I stole them myself. We had to move after that.

I was a stupid child.

Then as I got older, I began to realize that no, we're not normal. Normal people don't spend their lives trying to become villains. Especially when *none of them* are any good at it. And since I started refusing to help them, we haven't robbed as many banks or done as many evil deeds since they're basically useless without my powers.

Brandon drives past the small local bank on the corner and I look over at him.

"You passed the bank. You're supposed to park down the street."

"I will," he says.

"Brandon, what the hell? They have cameras outside the bank that are aimed at the street. If they see you cruising on by with us in our masks, they're going to identify us by tracking down your license plate." Sometimes I feel like I'm the only intelligent one in this family.

He pulls off and parks and that's when I realize what he's doing. He lied about what bank we're robbing. Instead of the small local bank, he thinks we're going to hit up The Beast. Okay, that's not what the bank is called, but that's what the supervillains call it since it's nearly impossible to break into, let alone get away with any money.

"Let's go," he says as he grabs a *Teenage Mutant Ninja Turtles* pillowcase that he's planning on stuffing the money into. I don't grab anything, because I'm not planning on touching the money.

"This is stupid. That bank has crazy reinforcements," I say, but it falls on deaf ears.

Brandon doesn't care as he rushes toward it as I grudgingly follow after him.

"I'm giving you five dollars' worth of help," I assure him.

He doesn't seem concerned. "Did you see that chick look at me as I walked past? This suit is the bomb. You should get one."

I glance around, wondering where this "chick" is. All I see is a confused middle-aged woman. "What? So we can be the Gimp Brothers? No, I'm alright. Thanks."

"Your loss. I'll keep all the ladies."

"You do that."

"I already said I would."

"With your ol' sock dick. You fuck them real good." This amuses me far too much.

Brandon looks over at me. "You know there are powers to make your dick look bigger?"

"Didn't a superhero blow up someone's dick the other day doing that?"

"Might have. But I think it's worth the risk, you know?"

"No, I don't."

"Why don't you try it out first? If your dick blows up, it's not as much of a loss, right? You're probably going to eternally be alone."

I nearly punch him because nothing sounds better at the moment. The only reason I don't is because Brandon is punch proof. I would break my hand if I managed any amount of punching.

"Here we go!" he shouts, like alerting everyone of our presence is the way to go as he turns to the front doors of the huge bank. There are cameras outside that are set to recognize people with their face covered because it's not uncommon for villains to try to break into locations like this. It makes the bank immediately go on lockdown. This means that as he tugs on the door, the door is already locked.

I just stand there, wondering how long he's going to pull and heave on it. Currently, we're going on about twenty seconds.

"Man, they're good," he says as he pants. He's not used to exercising.

"You're an idiot. Did you even *look* into the reinforcements of this place before deciding to rob it?" I ask.

He looks mystified. "People put shit like that up on the internet?"

I groan. "There is no way we are related."

"We have the same blood coursing through our veins, bro," he says as he gives me a hearty pat that sends me flying into the front door.

Smashed up against the glass, I say, "I wonder if they still practice bloodlettings anywhere."

Brandon finally lets go of the door and turns to me. "Are you going to help?"

I sigh and lift my hand. With my power of telekinesis, I'm able to maneuver just about anything. But what makes me ridiculously deadly is the power to precisely manipulate both small and large objects. This means that I could crush a human heart just with a lift of my hand.

But no one knows that but me.

If they did, I can only imagine the shit my family would drag me into. Instead of crushing any hearts, besides my own for falling back into my family's antics, I grab onto the door with my mind and simply open it. The locking mechanisms instantly break as I pull the door open and follow my brother inside.

Brandon barges in front of me, which is all fine and dandy since he wouldn't get hurt if he's instantly gunned down. "This is a mofo robbery, put your hands up and get on the ground!" Brandon shouts through his voice manipulator as we walk into the main lobby where everyone turns and looks at him in alarm. It's probably mortification over the words and voice he's chosen to use.

I pat his back. "Please don't use words like 'mofo.' I'm already horribly embarrassed by you."

"There are children around! I shouldn't cuss with children around," he says, like it's okay to rob a bank with children around but not say the F word.

This is the logic that exists in my family. My childhood was filled with: "You may break into the house after you're done eating, Landon, but you have to eat your peas first."

I sigh but step behind my brother as a security officer rushes forward and shoots him with a taser. Brandon doesn't even flinch and with a flick of my wrist, the security man is pushed safely out of the way.

He looks a little confused as he slides across the floor almost as if by an invisible force, shoes squeaking horribly loud as he moves. Once that's over with, Brandon rushes up to the desk.

"Give me your money."

And the woman opens the drawer painstakingly slow. She's killing time, it's clear, but Brandon doesn't seem to notice.

"Tell her to hurry up, we need to get going," I say.

"Honey, do you mind picking up the pace a little? I have a dentist appointment at eleven I'd really like to make," Brandon asks.

Oh my god. My brother is an idiot.

That's when a door opens leading to an office and a man steps out.

The last man I should ever want to see, especially while robbing a bank. Instead, I'm undeniably excited that he's here.

August Bell.

Also known as Chronobender since he can freeze time for short periods and has super strength. He's also the greatest superhero this city has ever seen. He's hot, powerful, and an attention seeker. Okay, maybe I made that last part up since attention kind of comes with the job. I know him, not only because of his superhero nonsense, but because we went to middle school together. I was the kid who sat in the corner and read my book and he was the one who was surrounded by flocks of people who giggled at everything he said.

I might have giggled a time or two as well.

"Chrono is here to save us!" someone shouts.

August looks around in confusion. Clearly, he was just here for something to do with the bank because he's busy licking his sucker and looking bewildered. "What?" Then he sees us and pops his sucker right out of his mouth. He turns to the woman huddled beside him and goes, "Hold my sucker."

And it's so damn hot.

I've never wanted to hold a sucker so much in my life.

"Earth to Leviathan," Brandon says. "A little help?"

My parents thought that Leviathan would be the perfect supervillain name because I could levitate things. Clearly, they had no idea what a Leviathan was, but it kind of made me sound like a badass, and it could've been horrible like my brother's supervillain name of No Harm-O.

But it snaps me out of staring at August. I wave my hand, using my telekinesis to push

Brandon to the front door, which he slams into. I really could have stopped him in time, but it was payback for *all* of this.

But now August is between me and the door and I really, *really* don't want to get caught. Even if it would be August pinning me to the ground with his super strength. I almost hesitate, because nothing sounds better.

Instead, I turn and run for the back and August, thankfully, picks my brother to go after. I jump the counter and run blindly as I look for a way out. Using my telekinesis, I force open every door because my power makes me a badass.

There is no one who can catch up to me when I want to get away. And that's when I finally tear open the door to my freedom. I look up in time to rip the security camera off the wall to keep them from watching where I go.

I step through, smug as can be because even August Sexypants can't catch up to me when I'm using my full power. And I wasn't even using a fraction of it.

"Meow?"

I look down just as a cat slips between my feet, tripping me. I fall forward, crashing down the three steps that lead into the alleyway, slamming down on my face.

"Ow, fuck," I whine as I roll onto my side. "Dammit, cat!" I yell, but the cat is nowhere to be seen.

I slowly push myself up to my feet, but the moment I put weight on my leg, pain tears into my ankle. What... the hell?

I hear a noise as someone runs into the alleyway. I raise my arms up, ready to beat up the man I don't recognize who is wearing a full-body superhero suit.

But instead of identifying me as a villain, the idiot goes, "Oh my god. Did the bad guy push you down?"

"Yes. He went... that way," I say as I point, and the wannabe superhero races down the alleyway.

The issue with crimes is that now everyone wants to be a superhero, so a ton of people show up every time there is a crime because they want a chance to join Superheroes United, an organization that pays the heroes for keeping the city safe. But it gives me a good alibi when my leg feels like it's died and gone to hell.

I pull my black sweatpants and shirt off. Then, with my face tucked, I switch to the spare mask I'd grabbed, a more simplistic white mask. And with my telekinesis, I send all of the clothes way up onto the roof just in time to see August turn the corner. He eyes me for a moment, but he probably didn't get a good enough look at me inside since I was hiding behind my brother in case someone got trigger happy. Under the sweats, I'd purposely worn a very tight outfit to make me look thinner than the bulk the sweatpants and hoodie gave me.

"Are you another wannabe?" he asks, clear annoyance dripping from his words. I don't blame him. I deal with stupid supers on a daily basis. I can't imagine dealing with them when trying to save lives.

"Me? God no. The mask?" I ask as I point to it.

"Yeah."

"No, that's just a fetish of mine. Are you kink-shaming me?" I ask, like I'm disgusted.

He looks alarmed. "Wait... what?"

"Are you kink-shaming me for wearing my fetish mask?" I ask.

His blue eyes search mine as his head cocks a little to the side. "I don't think so... am I?"

"Yes. You're making me feel uncomfortable."

"Me?" he asks. "I don't even know your name and you're going on about your naughty fantasies of having sex with superheroes."

"That definitely never came out of my mouth," I say with narrowed eyes.

He starts laughing. "I know. I'm joking."

"I didn't know the sweet and loving everybody's pal Chrono could joke."

"It's in my contract that I can't joke on TV. There's a list of words I can't use. Balls, knockers, hooha... that kind of thing."

"Makes sense."

"I'm also not allowed to say peanut butter for some reason. I just think the mayor doesn't like peanut butter," he says. "What are you doing?"

"Some dickwad blasted through the door and slammed into me, and I think I hurt my ankle, but I'm fine."

"Your hands are all scraped up too," he says as he rushes up to me and takes my hand. It's the hottest thing I've ever seen. "Are you alright?"

"I guess. I think I have whiplash from him slamming into me," I say as I look up at August's wavy blond hair. Clearly, with my mask on, he doesn't know that I'm the quiet kid from middle school who sat in the corner. He probably wouldn't remember me with the mask off either.

"Do you need to go to the hospital?"

"Oh, no. I just sprained it," I say as I put weight on it. It hurts, but I could walk if I needed to.

"How about I give you a ride home?" he asks.

"Aren't you supposed to be catching bad guys?"

"I caught the one. The other is probably long gone, but Superheroes United has a team looking for them. I'm off-duty and it's not like they harmed anyone. If I wasted my time on every little guy out there, I'd never get sleep."

So Brandon got caught.

Again. I'm not even surprised. Our oldest brother will have him out in no time, though, so I'm not too concerned about it.

"Sure."

What am I saying?

"I'd love to ride you. I mean with you."

Oh my god. My dick is talking.

"Oh..." He looks a little surprised.

Why is it when I'm around him, I'm just as stupid as my family?

I might as well just admit it to myself. I agreed to rob the bank because I hoped August would be the first one on the scene.

I think I need my brain checked.

CHAPTER TWO

"Do you need help walking?" August asks.

"Do I look like a damsel to you?"

I realize at this very moment I have two options. Suck up the pain and walk back to the car or ask for help. My leg would literally have to be hacked off before I would rely on *anyone* to help me. I probably would still figure out a way to drag my stump after me if that was the case, since I hate relying on others or looking weak.

I step forward and dramatically fall toward him. "Oh my god! The pain! The pain! I'm dying!" It sounds a bit dramatized, but I'm working with what acting skills I've got.

And instead of swooping in and grabbing me, August lets me fall forward, forcing me to slam down on my hurt ankle.

"What the hell, man? You were supposed to catch me." In your muscular arms and hold me up.

August quickly looks back at me with wide eyes. "I'm sorry, I just realized I left my sucker in the bank and got distracted."

"Your... sucker?" His sucker is more important than I am.

"She didn't want to give it to me because they're only for 'kids.' She said she'd only let me have it if I autographed something. I sold a piece of myself for that sucker," he says.

"You are the worst superhero I've ever met. Now help me to your car." Self-reliance is overrated when August is around.

"Right, sorry," he says as he steps up to me. Instead of giving me a shoulder, like I was assuming, he swoops me up into his arms so suddenly that I find myself in some type of wedding night bridal-style carry.

"This... wasn't what I was expecting. Do you mind—"

"Oh, I'm sorry. Do you want down? They teach us in superschool to just carry everyone because it makes us look good and sometimes I forget that it's not normal to carry people around, you know?"

"Oh god, no. I was wondering if you minded if I held on?" I ask as I grab onto his bicep and give it a nice squeeze.

"Do you want a fireman carry?" he asks.

"No, I generally prefer being carried like a princess, you know? Feeds my fetishes."

"Oh... do you... have a lot of fetishes?" he asks as he carries me.

"You know. Normal amount. You?"

"Not until now."

That's when the paparazzi come and start taking pictures, and I'm so blinded by August that I don't even make him put me down.

"Don't you need to strike a pose or something?" I ask.

"No, all of my photos are natural. I'm just very photogenic."

"That's impressive. Not that I look at pictures of you or anything."

"That's good. I hate the pictures, but what do you do, you know? When you're a symbol."

"Sex symbol?"

He looks down at me and raises an eyebrow. "No! A symbol of peace. Wait... you think I'm a sex symbol?"

I dramatically cringe. "No, gross. Gosh. So what color is your underwear?"

He nearly drops me with that one. "What?"

I start laughing. "It was a joke. You were talking about sex symbols and... ahhh the joke failed. I wanted you to laugh."

He smiles at me, and I feel like it's just as good. "Sorry. I get a lot of weird things, so I take too much literally sometimes. Some lady sent me her eggs the other day."

"Like... from a chicken?"

"No, like... from her body. Wanted me to fertilize them."

I stare at him in horror because he *has* to be kidding. "You're joking."

"No... I'm not."

"What'd you do with them?" I ask curiously.

"I had my PR people tell her that if she did anything like that again, she would be removed from the city. So I feel like a job well done!"

"So some days you get thank you letters and other days you get unfertilized eggs?"

He starts laughing. "Pretty much. Well... here's my car," he says as he walks up to a fairly boring four-door car. I expected him to be driving a Lamborghini around that somehow portrays "I'm hot as sin and better than everyone else." Instead, it's much more "I'm a first-time parent who is still struggling to hold on to my youth."

He sets me down gently and opens the door for me.

I get into the car and eagerly wait as he comes around to his side and gets in.

"So... what's your fetish name?" he asks as he waves to my mask. "I'm sure you don't have a superhero name since you're not a superhero."

"Uh... yeah, I haven't gotten that far yet. Just call me Landon," I say. I went by the name of Lan in middle school since my mom thinks she has to abbreviate everything, so I doubt he'll connect the dots.

"Just call me August, then," he says with a smile. "So, you have a power?"

There's no sense in lying about it; I have to carry an ID around with me everywhere that states what my power is. It helps that my card explains that I'm telekinetic, but they just have no idea how powerful I am since I managed to mess with all of their exams. They also think the supervillain me can only manipulate metal. It's the only smart thing my parents have ever done. They even went to the extreme of my family wearing metal in their shoes so if they're ever caught, they simply explain that I was able to move them so easily because of the metal. So supervillain me is a powerful metal bender and regular me can make papers occasionally flutter if I squint and groan like I'm constipated. They really need to fix their tests.

"I... do."

"So were you actually there to help with the bank break-in?" August says.

"I didn't even know the bank had been broken into. How'd you let that happen?"

"I let it happen?" he asks with wide eyes.

"Sounded like it. Where were you at when it happened?"

He looks a little embarrassed. "Um... something very important."

"You already said you were in the bank worried about a sucker." I just have the sudden desire to embarrass him more.

"I... might have been. Shush, you're not allowed to judge me. That's not included in a free ride home. Now where am I taking you?"

And that's when I realize that I have to give him an address of *some* kind.

"I was actually heading to the library."

"With a bum foot? You should go home and put ice on that. What's your address?"

"I forget."

"You... forgot where you live?"

"Yup."

"You can just direct me then."

"I got amnesia from my fall."

"Wow, that's awful. Why don't you want me to see your house? Is it some like villain den or something?"

"HA HA! You're so cute. No, it's just like... you're so rich and stuff, and you'll judge me for my quaint little sad house, you know?"

"No, I won't," he assures me.

Really, there's no reason why he can't know where I live. It's not like I have "Hey, I'm a villain" written all over my house. It's just a normal house.

"Okay, I'll direct you," I say. "So... what's it like being a superhero?"

"I love it. Yeah... fun... I guess," he says, but he doesn't look like he loves any of it.

He doesn't have the same smile I fell in love with in middle school, and I can't help but wonder why.

"Right here," I say, pointing at the house I live alone in. I moved out of my parents' place the very second I turned eighteen. Like I was standing at the door with my bags packed, waiting for the clock to strike midnight. My parents bought me a house for being their "favorite child," but I'm sure they just felt obligated to since all the money they had was from me as a naive child stealing it for them. I didn't *know* I was stealing it.

I was a stupid kid.

August looks shocked as he pulls into the driveway. "Here? *This* is your house? You were... you didn't want me to see your quaint house? Your house is twice as big as mine!" he says with wide eyes.

"Really? I assumed you live in a mansion," I say as I look at my three-story house... mansion... eh, words are meaningless.

"Yeah... no, I don't. I'm paid well but not *this* well. What do you do?"

"Oh, it's family money. My parents bought it for me." With the money my grandpa left us and maybe some money I stole for them as a naive child.

He parks the car. "I'm sorry to be a bother, but could I come in to go to the bathroom really quick?"

"Uh..."

As a supervillain, it's obligatory to let the superhero into the house to capture and torture him. But the only way I want to torture him is by tying him to my bed. My family would lose their minds if they knew I was letting August into my house with no plan on destroying him with anything but the power of my penis.

"Sure," I say as I get out of the car.

My ankle aches, but I'm able to walk on it as I lead him up to the house and unlock the door. As I step in, there is a loud burst of noise as everyone screams, "Congratulations!" and streamers are being popped in my face, confetti is flying everywhere, and my eyes lock onto the sign that says, "You're Officially a Supervillain!" while the world's fifth most powerful superhero stands behind me wanting to take a piss.

I draw my hand down so freaking fast, using my telekinesis to snap the banner down to the ground as everyone stops what they're doing and stares at August.

"What... the hell is going on?" I hiss.

"Did I interrupt something?" August asks quietly.

I would also like to know the answer to this question.

Mom cocks her head as everyone quietly stares at August. Everyone in the room is a supervillain of the... low caliber. Basically, they suck at it. But they get an A for effort.

"No... the bathroom... is right there," I say while giving my parents "the look." A look that says, "Do not start attacking Chronobender or you'll get your asses kicked, and it'll be unbelievably embarrassing."

August hesitates, then heads to the bathroom as my parents rush toward me. I'm sure they're coming with ideas of some way we could surround the bathroom and capture August. As a family, they couldn't even capture a squirrel that got into the house last spring, so I can't imagine how the capture of August would go.

"I'm so proud of you," Mom says.

I stare at her warily. "For?"

"You're already taking your villain position so seriously," she says as she pats me on the back.

"Doing?"

"You're planning on befriending him, right? So you can infiltrate Superheroes United and bring them all crashing to the ground!" Dad says.

"Yeahhh. Yep. That's my plan."

Not.

Mom rushes away before returning after a moment and handing me a piece of paper with my phone number on it. "Give it to him when he comes out. Flirt a little," she says as she starts fussing over my hair like that, out of anything, could make August interested in me.

That's when the bathroom door opens and everyone, from my family to my parents' half-hearted villain friends, turns and stare at August.

He stops and gawks at them before looking at me. I swallow the lump in my throat, strut over to him and hold out the paper with my number on it.

"You're super hot, call me some time, thanks, bye," I say as I shove him out the front door and slam it in his face.

"Honey, you need to work on your flirting," Mom says like she feels sorry for me.

"Do you really think that's the issue here?" I hiss.

"It's no wonder why you're still single. I thought it was because of that one long hair on your neck, but now I see that this is why," Mom says.

"What? I don't have a long hair on my neck!"

"You do," she says as she gives it a tug.

"What *is* this?" I ask as I wave to everything.

"We signed you up to join the Rebellion," Mom says.

The Rebellion is a group of supervillains who are *actual* supervillains. Like the kind that murder people and ruin lives. My eldest brother, who is standing next to my father with a bored expression on his face, is a member. I have no interest in ever becoming a member.

"What? I don't want to join—"

"And your final test was breaking into the Beast," Mom says. "You not only broke in, but you got away."

I have to be in the running for the world's most ridiculous parents. "I'm not joining! Get out of my house! All of you!"

"But your presents," Mom says as she points to a table filled with presents.

"Take your presents and go! I told you I'm sick of this, and I'm not doing it!"

Mom looks at the others. "Let's give him some time to process everything," she says. "You might want to open this present up, though." Mom picks a present off the top of the pile and holds it out to me.

I sigh, but who doesn't like presents? So I tear the paper off and open the box and look in at a wheezing cat. Literally, gasping for breath.

"Dammit, Mark, I told you to poke holes in the box!" Mom says.

Dad shrugs. "I thought it'd be fine."

Mom pats my back. "It'll be fine, honey, it wasn't in there that long. You finally get your villain cat! All the best villains have cats."

I look in at the ugliest blob of... skin and wrinkles, and grimace.

Mom shudders when she looks at it, so clearly, I'm not alone in my disgust. "It was *supposed* to be a Persian, but I sent your father out and I should've known better."

"The neighbor had a good deal on it," Dad says with a shrug. "He said it was called the Fugly Discount."

"Get. Out. Of. My. House," I growl.

"I told you to get the Persian," Mom snaps.

There are a few grumbles but everyone besides my eldest brother leaves. I set the box on the ground and pull the hairless cat out. It's not yet an adult, but close, so it's all gangly with wrinkled skin and big blue eyes that don't even help.

"It looks like an old man's ball sac," Nolan says.

It does. "Hey, Nolan," I say.

Nolan is seven years older than me at thirty-five. His power falls into rank B, since he has the power of telepathy. Supposedly, he has agreed to not read the minds of any member in the family, but when we were growing up, he was a complete dick. He was the first one to break the news to Mom that I didn't want to be a villain. Now that he's an adult, we get along better, besides the whole him-being-a-real-supervillain nonsense.

We look similar, with the same color of almost black hair, but he has blue eyes compared to my brown. He's also annoyingly taller than me, but I guess when I just sit on the couch and read a book, I don't have any need for long legs.

"Does this mean I can take my gift back?" he asks.

"What is it?"

"The new Sandy Simmers book."

"No. That's mine."

"They only had one left. I bought it for myself, but then Mom called and told me I *had* to bring you something," Nolan says. "So... I grudgingly gave it to you."

"Thanks. I'll cherish it. Also, Brandon's in jail. I'm not sure anyone cares, but you might need to get him out."

"I will. Before that, let's open these presents and see what we want to keep," he says with a grin.

I snort. "Deal." I set the cat on the ground and stare at it.

"My god, that thing is ugly," Nolan whispers.

"Why'd you get the pretty cat?"

"My cat's *so* much prettier."

The creature sits on its haunches and stares up at me with *huge* blue eyes and *huger* ears.

"Is it a boy or a girl?" Nolan asks.

"Good question," I say as I pick it up. It doesn't have a collar on, so I look at its rear end. "Uhh..."

Nolan leans in to inspect. "Hmm..."

"Umm..."

"Huh..."

"I have no idea," I say.

"Google it."

I pull out my phone. "According to Google... it has cancer."

Nolan starts laughing. "I think it's a girl."

"Yeah, sounds good," I say.

"What are you going to name it?"

"Wait, I have to keep it? I was just going to see if someone else would take it."

"No one wants your nut sac."

"No truer words have ever been spoken."

CHAPTER THREE

My phone beeps as I'm reading my book. I don't bother looking at it because no one messages me besides my family, and frankly, I don't want to talk to them.

What were they thinking trying to get me to join that shit show? I don't even want to see them for probably the rest of my life, if I'm given the option. They've already tried coming into my house uninvited, so using my powers, I've moved everything heavy in front of the doors so they can't push them in. It sounded much easier than changing the locks. I'm not lazy, I'm efficient. Efficiently keeping my family out by shoving a large piece of furniture in front of places they can look through.

The issue is, I'm running out of furniture. All I have left is my bookshelf, and I really don't want to chance any of my books falling and a single page being bent. That would be justification for murder.

The cat leaps up onto my lap and kicks my phone to the ground.

"Dammit, Balzac," I say as I pick the cat up.

She just purrs, telling me she's taking a liking to her new name. I tried giving her names like Daisy, Briar, and Loch Ness Monster, but Nolan's right, she looks like a ball sac. So Balzac it is.

She loves it.

I scratch her neck, glad she's at least soft as velvet. If I'm going to have the world's ugliest cat, at least let it be soft.

She bats at my hoodie strings as I lean over and scoop up my phone. I have fifteen texts. Six from my mom, three from my dad, four from Brandon, one from Nolan, and one from an unknown number. I skim them just to make sure no one has died.

> Mom: I kind of feel like you're mad at me for some reason.

I can't imagine how she came to that conclusion.

> Dad: Can you pay me back for the cat? It was $800. I'll give you until tomorrow or else.

I ignore that one.

> Brandon: Why didn't you tell Mom or Dad I got arrested? It took them three days, THREE DAYS to remember me!

> Me: Who is this?

> Nolan: How are you holding up? Hopefully, the cat's making things a little better.

> Me: Thanks. I already like her more than the rest of the family.

> Nolan: I don't blame you. How did we become so normal after being raised by THEM?

> Me: We're adopted. That's the only conclusion. Dad wants me to pay him back for the cat.

> Nolan: He stole the cat from that weird breeder down the road. He didn't even pay anything for it.

> Me: What a dick! Trying to make me pay him back!

And then the last text. A number I don't recognize.

> Unknown: This is August. You gave me your number. How are you doing?

My heart stutters, skips a beat, and I nearly orgasm right there.

"Balzac, he loves me," I whisper.

Balzac rolls onto her stomach and chews on my hoodie string.

I'm grinning as I start typing, "I'm doing super-duper good. How are you? I want to see you naked" before hesitating. If I bring August into my life, everything will go to hell. My family will become fixated on destroying him. Even if they're not very good villains, they're still villains. And I would be the worst one of all, deceiving him.

I delete the text and stuff my phone in my pocket. "Why don't we go to a pet store?" I ask.

Balzac doesn't seem to understand what that means, so I scoop her up and head to the door that is blocked by a large cabinet. I pull on my winter coat, since it's already getting pretty cold outside. With a wave of my hand, the cabinet slides to the other side of the room and I pass through the door and slam right into Brandon.

"Hey," he says as I hold the cat tucked under my arm like a football. I'm assuming that's how people carry cats.

"I see you got out of jail."

"No thanks to you," he says with a scowl. "I need your help."

Again? "NO!"

"But there's this really hot girl, and I told her I'm a telekinetic and I want you like hiding under the table making cool stuff happen. Maybe tug her shirt down a little or something. Just enough for a boob to pop out."

I stare at him as he grins at me, overly fond of this idea.

"Just think of how fun it'll be," he urges.

"If I can pull her shirt down, I get to pull your pants down so she can see your wee tiny penis," I say as I walk past him and get into my car. He hurries after me and taps repeatedly on the window.

I ignore him and set Balzac on the passenger seat. She puts her paws up on the middle console and looks around.

"Open up, Landon!"

I throw the car in reverse and quickly back up. The tire hits something and jerks over it before I realize that I ran over Brandon's foot.

"Whoops." Good thing he's invincible.

He still looks a bit shocked as I wave to him and rush out of the driveway.

"I stabbed him once," I tell Balzac as I drive. "Don't look at me like that. I'm a villain. A bit of sibling stabbery is good every now and then. He just bent the knife, so it wasn't like I hurt him or anything. He deserved it."

Balzac meows. She doesn't think arguments should be resolved with violence.

"What do you know? You're a fucking cat named after male genitals."

She meows again.

"You're so much easier to talk to than my family. They're all fucking nuts, you know? And sometimes I wonder if I'm just as crazy as them, but there's no way, right?"

And then I remember that I'm talking to a cat and decide to turn on some music.

I drive to the pet store and debate parking in the back. Growing up, we were taught to park in handicap spots. We are villains, after all. And then my mom would tell us to laugh at the elderly people as they had to walk the long distance up to the front of the store. That stopped after one elderly woman beat my mom with a cane. It was one of the best days of my life. My mom kept screaming for me to do something, and I was doing something! I was laughing. Very hard.

I grab Balzac and head inside. She might jump off and try to run away, but literally nothing can outrun me when I can drag it back with a flick of my wrist. I could do the same to August. He could never escape me and maybe even grow to love me.

Dammit, I'm thinking like a villain again, and I have learned the hard way that's not how you woo someone.

Balzac curiously looks around as I head inside with her in my arms. I really need to get a new job. Not because I lack money, I have plenty, but because it's probably not healthy to sit in the house all day reading books, and if I care about anything... it's not my health.

The aisles are filled with Christmas stuff for pets. Santa outfits, leashes with bells and bows, hats with elf ears. I never did much for Christmas. After a certain age, I started to despise it since it's my family's favorite time of the year to break into places because a lot of stores are closed. While most kids were unwrapping Christmas gifts, we would break into a local toy store where my mom would give each of us two minutes to pick out whatever we wanted.

Yeah, when you're five and stupid as shit, it's cool. But when you're twenty-eight and understand what stealing is, it's a bit of a bummer.

I walk down the cat aisle and over to the harnesses. I grab a blue one and pull it over her gray head and buckle it around her midsection. She surprisingly doesn't seem to mind it, even after I snap a leash onto it.

"Do you need clothes?" I ask. "Like... are you cold? You have no hair. You look cold and I feel sadistic over here in my puffy winter coat while you're basically a naked sac."

"What'd it say?" a voice behind me asks.

I turn quickly and look at August who is leaning with one arm against a display. *Clearly,* he took the time to pose there as he gives me a grin and a wink. It's all so cocky that my finger twitches and I use my telekinesis to make the leg of the display snap out from under it and the whole thing tips over. I hadn't realized he'd been putting *all* of his weight on it until he's falling with it, smashing down into a display of stuffed toys.

"I'm so sorry!" I cry as I run after him before remembering that I have Balzac on a leash which snaps her after me, causing her to fly through the air. Clearly, I'm a villain even when trying not to be. I decide that the cat is more important than August and drop to my knees before her.

"I'm so sorry. Are you okay?" I ask as I pull her into my arms.

"I'm fine, oh, you're talking to the cat..." August says as she purrs merrily in my arms.

I look over at August as I cradle Balzac, who seems completely unaffected. "Yeah, you're used to battling crazies, I'm pretty sure you can take on a display of stuffed toys." He's kind of struck this pose that makes me want to jump into the display with him and roll around until his clothes happen to fall off.

"I did this on purpose," he says, voice radiating sexiness.

"That's impressive." The sad thing is that I'm actually impressed.

"You ignored my text."

"I..." I should tell him that this can't happen, but now that he's before me sprawled out like a sex god on a large collection of dog toys... No! I'm better than that! I will say no. I'll say I'm not interested. I can do this! "I missed your text. Do you need help rolling around on the floor?"

He grins at me. "Are you volunteering?"

"No, but that lady over there with no teeth looks like she is," I say.

He laughs and gets to his feet before looking at the display he demolished with no help from me at all.

"Umm..."

"I'll clean that up," an employee says as she rushes up. "For an autograph."

"Uh... sure," he says. She whips out a marker and hands it to him. "What am I signing?"

She pulls open the front of her shirt and he nonchalantly signs the top of her boobs without even *hesitating*. There's a crowd gathering, but they keep a good distance, about ten feet from him, since it's the law. After some people nearly drowned when August couldn't reach them in time because of fans, a law went into effect that if anyone is caught within ten feet of any of the main superheroes in town without permission, they'll be arrested.

The woman swoons, then hurries off, seeming to have forgotten the whole reason she was here.

"She forgot her marker," he says as he walks toward me. "It's... oddly warm. I'm a little concerned where she got it from."

I yank my shirt up as he turns to me. "Will you sign my titties?"

"If you want," he jokes, but when I don't lower my shirt, we both wonder how far the joke will go.

He pops the cap off and writes something on my chest. "There ya go. Just for you."

"You're so sweet. You can go now. I'll see if anyone will be willing to buy my skin now that you've signed it."

"I have a few guys that might like to make it into a lamp if you're interested," he says.

I look down at my chest and see what he wrote.

-I like your face- August

"I like my face too," I say. "It's really good at 'I don't give a fuck' expressions. Let me sign you."

"Um... alright," he says as he passes me the marker.

"Turn around."

"Turn... around?"

"Yeah, turn around and drop your pants."

"People usually take me on a date before asking for that," he says.

He turns around but doesn't drop his pants, so I yank up his shirt and write, "You have a very nice face too" on his back.

"I can't read it," he says.

"I know." I hand the marker back and grab a Santa coat for my cat. I stuff her into it and nearly melt. "I've figured out how to make her cute! You just have to cover her entire body so you can't see her!"

"This is your cat?"

"Yes."

"What's her name?"

"Balzac," I say proudly.

"You... named your cat... Ball Sac?"

"No. Bal*zac*."

"Oh! Like the novelist! I thought you named her after a ball sac for a moment!"

"I did name her after a ball sac. Because she looks like one."

"Oh... um... I hope no one lets you name your children."

"I already have names picked out for them."

"Oh?"

"Thing one and thing two."

"Beautiful."

"What about you? Do you have kids yet? Did you fertilize any of those eggs sent to you through FedEx? Are you creating your own mini spawn army?"

"Not yet, but it's in the works."

That's when I remember that I'm not in my disguise.

"Wait a minute... how did you recognize me?"

He looks confused for a moment. "Oh, without your fetish mask on? You... do realize your mask only covered the area around your eyes, right? Like... your entire face and hair were showing besides the inch around your eyes."

"Were you checking me out?" I ask.

"Are you going to get me to say yes, then sue me for all of my money for being sexually harassed?"

"I might. Depends on how you answer."

"You have a nice... body... shape."

"Aw, that's the sweetest thing anyone's ever said to me. Thank you. You look beautifully human as well."

"Great! Now that that's out of the way, would you like to go out to lunch?"

I scrutinize him before grinning. "Are you asking me on a date?"

"Do you want it to be a date?"

"How much money do you have in your savings and what do your genetics look like?"

"Are you vetting me?"

"I usually make potential suitors give me hair, blood, and spit samples, and then they're allowed to perform a mating dance. If I'm impressed, I might give them the time of day."

"What time is it?" he asks.

I look at my watch. "Twelve—I see what you did there. Damn, you're good," I say with a grin.

"Clearly, I pass."

"I suppose. But I have my cat. I'm not sure if I'm allowed in a restaurant with my cat and it's too cold in the car."

"I'm the city's greatest superhero. I could take a pig into every restaurant in the city and no one would bat an eye."

"That's not a very nice way to talk about your mom."

"My mom left me when I was an infant," he says.

My eyes get really wide. "I'm so sorry!"

He starts laughing. "I'm joking. She didn't. Let's go."

CHAPTER FOUR

"Where would you like to go?" August asks once he has me in the car with him.

"This is how horror movies start," I say. "Naive person sweetly coerced into the car."

"You think I'm a serial killer now?" he asks.

"Are you?"

"Would I tell you if I was?"

"Probably not. You like my cat, so I'm going to deem you safe," I decide.

"Please don't make your decisions of who you should trust on how they like your cat."

I look over at him as he pulls out of the parking spot. "Aw, are you already telling me who I can and cannot go out with? You're already controlling, and we're not even on our first date yet."

He snorts. "I'm not... See that creepy guy there?" he asks as he points at a rank D supervillain strutting down the street. "You should trust him."

"He does look pretty cool."

"Wait, we got off topic."

"Honestly, I'm fine with anything for lunch."

"How about... Travelers?"

"Sure."

"Have you been there before?"

"I have, but it's been a while." The last time I was there, my dad put a glob of dog hair in his food so we'd get the bill for free. It was so embarrassing that I just paid, before quickly running. The really great part is that my parents don't even have a dog. I decide not to share that story with August. He still, mistakenly, thinks I'm an average human being.

He pulls into the parking lot and I get out with my cat and follow after him. He holds the door open for me, but as soon as he walks inside, all eyes instantly turn to him.

"Oh! Mr. Chrono, what a wonderful day to... be alive!" the hostess says, eyes fluttering, manic smile in place. She flings her hair back dramatically but gets her ring stuck in it and struggles to free it for a moment.

"I think she's having a seizure," I say to August who fights back a grin as the woman glares at me.

"Just one?" she asks as if I'm not present.

"No, the two of us."

"Hold tight for just one moment," she says before rushing off.

"Ooh," August says as his eyes hit on a jar next to the hostess's computer that's filled with suckers.

"What's with your obsession with suckers?" I ask.

"Who doesn't like suckers?"

I honestly don't know how to answer that, but the thought of watching August lick a sucker strangely turns me on.

The woman returns in a waft of perfume she must have poured into a tub and rolled around in like a chinchilla in a dust bath. Her hair is freshly done, which is *impressive* since she was only gone for about two minutes.

"Can I have one of those suckers?" I ask, pointing to them.

Her eyes narrow as her hand slaps down on the jar and she slides it away from me. "They're just for kids." Then she turns to August. "Right this way... *sir*," she purrs as she takes his arm and leads him off. I wander behind them like a third wheel and sit down across from August.

Once she finally leaves, August grimaces. "I'm sorry. I should have warned you."

"Oh, you know her?"

"No... for some reason people hate it when I'm with someone else and they instantly become horribly mean to them. It's... why I can never date anyone. The last guy I went out with was so harassed he told me it wasn't worth it."

"He sounds like a dick. Do you want me to beat him up?" I ask.

August looks strangely surprised. "What? No... he's the victim."

I glance at the hostess who is burning holes into the side of my head from her hostess station. If only she knew that I could crush her insides with a thought. "You think that little toothpick is going to bother me?" I scoff. Who does he think I am? Oh... that's right. He thinks I'm normal... ish. "Don't fret about me. It takes a lot to scare me off. Except for babies. Try to hand me a baby, and I'll be gone. It's my one weakness."

His eyes get wide. Clearly, he also understands my terror of small children. "People try to force me to hold their babies all the time. The other day, this woman shoved her baby in my hands and told me to name it. I said Snickersnorts and she literally named it that. It was a joke!"

"And you were making fun of Balzac's name?" I motion to the cat who has her paws on the windowsill as she looks out.

"I regretted it all day. Like... I mean, the kid has to grow up with that name now. I should have said something like Twinkleturtle or something."

I grin at him. "You're evil, and I'm digging it so hard."

He starts laughing. "Shush. You're not allowed to say that. It's in my contract that I have to be perfect."

"I'm surprised you're even allowed to go on a date."

"Oh, I wasn't dumb enough to let them rope me into anything ridiculous. Most of it's just... keeping up a good image in front of people. Like I shouldn't go on TV and be all 'I just fucked up those taint-licking no-gooders.'"

"If all news was like that, I'd actually watch it," I say.

He shakes his head, but I notice that he's grinning. "Me too."

We open our menus and look at the holiday specials they have. The restaurant has a variety of meals from multiple countries, and right on time for the holidays they just grind up some candy canes, sprinkle them on top, and charge an extra five bucks.

"I'm getting pancakes, what are you getting?" I ask curiously.

"Ooh, that sounds good. I might get that too. Do you need anything for your cat? If I told the hostess to get her cat food, I bet you she'd run out and get it."

"That's diabolical, and I'm loving it." Why's he so hot?

"Thanks," he says with a grin.

"But she'll be fine. She ate before we left."

We order our food and talk while we eat. He's so easy to talk to and funny, and I think I'm already losing my mind. I would move mountains for this man, and I don't even know his middle name. It's not my fault I had a baby crush on him for three years of middle school before my family viciously ripped me away and put me into a villain high school. And now that we're back face-to-face, that crush has just exploded into a bigger crush. Especially when I feel like a supervillain, who could be the world's best supervillain if I put my mind to it, shouldn't be saying things like "crush." Unless it's like, "I just crushed that man's neck."

The waitress comes with the check, which August instantly grabs. We have to return to the hostess to pay, though, which means we have to deal with more of her annoyances. I pick up Balzac and follow August up to the counter.

"Was your meal good?" she asks.

They're busy talking, so I glance at the sucker jar. It's an easy enough task that I don't even need my hands for it. Instead, I just will the latch of the jar that sits behind her to undo. It instantly does and the lid gently rises.

What makes me so powerful is that I can not only lift the lid with just my mind, I can keep it held up while splitting my attention on a second object, like the sucker. It floats out of the jar, I snap the lid in place, and the sucker flies over to me. I catch it before anyone even notices.

As we walk out to August's car, I give him a smile. "Thank you for lunch. I really enjoyed it. I was having a bad week, and this really did make my day better."

He smiles back at me and I feel almost giddy. "I'm sorry your week has been bad, but I'm glad I was able to make it better. Want to talk about it?"

"Nope. I don't want it tainting this."

He smiles. "I understand."

When we get into the car, I hold the sucker out to him.

His eyes get wide. "You got me a sucker?"

"I didn't know what flavor you wanted, so I got mystery."

"That is the most romantic thing anyone's ever done for me," he says as he takes it. "How'd you get it?"

"I have magic fingers."

"Ooh."

"If you're impressed by that, you should see me in the bedroom. I can make a mean bed."

He chuckles. "Do you fold the sheets under at the feet?"

"Oh hell no, only evil people do that."

"It's the first thing I fix when I get to a hotel."

I snicker. "And then check for bedbugs?"

"Yes!"

It's clear we're destined to be with each other. And then I remember that he's a superhero and I'm a villain and we are not meant to be. It's like Romeo and Juliet, but where I will not murder myself when he's simply sleeping.

Yes, he's Juliet in this scenario.

He may be taller, broader, and manlier than me in *every* aspect, but I'm Romeo.

He pulls up next to my car and turns to me. "I had a lot of fun. Would you want to go out again sometime?"

Nope. I should stop this now. Don't get invested. Realistically, there is no way for us to have a relationship. We are the sun and the moon. Romeo and Juliet. Destined to fail. Even if we become... something, he'll be devastated when he finds out who I am. "Yes, I'd love to."

He smiles and all those teeny-tiny meaningless worries I have pounding their way into my brain just vanish.

"Awesome. What if I call or text you? Sometimes I don't know my schedule with all the superhero-saving-people stuff—villains don't always seem to care about my plans—so spur of the moment works a little better for me."

"Yeah, call me whenever. I'm currently jobless and have nothing in my life, so I am there for you."

He looks concerned. He's *way* too sweet for me. "Oh... that's... too bad."

"Nah, don't fret about it. I like it this way. And I now have a cat to spend every moment of my life with."

"She's cute," he says as he scratches under her chin.

She instantly starts purring and kneading my leg which means she's maiming me with her vicious claws. "Don't lie to me. We both know she's hideous."

"Even when your children are ugly, you still have to tell them they're cute," he says.

"Is that what your mom told you?" I ask.

"You're evil."

I wink at him. "Thanks, it runs in my family. Also, I'm allowed to say that because I'm sure you already know how cute you are." I pick up Balzac. "Thanks for taking me out. And think of me when you're licking on that sucker."

"Oh my god," he says.

"What? Oh, you're so dirty. I just meant because I got it for you."

His cheeks turn slightly red, and I make it a life goal to make him blush. "Ahh... sure."

I grin as I get out of the car and rush over to mine. I feel like I'm walking on air with sunlight beaming down on me.

I get in my car, and that's when my phone beeps.

> Mom: Don't forget about the meeting tonight.

Well, for a couple of hours I was able to pretend that they didn't exist, but I guess it's time to go back to reality. Grudgingly. Kicking and screaming and whining a little bit.

It's not a pretty sight.

CHAPTER FIVE

"Now let's begin the SAVCGEM meeting!" my father says at the front of the room.

Yes, that is literally what they call it.

SAVCGEM stands for Super Awesome Villains Combined for the Greater Evil of Mankind.

I'm surrounded by idiots.

My mom guilted me into coming because that's what she's good at. I started the day off planning on barricading myself forever and ever in my house—until August texted—and my mom decided that I needed to come to their stupid little meeting.

I am the idiot for agreeing.

Balzac seems to be enjoying herself now that she's getting used to walking on the leash. She's currently sniffing around as I pull my book out, crack it open, and start reading.

"Before we begin, we'd like to welcome our newest member to the alliance!" Dad says.

Everyone whispers and looks around trying to see who the new member is. I'm excited because I'm hoping they can take my place and people will forget about my existence.

"Leviathan! Please come to the front of the room and introduce your cat to everyone!" Dad says.

There's clapping by the twelve people in the room as I stare at my dad like he's nuts. When I don't move, his eyes get wide and he points a finger at me before jabbing at the shitty little stage like he's going to force me to walk up there. When his superpower involves burning things only if he touches them, I'm not sure how he's going to pull that off. I could hold him at bay for hours with my power.

On the other hand, I know that this will end sooner if I just get it over with. I groan in annoyance but get up and walk to the front of the room with Balzac by my side. She's looking undeniably cuter the longer I've had her. Right now, she's wearing a flannel shirt and it might be the cutest thing I've ever seen as she proudly trots along at my side.

Dad heads past me and we meet on the step leading up to the stage, where he grabs my arm. "You better pay me back for that cat."

"Or what?" I threaten.

He smiles and pats me on the back. "You're so good at threats," he says approvingly. "You've taken after your mother, and I couldn't be prouder. Did I ever tell you about the time that she threatened me into marrying her?"

"Only a million and one times," I say, which seems to satisfy him because he smiles fondly and heads over to his seat. I walk up to the podium, pick my cat up and look at the crowd. They're all wearing their "villain" outfits and masks as if we don't know what each other looks like. Most of them were at my "villain" party, so I'm not even sure why I have to show the cat off since they've already seen her.

"This is my cat. She's ugly and her name is Balzac."

Baker, a little old man who took to villainy late in life, starts laughing, but everyone else just stares at me. Even my parents.

"Thank you," I say, then walk back to my seat with my little cat trotting by my side. I sit back down, crack open my book *again*, and start reading.

"Thank you, Leviathan. Next up, it's Baker's turn for our weekly bad deed," Dad says.

The elderly man grabs his cane and shuffles up to the front. None of us help him onto the stage since that would be the "hero" thing to do, and it takes him like ten minutes. But he's all smiles as he reaches the microphone.

"What if..." he says, pausing for dramatic effect, "we change all of the local restaurants' ketchup to hot sauce!"

"That's villainous!" my mom shouts and everyone claps.

This is my life.

My phone rings and I nearly leap out of my chair when I see who it is. I scoop up Balzac and start running for the door.

"He's so excited, he's already getting started!" Baker says.

"Hello?" I answer as sexily as I possibly can, keeping my voice low and seductive.

"Oh, I'm sorry, were you asleep?" August asks.

I sigh. "No... I wasn't."

"Do you... do you think we could meet?"

"Yes!"

"Bring your fetish mask. I don't want people seeing us."

"I already have it on!" I say as I run for my car. "Where am I going?"

"Come over to Park Street and park in the McDonald's parking lot. When you arrive, let me know, and I'll try to direct you. I don't want to come down and get you, because I finally lost my stalkers... I mean, fans."

"That's okay. I'm a big boy, I can take them on."

He chuckles. "Are you going to fight for me? Generally, I'm fighting for other people."

"I'll fight for you. I took two weeks of karate when I was ten. After I spend five minutes trying to remember the moves, or YouTubing them, I'll be able to save you."

He chuckles. "Thanks."

I stay on the phone with him for the whole drive, even though it's only about five minutes from where I'm at. "I have Balzac with me again."

"She can come. You have her leash?"

"I do."

"I'm up on the roof... I just don't want her falling off or something."

"Wait a minute, I thought you were a superhero. You can't fly?" I joke.

He chuckles. "No, I have to drive, but I get a siren."

"Wow, ain't you special," I say as I get out of my car. I put Balzac on the ground, and she trots after me. "Where are we going?"

"Why does your cat act like a dog?" he asks.

"Are you watching me?" I ask, weirdly excited about that.

"Maybe."

"Do you like what you see?"

"You look really tiny, but I'm going to say yes."

"Thanks. Where are you?"

"Look up," he says. I do and see him way at the top of an apartment building.

I grab the bottom of my shirt and yank it up, flashing him my shockingly white chest. "Did you like that?" I purr.

He starts laughing. "It was just like a flash of light in the darkness. I thought it was a bright light at first."

"No, it's because my stomach has never seen the sun."

"What are you talking about? I've seen it twice now."

Even the goofy things he says makes me grin. "Oh? You think you're like the sun now?" I ask with a snort.

"Nah."

I cross the street, then crane my neck up. "Now how do I get up there?"

"What? Can't fly?"

"Nope. I could try crawling up the side but I'm not sure my cat will make it."

"True, we don't want the cat to get hurt. Just go inside, there's a staircase right in front of you once you're through the door. Take that all the way to the top. The passcode into the building is 5274."

"Alright, I'll be right up."

I hang up and hit the passcode before pulling the door open and casually walking in with my mask and cat, who is still trotting beside me on a leash. The stairs are easy to find, so I head up them as Balzac trots by my side, happy as can be. She's fucking weird. That's all I have to say about it. But *maybe* I should give her a nickname. Not because Balzac isn't a superior name, but because I feel like maybe it'd be more shocking if I only pulled it out when I needed to.

"How about Zacia?" I ask the cat.

She ignores me, which tells me she loves it.

"Alright, Balzac, Zacia it is!"

She glances up at me. She loves it.

About halfway up, I wonder if I even really want to see him this badly. I've been walking for miles and my legs are reminding me that my pastime is sitting on the couch and reading books. And when I do decide to be evil, it's not like I actually fight. I just flick my hand and wicked things happen. By about the sixth floor, Zacia is leading the way and I'm dying.

My phone rings, so I stop and pull it out before seeing that it's August. "Did you get lost? Or abducted?"

"I... wish... I... was abducted," I pant. Okay, maybe I'm being a bit dramatic. Sue me. Villains love drama. "Where's the elevator?"

"It doesn't go up to the roof." He starts laughing. "Are you out of shape?"

"I read books all day, yes I'm out of shape!"

"Want me to come down and carry you up?"

"Yes. I do."

He laughs. It's such a cheery sound.

"I'm serious. Come carry me."

He hesitates. "Seriously?"

"Yes."

"Um... okay? Sure!"

He hangs up and after a few minutes, I hear footsteps before August comes around the corner, decked out in his superhero uniform. It's made of a pair of tight blue pants and a white spandex style shirt. It's mostly covered by a matching jacket, so he doesn't freeze, and a red cape. It's the ugliest outfit I've ever seen, but on him, it's beautiful. Maybe even designed by the angels.

He gives me this crooked smile that melts my cold villainous heart. "Hey," he says.

I'm smiling wildly when I say, "Hey. Did you come to rescue me?"

"I did. From these evil stairs."

"How are you going to do it?" I purr.

"By being motivational. You can do it! Come on! Follow me!" he says, taking on the voice he uses when he's doing something with kids. Instead of helping to motivate me, it makes me start laughing.

"No! I wanted you to carry me!"

"Seriously?"

Yes. "Nah, it's fine. But I want you in front of me as you walk up the stairs."

He raises an eyebrow. "Why?"

"Just seeing you being awesome makes it easier for me to walk up the stairs."

He narrows his eyes, like he's trying to think about it. "Oh, I thought maybe you wanted to look at my ass or something."

"It's the only good thing about that hideous uniform."

He starts laughing as he begins walking beside me. "You don't like my uniform?"

"If you'd like, I'll design a better one for you."

"I have a feeling I'd be in fishnets and booty shorts."

I chuckle as I scoop up Zacia. "At the very most."

"Oh? You'd have me in something skimpier? But I get cold easily."

"I was thinking like a vest with only one button so we can see your chest and abs."

"I already get harassed in this. Can you imagine if I was walking around in a vest with my nipples and abs showing *and* booty shorts?"

"You'd pick the person up to save them and they'd orgasm on the spot."

His face scrunches up. "Oh gross. I would probably stop saving people," he says as we finally reach the top. He holds the door open for me, and I realize that I'm going to taint this innocent soul and I'm going to love it so much.

He walks over to the ledge and sits down, so I sit next to him with Zacia in my arms.

"So?" I ask.

He looks over at me. "So?"

"What's going on?"

He gives me a smile, but it's not genuine. It's the smile I see on TV, not the smile he had when he was younger and not the smile I get when I make him laugh.

"What do you mean?"

"You're upset about something."

He shakes his head. "No, I'm not. I just wanted to spend the evening with you."

39

"Do you always hide your feelings?" I ask curiously. "Is that because you have to or you feel like you're supposed to?"

He's quiet for a moment as he looks away from me and out at the city. There's more wind up here, but it's not too horribly cold tonight; even so, I stick Balzac under my coat so just her head is peeking out.

"I'm fine, honestly. I'm not going to just... let's enjoy our second date!" The second part is said with fake cheer. He wants me off the conversation because he doesn't want to face what's wrong.

"Sometimes I hate the path that has been chosen for me," I say. "Your turn."

He hesitates before saying, "Sometimes I also hate the path that has been chosen for me."

"I feel like everyone wants me to be something I don't want to be. But I continue to do it because I feel like they won't care about me or want me if I don't."

He takes a deep breath. "I feel like I constantly have to be happy and smile, and trudge forward even when I'm surrounded by people who get hurt and people who I can't rescue in time. There is this huge weight on me, but I'm only one person."

I catch his blue eyes. "See? Doesn't that feel better?"

He nods. "Yeah. I wish I could be honest with more people... but I've gotten so used to having to keep it to myself, that sometimes I forget how to be. So thanks."

"I wish I could help you with more, but I don't know how."

"You making me laugh helps a lot. I was called in on a fight today, but I didn't get there soon enough and the woman is in the hospital. But it's like... the police weren't but five minutes from her. Why didn't they get there sooner? Why does everything fall on me? It's *my* fault if she doesn't get rescued in time because I'm everyone's savior! I didn't want to be anyone's savior. I wanted to be a teacher. But I can't rightfully sit in a classroom and teach literature when I have the ability to save people."

"You can. Tell them tough shit. You could even laugh at them," I say.

He snorts. "They'd think I lost my mind. They just tell me that I need to demolish the villain organization, but there's no fucking way I can go up against an entire *team* alone. At least I'm able to keep them back for now."

He doesn't think he could beat them? Interesting. I'm sure they'd *love* to know that. Not the villain group my parents belong to, no, he could smash them with a flick of his finger, but the one my parents *signed me up for*. The Rebellion.

He leans into me. "You alright? You look enraged all of a sudden."

"That's just how my face looks when I'm with a cute guy," I say.

He chuckles. "I'll take it. Oh, by the way, your cat is adorable."

"You need glasses."

"I have contacts in. It's hard to wear glasses with this mask on. It's like, do the glasses go under or above? Neither works. It's a mess."

I think I suddenly have a glasses kink. "I want to see you with glasses on."

He grins. "Alright, I'll wear glasses the next time I see you."

"Is that all you'll be wearing?" I ask.

"I deal with some *very* forward people on a daily basis, but you might be the most forward," he says.

I grin at him. "They're all just jokes... unless you want to... then I won't complain. But I'm not like sexually harassing you or anything. Unless that's your thing. Then I can get into it if you want."

"How about we start with the glasses and see how it goes from there? I might take my socks off or something for you."

"Oh man, you know your way right into my heart."

"So... what's your superpower?" he asks. "If you don't mind me asking."

"You didn't look it up? I'm sure you have access to all the data on the superhumans in the city."

"I do, but I'd never look it up without permission," he says.

"Super low-end telekinetic," I say as I hold my hand out and pretend to fixate on a stray nail. I could literally send my car flying with just a glance, but instead, I squint and fixate on it and make it shudder a little before slowly lifting. I let it tumble before it's two inches above the ground.

"That's neat! I have super strength," he says.

"What! You do?" I say as if not everyone in the city knew that.

He chuckles. "Yes... and I can also freeze time," he says.

41

"I don't know much about your time freezing. Is it endless?"

He shakes his head. "Oh, no. I can stop time for about one minute at a time. And only maybe three or four times a day. I can for a little bit more if I really, really push myself. The limitations of it forces me to decide when I should or shouldn't use it."

"That makes sense." I look around at the view the top of the building gives us before glancing back at him. "Do you live here?"

"No, I used to when I was a kid and they never changed the passcode, so I come here whenever I want to be alone."

"I'm here, so you're not exactly alone."

He gives me a smile. "I changed my mind."

"It's because I'm awesome, isn't it? And my cat is amazing."

He gives me a true smile this time. "It is."

We talk well into the night, never running out of things to share. And while I know that what I'm doing is wrong, it feels so right. And I can't seem to talk myself out of it.

CHAPTER SIX

My phone beeps and I snatch it up, hoping it's August. We've texted throughout the week but haven't been able to meet up with each other because he's been busy doing hero stuff. I am literally about ready to beat the shit out of the next person who tries to mess up our date by making him busy.

Instead, it's Nolan.

> Nolan: The Rebellion is having a mandatory meeting tonight.

> Me: Have fun?

> Nolan: You're part of the Rebellion.

> Me: I am not! Mom and Dad signed me up. Not me.

> Nolan: It doesn't matter, you're part of it now.

> Me: Then I'll withdraw.

> Nolan: You have to go to a meeting to withdraw. I'll pick you up at seven.

> Me: You better buy me fucking ice cream.

> Nolan: I didn't know ice cream could fuck.

> Me: That's where Neapolitan comes from.

Now I'm pissed. My mood turns sour and the rest of the day I grump around unless August texts. Then I'm all smiles and giggles. If only the Rebellion could see me laughing at everything August says like he's the greatest thing that has ever been put on this earth.

When Nolan shows up at seven, I head out with Zacia and get into his car.

His eyes drop to my lap. "You're bringing your cat?"

"Yes. Have a problem with it?"

"What's it wearing?" he asks.

I give him a wicked grin. "I went to the pet store and they have these superhero outfits that look exactly like Chrono's supersuit. I thought it'd be fitting for the meeting. Since I have to wear this stupid suit, she can wear her suit too."

He starts laughing as he reaches over and pets the cat. "This is why I love you. Most people are nervous and excited to show up and you're just going into this from the complete opposite direction."

"Thanks. Now, the more concerning question. Where's my ice cream?"

"We'll swing through and get it," he says. "Are you sure you don't want to join? I mean... this is what villains dream about."

"I don't mind the nonsense Mom and Dad do, but no, I don't want to be a supervillain. Unless supervillains read books all day, I'm not interested."

"I get it, but you can just tell them you don't want to do some of the darker jobs. Like, I don't do anything really bad. They just use me for reading the minds of people. Last week, I read the mind of a politician to find his dirty little secret to make him resign. The country's better off without him."

"I get that, but I just... really only want to read my books."

"And stare at cute boys?"

I grin. "Depends if they're in the bookstore because I really don't have the energy to go looking for them."

"What about August? I saw the pictures of you with him online. People were going nuts trying to figure out who the man he was carrying away from the bank was."

I snort. "Yeah, it was fun, but that's all it was," I lie. I can trust Nolan *way* more than the others, but there's a possibility he'd tell the family and I already lied and told them August hadn't texted again.

"He really never sent you a text?"

"He did... but I ignored it. I don't want to deal with it. You know Mom and Dad would try to get me to do something stupid."

"True. But... you could have at least like... tainted him a bit first or something."

I laugh. "He is *really* cute. And I think he should get a little tainted."

Nolan shakes his head as he pulls up to the only ice cream shop in town that stays open for the winter. "What do you want?"

"Hot fudge sundae," I say, so he orders at the drive-thru and pays for it.

"I think getting out and finding someone would be good for you, though. You let the family dictate your life," Nolan says after he pays. "They see you as powerful and they want to use you. You shouldn't let them use you."

"I know. But sometimes, I feel like that's the only reason they want me."

"Of course it's not," he says as the lady comes to the window and hands us our ice cream.

We talk some as Nolan drives to the meeting hall just outside the main part of the city and then parks. I've always liked hanging around Nolan because he treats me as an equal. Not some overly powerful furniture mover.

I get out of the car and follow him inside. He glances back at me and gives me a reassuring smile. "I'll introduce you to the others."

There are three people inside when we enter. Two I recognize—Darknight and Racer—but the other I don't.

"This is Marauder. He's the leader," Nolan explains.

The man isn't even wearing a mask, like the others and me... and my cat.

Instead, he's wearing normal clothes and a soft smile. "Nice to meet you," he says. "As your brother said, call me Marauder." He holds out his hand, so I give it a good shake.

"You can call me Leviathan. I'm sure this isn't normal, but I actually didn't sign up for this and want nothing to do with being here. So I'd like to resign."

"Oh my goodness. Your cat!" he says, then starts laughing hard enough he's grabbing his stomach. It really isn't *that* funny, but I smile and nod. "The outfit! It's priceless."

"Ha. Thanks. So... I'd like to leave? Do I just walk out? Run? Do we hug? Am I making this awkward?"

Marauder seems unfazed by my questioning. "Now, Leviathan, this is a huge privilege being here," he says.

"I understand, *buuuut* I'm not interested."

"People *kill* for this opportunity. The least you can do is stay for one meeting. If it's still not up your alley, we'll take you off the roster. But remember, once off, you can't come back. And you have to wait for your brother to drive you home anyway!"

I look over at Nolan who is watching me closely. "True... fine. One meeting, but you're not going to change my mind."

"That's alright. God, I love that cat."

"Thanks."

"Have a seat. Sparx will be here shortly."

He leads me over to a large round table and pulls out a chair for me, which I sit in. While I wait, they talk, but I notice I have a text from August, which I deem much more important.

> August: I finally got home. Are you free tonight?

> Me: Maybe later. I'm at this stupid thing with my brother. But you should see what I have Balzac dressed as.

> August: I can only imagine. Do you take her everywhere with you?

> Me: Pretty much. I should ditch my brother for you.

> August: I can wait.

> Me: I have no patience. None. I've been here for one minute, and it's been the longest minute of my life.

> August: A minute does sound awful. Want to know what I did today? A press conference, but it started an hour late.

> Me: And you just... waited?

> August: I did.

> Me: Did you have a sucker?

> August: Were you watching me?

> Me: No, I only like watching you when you're at home because that's much creepier.

> August: Haha! I'll strike a pose for you the next time I'm in the shower.

Then I'm thinking about August in the shower, which is so much better than staring at these fools. That's when someone walks in and Marauder calls the meeting.

"I would like to start by introducing everyone since we have a new member today!" he says. "I will begin. I am Marauder, I am the leader and creator of the Rebellion."

The woman to his right, who just showed up, nods at me and says, "I'm Sparx. I can control electricity."

The next man who is wearing an all-black suit says, "I'm Racer. I can move so fast you can barely see me."

"I'm Darknight," the next says, with no explanation at all on what he does.

"Obviously you know me," Nolan says.

"Sometimes I wish I didn't," I say, which makes a couple of them chuckle, but Racer just stares at me with narrowed eyes. "I'm Leviathan." End of story.

"What's your power?" Racer asks.

"The power of laughter," I say as dryly as possible while petting my cat.

"You haven't made me laugh yet," he says.

"I don't have a mirror."

He stares. I stare.

The difference is that my staring could fuck him up so hard.

Everyone else laughs.

"On to our meeting!" Marauder says.

I really should have brought a book.

They talk about mundane things like politics and city nonsense, then start talking about darker shit that catches my interest. Not because I'm interested in it, but because I'm interested in not being a part of it. Especially because I know that if I hear it, if they tell me it, they're not planning on letting me out of the Rebellion.

"Well, we all know that the way to Mayor Wyatt's heart is by taking care of his daughter," Sparx says.

I stand up. "Well, this is boring. I'm going to wait in the truck. Thanks again for inviting me, but it's going to be a hard pass."

"Sit," Marauder says, voice stern.

"No, thank you," I say.

It's clear Marauder isn't used to people going against him because he cocks his head and just watches me. "Landon, sit down."

"I am not interested. Thank you for your time," I say as I set my cat on the ground.

"Landon, please, I think you should just sit down," Nolan says, looking concerned. He's worried about what I'm doing, but I know that if I give in, this will become my life. And I'm not murdering the mayor's daughter.

"No. Thank you for having me. I'll be leaving."

I start walking toward the door when Racer rushes in front of me, keeping the entrance blocked.

"Landon, have a seat," Marauder repeats.

I casually look back at Racer. I've never gone up against a supervillain before, and never any as powerful as one from the Rebellion, but I'm leaving this fucking building one way or another.

"Move," I growl as I stand my ground. He may tower over me, but when you have a power like mine, it doesn't take height to put someone down.

"Sit in your fucking seat," Racer says.

"I'm not asking again," I warn.

And as quick as that, he snatches Zacia off the ground, grabbing her by the neck.

"You're going to regret that," I growl as I grab onto Zacia with my telekinesis, lifting her into the air as I force Racer's hand off her. Once cat and asshole are separated, I grab onto Racer's body with my mind and draw my hand to the side hard. He slams into the wall hard enough that his shoulder punches through the drywall. "Do not *ever* touch my cat again."

I hold my arms out as Zacia floats over to me and into my arms. She sinks her claws into my jacket, clearly concerned. But Racer isn't finished. He rushes at me so quickly that I nearly don't have time to react, but I grab onto him with my power, wrapping it around his throat.

I begin closing my hand, even though we're feet from each other, and the man begins gasping and flailing as his legs lift off the ground. He's clawing at his throat even though nothing is there for him to pull away. And just as his arms begin to slow, I throw him to the ground.

"Try it again, and I'll pop your fucking head off," I growl, even though I really wouldn't. I'd probably start vomiting if I just popped his head off and that wouldn't look very supervillainy. There'd be blood and throat stuff everywhere and I'm not sure I could handle that.

He stays on the floor this time and no one says a word as I strut through the door. I debate going to Nolan's car, but instead, I stuff Zacia under my shirt and start walking. I can tell she's upset because she generally starts purring the moment she's under there, but this time, she's quiet.

"I'm sorry, baby. I won't let anyone touch you again."

My phone beeps as I walk down the road, and I jump. I pull it out and see that it's August and relief instantly washes through me. I feel like the tension leaves my body and I'm able to breathe again. I didn't realize I'd been so tense.

> August: Are you still surviving?

> Me: Please come get me.
>
> August: That bad, huh?
>
> Me: Seriously. Come get me.

My phone starts ringing, and I answer it immediately.

"What's wrong?" he asks, voice soothing me further.

"I want you to come get me." It almost comes out as a plea. Yeah, I'm powerful as fuck, but right now, I just want him to block me from the shit this world has to offer.

"Where are you at?"

I don't want him near that hell, in case they decide to follow me, so I try to think of somewhere within walking distance. "Meet me at Riley's Auto store."

"Okay, I'll be there in ten minutes."

"Thank you."

"Is everything okay?"

"Just... family shit."

"I'm sorry."

"Nah, don't worry about it. I'm fine. Better now that you're coming. And you better be wearing your glasses."

He chuckles. "I can do that."

"Good. Maybe like a Speedo too, and that's it."

"I don't own a Speedo."

"Dammit."

"I'll see what I can do," he jokes.

I'm the world's worst supervillain. Even I need the superhero to come and save me.

CHAPTER SEVEN

August is already there when I walk up. At least Zacia is purring by then. I had ditched my supervillain shirt alongside the road since he could tie it to the supervillain me, and left on the dark pants and my regular coat. When I reach the parking lot and August gets out of his car with his plastic-framed glasses, I forget about everything that has ever ailed me.

He gives me a smile. "Hey."

"Wh-Who are you?" I ask in alarm as I step back.

"What?" he asks with a cock of his head.

"It was a joke... get it? In the comics, Superman hides his identity with just glasses."

He chuckles. "Ah, I get it."

"I love them. They make you look very sophisticated." And sexy. Although he could walk up with a paper bag on, and I'd still be ready to let him bone me.

"Thanks. Are you doing alright?" he asks.

"Better now that you're here," I admit.

"You're such a flatterer."

I grin and head around to the passenger side. "Oh! I forgot. Look at Balzac," I say as I pull her out with her Chrono superhero outfit on.

"Oh my god." He looks as amused as I was when I bought it.

"I know, right?"

"First off, it's so weird that they sell this stuff... and kind of hilarious you got it for your cat."

I grin. "I felt like what better way to get your attention?"

"You don't need to dress up your cat to get my attention."

My grin immediately widens. "Are you flirting with me?"

He runs his fingers through his blondish hair. "I've been trying to, but I'm not really sure what works with you," he says.

"The glasses are working. Really, you don't have to try too hard. You could just stand there, and I'd be into it."

"Do I need to pose?"

"You don't even need to pose. I'm already digging it."

He chuckles as he starts driving. "I guess I didn't ask where you wanted to go. I was just taking you to my house."

"Are you kidnapping me?" I ask.

"Do you want to be kidnapped?"

I look over at him as he glances over at me, looking amused. "When you're wearing those glasses, I'll agree to about anything."

He starts laughing. "No! Now I sound like a creep!"

"You can be a creep. You can creep all over me if you want. Yes, I'd like to go to your house even if your plan is locking me in your dungeon."

"I don't have a dungeon... yet."

"Ooh."

He shakes his head. "You're making me sound even creepier."

"I love it when I'm the least creepy person in a room," I say. I unzip my coat now that the heat of his car has warmed me up. "I can't believe it's so cold already. Although, that's the best time of the year to read."

"Thanksgiving is next week already. You know... the other day when I was complaining about... stuff? It's times like Thanksgiving and Christmas that remind me why I'm so thankful for this job."

"What do you mean?" I ask curiously as I look over at him.

He glances at me for just a second before turning back to the road. "We were *poor*. Like... we got one gift at Christmas, and it was usually something very practical."

"Oh..." I never got that impression while we were in school. He always seemed so happy and was very popular, so my childish brain assumed he had it all. I was *jealous* of him, but more than anything, I just wanted him to like me.

"You didn't notice?" he asks. "It's like, when you're that age, you feel like everyone notices."

"What do you mean?" I ask as I watch him closely.

"When we were in school—"

"Wait... you remember me?"

He snorts as he looks over at me again. "Oh my god. You... what? Did you not remember *me*?"

"Of course I remembered you! Your face is on every billboard and bus bench. Do you know how many times I've sat on your face?"

"You have a very peculiar way of sitting on benches."

I grin. "Maybe."

"So did you actually forget?"

"I couldn't forget you if I tried. My August shrine in my bedroom doesn't help."

He chuckles. "I hope that last one was a joke."

"I guess you'll have to come over sometime and find out."

"I'm not sure if I want to now. Will I be tied to the bed in this scenario?"

I snicker. "If you want to be. Anyway... how long have you known it was me?"

"Since the bank... Landon, I had a *huge* crush on you in middle school. So when I saw you, of course I knew it was you."

"You're joking. I was the weird kid who sat in the back of the room peering at you from over my book," I say. I can't believe he even *noticed* me back then.

"Wait... you had a crush on me?"

"Of course I did! Didn't everyone? You were funny, and nice, and cute."

He's beaming now, and suddenly I want to feed him more words about what I thought of him to see how much wider that smile can go. "That's hilarious. If only we'd have just... talked to each other."

"I just... why would you have a crush on *me?* Me of anyone! I just read books! I didn't even bother talking to people, since I really didn't care about anyone other than my small little circle."

"It all started with that project on pollution we did with each other."

My mind is reeling as I try to process this. "In sixth grade?"

He nods vigorously. "Yeah! You were really nice and funny, and then I had this huge crush. Do you remember when I got in *big* trouble because I picked up that huge container of balls in gym?"

The memory comes flooding back to me. "Yes! You tripped while carrying them and they went flying everywhere. Didn't the weight of the container punch a hole in the floor?" Of course I remember that.

"I was trying to get your attention. Everyone else was so impressed by my superpowers, I thought you would be too."

I start laughing as I stare at him in disbelief. "Are you serious?"

"Completely serious. I can't even *tell* you all the stupid things I did in front of you to try and get your attention."

"You're killing me. Suddenly, my crush on you seems very low-key. I just thought you were so far out of reach that I didn't even *try*."

"Remember the time I picked up the teacher's car and put it behind that tree where he couldn't get it out? That was because he was being mean to you."

"Why did you literally do *everything* but talk to me?" I ask.

He starts laughing as he shakes his head. "I don't know! I was a stupid kid! It sounded terrifying to walk up and talk to you and it was just so much easier to—"

"What, carry cars around and throw containers?" I ask.

He nods. "Yes!"

"That's hilarious."

"I was devastated when I started high school and you weren't there... I had finally decided I'd talk to you. I even wrote up what I was going to say."

My eyes get wide as I realize what that means. "You wrote a speech to woo me?" I ask. "Oh my god! I want you to give it now."

"I don't have it!"

"Speech! Speech!" I chant.

He shakes his head. "I really, really don't have it!"

"You have to remember it."

"I don't."

"Boo... I don't know if I believe you."

He looks amused. "Why'd you leave?"

I grimace at the thought. "My parents put me in this stupid charter school... it was awful, and I hated it so much." It was a school for supervillains and I hated everyone there. We didn't learn anything because it was basically a school of bad kids insistent on doing bad things. Most of the teachers were just normal people who grew to hate us.

"That sucks. It wasn't long after that I was pulled into Superheroes United. Before long there wasn't even time for me to go to school. I was just given coursework and a tutor. I didn't have time to do anything else, but for the first time in... ever, my family had money."

"I never realized your family was hurting for money," I say.

"I didn't know your family was rich."

Suddenly, I feel very guilty about my house and the money my family "owns." Quite a bit of it came from my grandfather, who has since passed, and was a true supervillain. Not that I'm perfect and follow every law, but I haven't actually stolen anything for a long time. A lot of my shift from evil to good revolved around August.

I wonder how he'd feel if he knew he was the reason for me quitting the path I was headed down. I was still sporting my crush when he became a superhero and I started to question what he'd think of me if he knew what I was doing.

"What are you thinking about?" August asks.

"Being a supervillain," I say.

He starts laughing. "Is that your goal?"

"Well... I was just thinking about how fun it'd be for you to chase me and tie me up," I say.

"Oh god. Alright, please don't become a supervillain for that. I am more than willing to chase you around and tie you up now," he says.

That makes me laugh, especially because it's hilarious thinking of August doing it. Oh, but I'd dig it so hard.

"How much do you charge for this service?" I ask.

"For you? It'd be free."

"Ooh. Guess what we're doing when we get to your house?"

He snorts. "Oh man. You can't even make it up the stairs without my help, so it's not going to be much of a race."

"Shit. I forgot about that. What if you were like... in bondage or something? That'd slow you down and up your sex appeal all at once."

"Huh... you have some unusual hobbies. Back in middle school, you were so quiet and innocent and now? What *happened* to you?"

"Oh, I was just a closet pervert back then. Now I share my perversions with anyone who's interested in listening."

"So... mostly your cat?"

I start laughing about that one. "Only my cat."

He grins and shakes his head. "Hey, at least someone will listen to you."

"That's true. That's why I keep her on a leash, so she can't get away. I'll do the same to you if you try to escape."

"Nah, I like you. You don't need to keep me tied up... unless you really want to." He turns into the driveway of a very nice two-story house that is slightly smaller than mine. "Here we are."

"Ooh, do I get a tour and then a chance to snoop around?" I ask.

"You can do anything you'd like. It'll be pretty clean since my mom cleans it when I don't have time to. I used to feel guilty about that, but I've bought them a house amongst many other things, so when she insisted on helping me by cleaning the house, I didn't even hesitate. I threw the keys at her so damn fast."

"Did you have to hide all your sex toys from her?"

"Yes, I keep those in their own special little fireproof box."

"Special box made just for one, right?" I tease.

"You're evil."

"Thanks. It runs in the family."

He chuckles and parks the car before turning it off.

"I can't wait to see your house. The house of the infamous Chrono. Do you have pictures of yourself in your supersuit hanging on every wall that you touch yourself to?"

"Every day."

"And a room full of all the people you save that no one hears from again?"

"I literally could just open my door and they'd willingly flock in and lock themselves up."

"It's a good thing I'm not in your position. I'd invite them over to do things for me like clean, cook, buy me books. I'd never have to leave my house. I could be the ultimate recluse," I say as I get out and take Zacia over to the yard. She, of course, chooses his flower bed to start digging in.

"Your cat is trained to go outside?" he asks.

"She's awesome... besides trying to dig up your flowerbed."

"That's alright. I hate flowers."

"That's hot."

He starts laughing. "How is that... hot?"

"It just automatically is."

"Alright. I'll take it."

He sets a hand on the door *just* as his phone begins ringing. "Shit."

"What's wrong?" I ask as he looks down at his phone.

"An armed robbery on Tanger Street. I have to take this. Just... go inside my house and snoop while you wait for me. Look for all my paintings that I touch myself to."

While that *does* sound awesome, I don't plan on leaving him just yet. Especially when there's excitement in the future. "I'll go with you."

He shakes his head. "I'm not taking you with me."

"I can drive as you change into your supersuit. It'll save you time, and when we get there, I'll wait in the car."

He hesitates, but I've already grabbed the keys out of his hand and am heading toward the car after snatching up Zacia. He rushes after me and gets into the passenger seat as I back out of the driveway.

"I was going to tell you that you can speed, but the way you shredded an inch of rubber off my tire as you flew out of the driveway, I don't think you need help," he says.

I grin. "I'll get you from point A to point B as fast as you'd like to go."

He climbs into the back seat and I glance at him in the rearview mirror as he pulls his shirt off.

"Don't wreck because you're peeking at me."

"Gosh ew, gross. I'm not a perv," I say as I peek at him again. He's grinning at me, which makes me laugh. "I'm sorry!"

"Oh, you don't have to be sorry. I just don't want you to die. I'm semi-invincible, but I don't think you are."

"My heart is."

"Well, who needs an intact head when your heart can just keep beating?" he asks.

"Sometimes the stuff you say is so fucking sexy that I don't know what to do about it."

"I can give you some of the quotes Superheroes United feed me. Maybe that'll help?"

I glance back at him, overly excited about the private show I'm about to witness. "Yes!"

"Together... we can save them all!" he says in his "superhero" TV voice.

"Oh yes!" I moan, and he starts laughing, but I keep my face completely straight as I zoom around a slower fucker going sixty-five. "More! Give me more, August!"

"Umm.... We are strongest united!"

"Oh yeah, baby. That one went right to the groin."

"I would love to see you reading these lines."

"There is no way in hell I'd read any of that shit. I'd be like, 'What's up, assholes? Be good or I'll come fuck you up.'"

"Threats, huh?"

"Yes." I look back and see that he's fully suited. "I missed you changing your pants," I realize.

"Really? I even pulled my underwear down some in the process and stuffed the excess between my ass cheeks so it looked like I was wearing a thong."

"You're so majestic."

"Thanks," he says as some huge boat of a car leaps out in front of me. The grandpa driving it clearly hadn't looked either way. I slam on the brakes to keep from hitting the car as I pin Zacia against me but kind of forget about August, who had been climbing back into the front seat.

For a superhero who doesn't know how to fly, he takes flight, head slamming into the dashboard as I narrowly avoid the asshole's car by jumping the curb. I come to a stop right in the parking lot of the gas station that's currently being robbed.

"Are you okay?" I ask.

Silence.

Ohhh fuck.

I pat the side of August's face and he groans, but he's out fucking cold.

"You gotta be a superhero now!" I urge as I pat his head while looking into the gas station where people are being held hostage by a man waving his gun around. And I have just knocked unconscious their only semblance of help.

"Well... this is awkward," I say as he makes some groaning noise.

The gunman charges for someone with his gun raised as I think about what I should do. I could probably just... leave. I mean, August needs a day off every now and then, right? Let the cops handle it! Or there *are* other supers.

"Help!" someone screams.

"*Fuuuck,*" I cry as I grab the mask out of August's hand and jump out of the car while yanking it on. I reach out to the gas station door with my telekinesis and pull it open, snapping the lock. The gunman turns to me.

"Get on the fucking floor or I'll put a bullet in this girl's head," he howls as he aims the gun at a girl cowering on the floor with her friends.

Clearly, I don't react quickly enough because he pulls the trigger. I throw my hand up, pushing the bullet straight up into the ceiling, then fixate onto the gun, grabbing it with my powers and switching the safety on. I drive the gun back, forcing him to punch the butt of it into his face so hard that he staggers and drops to his knees. One of the men closest to him rushes forward and pins him to the ground as I look at the people staring at me. Several of them pull out their phones, like they're going to record me saying one of those stupid fucking "I'm a hero" lines. Instead of saying anything, I crush all of their phones with just a thought before remembering that I'm probably being recorded by security cameras, so I murder those little fuckers too.

"If any of you say anything about me being here, I will hunt each and *every* one of you down. And I will make your life a living hell," I growl. "When the police come, tell them that Ronald McDonald saved you."

I grab a Caramello off the counter, then think better of it and grab the whole box. I am technically a supervillain. "Now was I here tonight?"

"No," a few say.

"Good."

Then I see a box of suckers and take the entire box. "Thanks for the treats."

"Take all you want! Thank you for saving us!" the cashier says.

And suddenly, the gas station is filled with applause...

For me.

I stare at them like they're nuts. All I did was make a guy pistol whip himself.

"You saved my daughter's life!" a woman says. "Thank you!"

"Thank you!" a man says.

This is fucking weird.

And it makes me feel weird.

I quickly rush out to August's car, cradling my box of suckers and candy bars to my chest. I don't even know what to think of the whole ordeal. I mean... I really didn't even break a sweat and it took me all of what? Twenty seconds?

As I'm pulling away, August groans as he sits up. "What... happened?" he asks.

"You went in, you kicked their asses, they told you they'd like to carry your babies. It was a guy saying it, so it made it a little awkward, but I think you handled it well when you told him that you were in a committed relationship."

"I'm in a committed relationship?" he asks, sounding very, *very* confused. Why he thought that was the only strange thing out of the bunch, I'm not sure.

"W-We're married... oh my god. Did you forget that?" I ask as I grab my chest. "How could you treat me like this?"

"I'm sorry! It's okay!" he says as he pats my cheek, then sits in silence for a moment. "Wait... what? We're not married. You were driving like a maniac... that guy pulled out, and I smashed my head against the dashboard. Wait! Those people!"

"They're fine, the police got there first."

"Really?"

"Yeah, the gunman's been stopped."

"Why are you wearing my mask?"

Shit. I've gotten so used to wearing these dumb things that I forgot. "Fetish."

"Ah... your... mask fetish. I forgot."

"It smells like you."

"Oh god."

I start laughing. "Turned you on, didn't it?"

"I don't even know what's happening anymore, but I'm going to say yes?"

"Good. I like it when you're confused."

"I like it when you like it... yes."

"Should I take you to the hospital?"

"Oh god no. I'm fine. Do you want to know what else is fine? You're fine. Very fine. More than fine. I feel like I have no filter," he realizes.

"I feel like the right thing to do would be to take you to the hospital."

"I'm fine. Everything's coming back to me. I remember you checking me out and telling me to take my underwear off."

"That... never happened, but if you're interested, it could."

"Yes. Would you like to see my butthole?"

"I think we need to go to the hospital."

"Where'd you get all of these suckers?" he asks with wide eyes.

"I got them for you."

"Oh my god. You're the sweetest person I've ever met." He pulls a wrapper off. "Do you wanna lick my sucker?"

"Don't tempt me."

He starts giggling and I realize that I have broken the world's fifth-greatest superhero by smashing his head into the console. Eh, but he's still asking me to suck his sucker, so I'm digging it.

August assures me he's fine besides the slight headache, so I drive him back to his house. As I put the car in park, my phone buzzes, so I pull it out.

> Nolan: I'm really sorry about what happened tonight. I should have stood up for you. It wasn't fair of them to corner you like that when you clearly want nothing to do with it. I've talked to Marauder and he has agreed to withdraw your name from the group. You don't have to worry about it anymore. Okay? Again, I'm sorry.

I feel a small burst of relief. I hadn't realized I'd been upset about it until I got the text from Nolan. It was just that I knew, deep down, if I was caught up in their shit, it would stop me from ever getting to be with August.

> Me: Thank you. I'm glad you were able to talk him out of it. It's just not the right path for me.

> Nolan: The only path for you is filled with books.

> Me: Exactly! You know me so well!

> Nolan: And a hideous hairless cat.

> Me: She's growing on me.

> Nolan: Oh no. You're becoming love blind. Like severely blind if you think that thing is anything but ugly.

> Me: I feel the same way about my love for you.

CHAPTER EIGHT

My phone buzzes as I lie in bed curled around Zacia. The plan had been to stay in bed all day and pray that no one finds me. My parents already bugged me all morning, but my furniture blockades seem to be doing the trick.

> August: Happy Thanksgiving!

I can't keep the smile at bay as I stare at my phone.

> Me: Happy Thanksgiving to you too.

> August: What time are you meeting with your family?

My family doesn't "do" Thanksgiving. Instead, they get together with all of their supervillain friends and do stupid shit that has nothing to do with being thankful and a whole lot more with being greedy.

> Me: Just me and Zacia today. You?

> August: When do you guys do Thanksgiving?

> Me: We don't really have Thanksgiving. My parents are… strange. That's a kind way of putting it. They very strangely do weird stuff on Thanksgiving that I want no part of.

> August: Like a swinger's club?

> Me: Gross. No!

> August: Good, for a moment I thought I was going to have to join a swinger's club to save you.

> Me: Don't make me laugh. That was gross. No. Yuck.

> August: I'll pick you up at eleven for Thanksgiving at my house.

> August: If you want.

> August: That wasn't an order. I just want you to come.

I stare at the phone. He… wants me to come to Thanksgiving? With his family? That's a big jump. That's like… me having to be normal in front of *parents*.

My phone starts ringing, and I see that it's August, so I accept it.

"Hello?"

"Have I terrified you or turned you on by ordering you to do something?" he asks, actually sounding worried.

"A little bit of both. I'm not going to crash your Thanksgiving!"

"I… didn't think you would. I thought you'd come over, eat some turkey, drip gravy all over your hot body, scarf down some dessert, and play some board games."

"One of those was not like the others," I say. "What type of board games?"

He starts laughing. "Anything you want. Will you please come?"

"Shouldn't it just be for your family, though?"

"Maybe I want you there too."

I nod even though I'm on the phone in bed and he clearly can't see me. "Okay. Yes... I want to go. As long as you're sure and your family doesn't mind."

"My family doesn't care at all."

"Okay. You said eleven?"

"Yep."

"Do I need to make something?"

"Nope. I have that covered."

"Can I bring my cat?"

"I didn't know you could leave the house without her. Of course. My sister will love her."

We hang up and I get out of bed and take a shower. Then I fret over clothes since I hadn't planned on ever meeting August's family. I don't know if I have an outfit that says, "I'm a perfectly normal human being who wasn't raised by supervillains."

I pull on some black pants and start flipping through my button-ups. Since August could literally have just about anyone in the city, I feel like I need to look the best I can. Most of my clothes range from black to blue, so I find a lighter blue that looks a little more cheerful than the darker colors. Then I turn to Zacia who is looking a little boring in her pink and purple pajamas. It's not my fault she was born with no hair and as ugly as sin. Any time I take the clothes off, she finds the nearest heater vent and huddles on top of it until I cover her with a blanket. I find her a shirt with a pumpkin on it and pull it on. It even came with a little headband, but I'm not that sadistic.

When eleven comes around, the two of us are huddled in front of the door waiting for August's arrival. As soon as he pulls into the driveway, I rush out before realizing that I don't look very sexy running for him. I kind of look a little needy, if I'm being honest. Especially since I was already sweating a little from being bundled up extra early in my eagerness.

I slow down and strut out to the car like I think I'm hot shit, as he gets out of the car and comes to my side. Clearly, it's sexy enough that he's going to stop what he's doing and pull open the door for me.

"Did you hurt your foot?" he asks.

"Nope. Just my pride," I say as I scoop up Zacia and put her in the car.

He starts laughing. "It was a very sexy walk."

"Thank you. I try."

He closes the door before rushing around to his side like he can't be away from me for a moment. Or maybe I just don't want him away from me longer than a moment.

"Did you ask your parents about me coming?"

"I told them you were coming, and they got all excited."

"My parents would be really excited if you came over too." But they'd probably try locking him up or torturing him in some way. I can only imagine how disastrous that would be.

"I'll have to meet them sometime."

"Nah, you'll be better off without them in your life. Trust me. So... anyway. I dressed my cat up."

He chuckles. "You both look very nice. She's pulling off the no pants thing better, though."

"Ah, I can lose the pants, if you insist. I'll tell your family that you forced me to take them off, and I bet they'd instantly love me."

"And hate me."

I chuckle. "Fine. I suppose I'll keep them on."

"I *want* you to keep them on in front of my family."

"Now you're saying you don't want to see me without pants on? Am I not pretty enough for you?" I ask.

"You're too pretty, actually."

"Aw, you're cute too," I say as I pat his leg, letting my eyes run over his button-up and dark jeans. "You look handsome yourself. Did you dress up for me?"

"Well, I'd been planning on wearing sweatpants, so I'm going to say yes."

"Aw, Balzac, he likes me," I say.

"I do," he says with a grin. "You know that robbery the other day?"

"The one you napped through?"

"I didn't nap through it, you smashed my head into the dashboard."

I shrug like none of it was my fault. "You should have been sitting with your seat belt on."

"Probably. Anyway... you said the police handled it?"

"Yeah... I mean... I think?"

"The police said it was already handled by the time they got there."

"Hmm... That's weird. I just saw some guy pinning the robber down and assumed it was the police. Was it not? Ooh. Did something happen? I'm nosy. Tell me," I urge in the hopes of getting him off questioning me.

He shrugs. "I don't know what happened, you smashed my head into the dashboard."

"Yeah, well you asked if I wanted to see your butthole, so we're even."

He looks away from the road to give me a look of horror. "You're joking."

"No, I'm not."

"Did I?"

I start laughing. "Did you show me your butthole?"

He gravely nods.

"No, I gave you a sucker instead, and you were *mesmerized* by it. You kept asking if I wanted to suck your sucker then."

He looks mortified and I'm loving every moment of this. "*No!* Please tell me this is a joke."

"Nope. I'd never joke about anything as serious as sucking someone's sucker."

"Why did you even want to come with me today?" he asks. "I would never have been able to face you again if I knew this happened."

"I enjoyed myself even if you didn't," I say.

He's now more mortified about having asked me to suck his sucker than worried about anything to do with the mysterious person who stopped the gunman. So job well done by me.

"I've never done this," I say.

"Destroy someone's self-image?" he asks.

I start laughing. "No, I've done that. And how did *I* destroy your self-image?"

"You could have just pretended none of it happened or something. Let me live with this image of me spending a fun-filled time with you. What were you talking about?"

"Are you trying to distract me? Ah, that's alright. I was talking about meeting family or like... going to some gathering like this. You know, because my parents go to that swinger's Thanksgiving where the only hole they're stuffing isn't their mouth hole. Well... it could be, I guess," I say.

"Oh my god. You went from being disgusted to diving in."

I grin at him. "I know, right? Maybe I can get your parents to join."

That makes him look horrified all over again. "Nope. No. Gross. Disgusting."

"Hey, you're the one who said my parents were into it," I remind him as he pulls into the driveway and parks his car behind a few others.

"Never said that," he lies.

He gets out and I follow after him as I realize that I'm strangely kind of nervous. I'm rarely nervous.

Break into a bank?

Sure!

Battle off a crazed supervillain who has my cat?

No problem!

Take on a gunman?

Why not?

Face August's parents?

No thanks.

"Something wrong?" August asks.

"Are your parents evil?"

He grins at me like I'm cute for asking. "No, they're really nice."

That's the issue. I'm used to hanging around evil people. I feel more comfortable with evil people. This is a disaster!

"Hey," he says with a gentle smile as he caringly reaches out to me. "This will be fun. They'll really like you."

I nod. "Okay," I say, while wondering when he became a big fat liar. At least he's a sexy big fat liar.

He slides his hand into mine and gives it a gentle squeeze. Suddenly being involved in a dream I've had since middle school makes me forget about everything else as he grabs a bag and then leads me up to the house.

"I probably should have left the cat at home. Normal people don't bring cats to meet parents, do they?" I realize.

"You'll win my family over with the cat alone."

"Good. I use her like a shield," I say as I pull her close to me with one arm. The other is preoccupied with squeezing tightly onto August's hand.

August pushes open the door and it's like everyone's head is on a swivel as they turn to stare at us.

"August!" a teen of about fifteen or sixteen shouts. "I just volunteered you to mash the potatoes."

"When I wasn't even here to defend myself?" he asks.

"Look at the kitty!" she says as she rushes over to me and promptly forgets about August. "Can I pet her? Him? It? Whatever it is?"

"Sure," I say.

"Landon, this is my little sister Victoria. Mom, Dad, this is Landon. Landon, this is my mom Catherine and my father Arthur."

August definitely looks more like his dad. They share the same blondish-brown hair, although his is shorter, and dark eyes. His dad is wearing glasses and it reminds me that I should make August wear his glasses again. His sister has brown hair that looks like his mother's. It's almost fluffy with a light wave to it. But she still shares some features with her brother to the point where you can tell they're related.

"Nice to meet you," Arthur says as he comes forward and reaches out to shake my hand. My hands are preoccupied with the cat Victoria is fawning over and August's hand, so I grudgingly let go of August and shake Arthur's hand.

"Nice to meet you too," I say.

August's mom comes over and smiles at me. "Nice to meet you too. We've heard good things about you."

August talks about me to his parents? Why does this surprise me so much? And makes me almost giddy. *Me!* Giddy. Imagine if the supervillains saw me now.

"And what is this little cutie's name?" Catherine asks.

"Bal—Zacia!"

"Balzaci?" she asks in confusion.

"He named the cat Balzac but seems to be embarrassed by the name at the moment," August teases.

"Shush. I want them to think I'm normal."

"Because she looks like a ball sac?" Catherine asks, then starts laughing. "I guess she kind of does."

"I call her Zacia around other people, though. So... you can call her that."

"Can I hold her?" Victoria asks.

"Sure," I say as I pass her off. Zacia is purring and doesn't seem to mind, so I leave her with Victoria. I follow August and his parents into the kitchen that is filled with wonderful smells.

"We're almost ready," Catherine says.

I try to help August set the table but he just smiles at me and tells me to have a seat. I feel like I should be doing something at the very least, but I just watch him work and before long, we're all seated at the table with plates laden with food.

"So where do you work?" Catherine asks me as I cut into the turkey on my plate.

"Uh... I'm currently looking for a job."

"What kind of job are you looking for?"

"One where I can read books all day would be very nice. But I'm not sure yet. I'm not... hurting for money, by any means, so I'm just waiting for the perfect opening. Being picky, I guess."

"He lives in a mansion," August inputs.

"It's not a mansion!"

"When I helped him a bit ago he was all, 'I don't want you to see my quaint little house.' And then I pull up to this massive mansion."

"You're such a liar! It's not massive *or* a mansion. It's a house. Yeah, it has three stories, and this huge yard, and a hot tub, but it's still just a house."

He grins at me. "Uh-huh."

"You guys were in school together, right? Didn't you say that, August?" Arthur asks as I take a bite of the turkey. Why the hell my parents would prefer to run around like idiots when they could be eating food this good, I have no idea.

August points his fork at his father. "Yes! We both had crushes on each other, and Landon showed that by creepily staring at me when I wasn't looking, and I showed it by stuffing a teacher's car behind a tree."

"Oh, I remember that. That was a mess," Catherine says. "The teacher tried getting you suspended, and you were crying so much you could barely see to get the car out from behind the tree."

I start laughing. "Hold on, I didn't hear this side of the story. Go on, go on."

"Nope, that's enough," August says as he grins. "Let's keep playing twenty questions with Landon. Where were you born? How big were you?"

I snicker, especially because Catherine is playfully glaring at him.

"Since it's Thanksgiving, you should be thankful we've even included you," his mom warns him.

"Ooh, your momma's setting you straight," I say. "I like her."

"Just don't set me too straight or my interest in Landon will plummet," he says. "It's already plummeting since he's taking your guys' side."

"Hey, I haven't even been mean to you yet!" Arthur says.

August points his fork at him. "Yet. Right there's the word."

"Wait until we play board games. I'll demolish you. Do you like board games, Landon?" Arthur asks.

"Yeah, I guess. I never really played them a whole lot. My parents were more into like... cops and robbers and things like that." Like real cops and robbers. Where we were the robbers and the cops were trying their damnedest to stop us. It wasn't very hard when I could practically do anything with my power. I decide to keep that to myself. No better way to make the parents of the man of your dreams suspicious than by telling them any of *those* stories.

"Our goal when playing board games is to make August lose because he is suspiciously good at games. We're convinced that he's stopping time to cheat," Catherine inputs.

August innocently raises his hands up and it makes us laugh. "I would never waste my power of stopping time to cheat," he says, and he almost says it with enough conviction that I believe him. *But* I've lived with cheaters and liars and I know how to read a liar even if it's a little fib.

Interesting.

My little August isn't as perfect as he's leading us to believe.

Why's that make him so sexy?

Once lunch is over, they clean up the table and Victoria comes waddling into the room with a stack of board games. "What do you want to play first?" she asks.

"Yahtzee!" August decides, before leaning into me. "I'm really good at Yahtzee."

"Because he cheats," Catherine says.

"I would *never* cheat."

"He cheats."

"Once. I cheated once, and they'll never let me forget it. I was like five."

"It was a week ago," Arthur says. "A week."

"Don't listen to them," he says as he hands me a piece of paper.

"I've never played this," I say, and they all gasp at me like I've told them I'm a supervillain.

So they explain the rules by all three of them trying to explain at once, but I get the gist of it. August makes the first roll, and of course, he rolls three fives on the first try.

"I'm just naturally talented," he says as he puts two dice back and rolls again. One comes out a five and the other a three. The last try gets him a two. "See? Not perfect."

"Uh-huh," Arthur says. "I've got my eyes on you."

We play about a third of the game before I realize that August is either insanely lucky when it comes to this game or he's freezing time.

As his dice come tumbling out, I flip each of them with my mind until they're all on different numbers.

"Ha! Looks like your luck has run out," Victoria says as he scoops them all back up and puts them inside. When he throws them again, I flip them.

We do two rounds of this where I manipulate his dice yet leave everyone else's alone, making his winning streak take a severe nose-dive. Then on his third round, he tosses them down and when they all land on the very numbers he doesn't want, he turns to me.

"Someone else is cheating now," he says.

"Someone else? Does that mean you were cheating before?"

"No! I just mean because they kept *blaming me*. You're rolling the dice, aren't you? With your mind."

I grin at him. "No idea what you're talking about."

"You are evil!"

I give him a wink. "I'll take that as a compliment."

Victoria's eyes get wide. "Ooh, you're cheating to make August lose? Try harder. Make him cry. When he loses, he cries."

"I cried once when I was like two."

"It was last week," Victoria jokes.

"That one is not true. And I'm not cheating! I don't know why I'm so good at this game! I'm actually not cheating!"

Everyone stares at him, clearly suspicious.

"I'll admit, when I was younger, I did cheat *occasionally,* but I really haven't since I realized how amazingly good I am."

"Demolish him," Victoria says.

I start laughing as August flails around a bit, like waving his arms about will help prove his point.

"No! I don't want to be demolished! I'm being truthful!"

"Hmm..." Catherine says, and everyone starts laughing because she sounds very suspicious. "Let's tie him up. If he's tied up, and he freezes time, it'll be harder for him to do anything."

"Then how will I roll the dice?"

"One arm free," she decides as Victoria runs off. I grab Zacia's leash, more than happy to hogtie him if needed. I honestly couldn't think of a better way to spend the day.

"I feel like you guys are ganging up on me," August says.

"What are your guys' thoughts on a gag or tape over the mouth?" I say.

Victoria's eyes nearly sparkle at the thought.

"NOPE! Your Christmas present will vanish if you even try."

She sighs but wraps the rope she found around him a couple more times. But of course when we start up the game again, he keeps winning everything.

My phone beeps and I look down at it.

> Dad: Where are you?

> Me: At a real family's Thanksgiving.

> Dad: Sounds awful. When are you coming? We need your help.

> Me: I'm not.

I set the phone down and it immediately beeps again.

> Brandon: Why aren't you coming? We need your help.

> Me: Don't you ever just want a real Thanksgiving?

> Brandon: This is real. A real lot of fun! HAHA!

> Me: I hate you.

> Brandon: Come on.

I ignore him and that's when my phone beeps again.
"You're very popular," August says.
"All my men. Are you jealous?" I ask.
"Nope, because you're with me instead of them."
I grin at him. "True."

> Nolan: Mom and Dad are telling me to force you to join us. But whatever you're doing has to be better than this.

> Me: It's much better.

> Nolan: Have a good Thanksgiving. Eat enough for me. Right now, we're just starving because Wild Bill forgot to bring food even though it was "his turn."

> Me: I'm so full I can't even move.

> Nolan: You're the worst brother ever.

"My brother is starving to death."
"Your brother is going to the swinger's party *too?*"
"Both brothers."
"Your family is into some super kinky stuff."
I start laughing. "That they are."

August pulls into the driveway and puts the car in park.
"Do you... want to come in?" I ask.
He smiles at me. "I do."

I lead him inside and let Zacia loose. She trots off to her food bowl as I look over at August.

"Want to watch a movie?"

"Sure," he says as he follows me into the living room. I sit on the couch and pat the spot next to me. He sits down beside me as I pick up the remote, but I don't turn the TV on yet.

"Thanks for inviting me. I had a lot of fun," I admit.

He gives me a huge smile that makes me want to smile back. "Me too. I can't believe you cheated while playing Yahtzee!"

"I didn't like you demolishing us. I wanted to even the playing field."

"You did more than even it."

"Says the person who *still* won."

He looks extremely smug as he watches me.

"Don't give me that smug look." That's far too sexy.

He bites his lip and my eyes are drawn down to them. I want him to kiss me or do something more than the occasional platonic hug. I lean into him, in case he's just being overly polite and I'm not giving enough signals that I want him to devour me.

He leans toward me, hesitates, then just smiles at me. This man is driving me crazy.

I swing my right leg over his lap and sit down on him, facing him. "What do you want to do?" I ask.

He sets his hand on my thigh, then slides his fingers up, making me ache for more. "I want to kiss you."

"Then why don't you?" I ask curiously.

"I don't know. I feel like I've just blocked myself off from people for so long that I don't know what to do. The last few relationships I've had have been disasters. Not that I think you're in it for the money, since you're rich, or for my superhero status, since you don't seem to care about that. It's not you, it's me being an idiot and overthinking things."

I cup his face in my hands. He leans into them, thinking I'm here to caress his face. Instead, I give it a good shake.

"W-What the hell?" he cries.

"I don't want your money, and I don't want your fame."

"I'm honestly not concerned about that at all. I meant more that I didn't want to screw it up because I've been surrounded by these idiots."

I swallow hard because I can't help but wonder if I'm worse than them. I want August for who he is, but aren't I also lying to him? But what if I never go back to that life? What if I never do any of that shit again? I'll get a real job, and I'll tell my family I'm done with it for good. I've been teetering on that edge for years. This is the push I needed. So now I'll be done. I'll stop it all just for August. The only reason I've still done what I have is because I felt like it helped me fit in. If I didn't do all this villain stuff, would my family even care about me? The only time they treat me special is after I've done something wrong or bad.

"What's wrong? Now suddenly you look like you've seen a ghost," he says.

I lean forward and tuck my face against his neck. "I think I'm so deprived of normal human interactions and attention that whenever I'm with you, I want to give up everything else." *Just so I can be the person you think I am.*

He pulls me back so he can look me in the eyes. "Never change, Landon. What has drawn me to you all of these years was *you*. I don't want you to be like anyone else."

I nod, even though I want to tell him he doesn't know the real me. But maybe he does? Because when I'm with him, I feel like I don't have to try and be someone else.

"I think you should just take your shirt off or something because this shit has gotten heavy," I say.

He snickers. "Is that how you handle things? By making people whip their shirts off?"

"It is."

He shakes his head and leans in to kiss me. I press my lips gently against his before needing more of him. I open my mouth and feel his tongue brush against mine. Back in middle school, I dreamed of kissing August. Of course back then, my idea of a kiss was a little peck on the lips. And in these weeks since I met up with August again, I never imagined how good it'd feel to finally have his lips on mine. We're both pushing into each other, *needing* each other. It's like we can't get enough as our lips touch. My hands slide up his arms before one wraps around his neck and the other slips into his hair.

He pulls back and I want to complain, but I also feel a little breathless. He showers me with soft and gentle kisses until Zacia leaps onto the couch and squeezes between us. I grab her and pick her up so she's head level with August.

"My Balzac wants kissed," I say.

He snickers. "Oh?"

"Kiss my Balzac," I say.

He leans forward and kisses the top of her head.

I snicker and slide off his lap. Not that I don't want to go further, but because I feel like I need to tell him everything about myself before I do. But I'm not sure I'm prepared to do that today.

"I'm going to tell everyone you kissed my Balzac," I say.

"It was very soft."

"Thanks. I like to touch it every chance I get."

He starts laughing. "What else do you like to do with it?"

"I play with it," I say as I run my fingers along the couch and Zacia bats at them. "I also like to cuddle my Balzac while I sleep."

"You're a naughty boy."

That puts me over the edge and suddenly, we're both laughing. All previous worries have vanished as I make Balzac jokes that aren't even that funny, but he laughs for some reason, so I keep going.

I turn on a movie and he wraps an arm around me. We spend the next few hours watching movies and eating popcorn, and I'm honestly not sure if I've ever had a better day.

CHAPTER NINE

"No," I say the moment my mom walks into the house.

"You didn't even wait to hear what I had to say," Mom says.

"It's already a big fat no."

"Nolan told me about how you spent Thanksgiving," she says as she sits on the couch next to me.

I slowly lower my book. "And?" I stare at her with calculating eyes.

"I think it's great. I know we don't do things traditionally, but it doesn't mean you can't. So I thought it could be fun to do something as a family today," she says.

"What... kind of thing?" I ask warily. So very wary.

"Lunch."

Suspicious. "With a side of bank robbery?"

"No bank robbery."

Very suspicious. "A dash of car theft?"

Mom chuckles but shakes her head. "Nope. Just some good family bonding time."

I narrow my eyes. "Are you dying? Is this your last wish?"

"No, I'm not dying."

"Oh my god, you're dying."

"No. I just thought it was a good idea. So get dressed in something that makes it look like you're not homeless," she says.

I look down at my jeans and T-shirt. "What? What's wrong with my clothes?"

"They don't look cute on you, hon."

I glare at her before heading off to get changed. I pull on something a little nicer before rushing down the stairs. "I can't believe we're actually going to do something as a family that's normal. Where are we eating?"

"Where do you want to eat?" she asks as she leads me toward the door.

Zacia meows at me, but I decide it'd be best to leave her behind since, without August, most restaurants frown on her entrance even when she's wearing her flannel shirt. Which I think is ridiculous. So I give her a scratch behind the ears and continue on my way.

"I get to pick?" I ask in shock. I don't even get to pick where we eat on my birthday. Especially because last year for my birthday, they thought it'd be funny to have someone kidnap me. They only came out to tell me it was a joke after I nearly maimed the man. Once I set to work on maiming my family, they realized that maybe it wasn't the best joke after all.

"Sure!"

"Ooh. Like fast food or sit down?"

"Something nice."

"Steak house! I want to go to a steak house," I say.

Mom smiles, reaches over, and squeezes me to her. "You're buying, right?"

"Sure," I say.

She laughs and leads me out to the car. I get into it as my mouth waters at the thought of the steak and the delicious rolls the steakhouse has. "Is it just us?"

"No, your father and brothers are meeting us there."

My phone beeps.

> August: What are you doing?

> Me: My mom's actually taking me out to eat. Like this never happens.

August: I really want to meet these parents of yours.

Me: You're not allowed. What are you doing?

August: Waiting at the broadcasting station. I have to give a speech about peace.

Me: Can I write it for you?

August: Sure.

Me: Alright. Start off with: What's up, assholes? Y'all better straighten the fuck up or I'm bringing my crop next time and spanking asses.

August: You'd be the first one to do something wrong.

Me: Maybe that was my plan? To get you to spank me.

August: Anyone ever tell you that you're awful at speeches?

Me: How?! Fine. For real. Walk up and say: Yo, motherfuckers, I'm top man in this house. Any of y'all even look evil, I'm gonna rearrange your face.

August: You'd be the worst superhero ever.

Me: You don't even know.

August: But everyone would love you anyway because you're sexy.

Me: Aw. And when did you pick up lying? I thought you were saintly. I'm actually about ready to pass the broadcasting station. I'll moon you as I go by.

August: Wait until I can see!

> Me: Too late! This hot guy locked eyes with my butt cheeks. He's proposed to me. He's so rich. We're getting married tomorrow.

Mom clears her throat and tosses something in my lap. When I look down, I realize it's my villain suit. "You better put that on if you don't want to get recognized."

"Wait... what?" I ask as I look over at her. During my distraction with August, my mom had pulled her mask on and is now shedding herself of her outer clothes so she can pull her villain outfit on over her camisole. "I thought we were going out to eat?"

"Ha! It was a joke. We're meeting up with the gang to—"

"What the fuck?" I ask in disbelief.

"Oh, you should have seen how excited you were. Now get your outfit on unless you want to get your picture taken, and then that'll be everywhere."

"What?" I ask as we pass the broadcasting station. Instead of joking with August, I'm now overcome by these... stupid feelings.

Mom reaches over and tugs my mask onto my face. I can't even see because it's crooked, but I right it so I can glare at her. "We're going to have so much fun! Craig has this whole evening of fun planned. But it starts with breaking into this store and you're the only one with the power to do it."

"You just want my power?" I ask, voice rising. "That's all you want?"

"Honey, you're so powerful, and we couldn't do anything without you. I have the power of luck. How good is that when you can pick up cars and move things with your *mind*?"

I swallow hard as this sinking feeling hits my stomach. They have proven to me *again* that they are not a family. They just want to fucking use me and my power.

We're at a stoplight, so my mom reaches over and starts forcing my villain jacket on me. This one even has a cape that I can't stand.

"Why?" I ask.

She smiles at me. "I already told you! We're going to have so much fun!"

I'm overcome with so many emotions that I have trouble choking them all down like I always do. "Why don't you want me for me? Why do you only ever fucking want my power? If you drive me there and I do this for you, I will never *ever* do anything for you guys again."

She just chuckles. "You say that all the time," she says. "But you always come back because you secretly love it!"

That's when I hear a horrible noise and Mom slams on the brakes. I turn to look behind me as smoke rolls out from behind some buildings.

"Did a bomb go off?" Mom asks. "They did say that Chronobender was making a speech today. I wonder if someone bombed the station."

Panic fills me because August is in there.

I yank the door open, even though the car isn't completely stopped yet, and jump out. I stumble when I hit the moving ground but keep my feet under me, then run for the station that's about a block away. Smoke is rolling out as debris litters the street. Some people are running in terror, while others get out of their cars or nearby buildings and run for the broadcasting station, but I'm not sure what's left for them to do. The two-story building has caved in. The second floor is now almost one with the first and there's no way to enter the wreckage. Parts of the building are already on fire, and I know that I need to do something.

I yank out my phone as I run and quickly click on his name as my hands shake. I put the call through, but it rings and rings. When it hits voicemail, I pull up our chat.

> Me: Are you okay?
>
> Me: August?
>
> Me: August, please.

No, no, no. The only person who cares about me, who cares about who I am and who I want to be, can't die. But he's Chronobender, right? Surely he can't die just from this. But... it was a bomb. He's not like Brandon. He's not invincible. He could die. He could die so easily.

At first, I don't know what to do. I'm standing there, as unsure as the rest of the people, until someone shouts.

"It's Leviathan, I bet he bombed it!"

Me? They think *I* bombed it? Why?

Oh... that's right. Because I'm a villain.

I am nothing more than a villain.

"Get back," I shout. "Everyone get back," I yell as I hold my hand out.

I'm nervous. If I grab the wrong piece, will the rest of the building collapse and crush them? But I can't just sit here as the fire begins to worsen.

With my mind, I lift a piece of the roof and let it drop in the parking lot next to the building. It crushes a car, but I can't imagine anyone caring about that when there are lives at stake. I lift another slab, but it makes the support shake, so I grab onto the support with my mind, splitting my power between both of them as I lift them up and toss them into the parking lot.

I run toward the building now that I've cleared enough of a path to see. "August!" I shout, but I can't hear anything over the sirens and the people. A woman standing nearby is screaming something, so I reach out to her. "Do you work here?"

She cowers in fear. "Don't hurt me."

"I'm trying to get them out! Answer me!"

She nods. "I stepped out for a break."

"Was there anyone on the second floor?"

"I don't think so. Everyone came down to see August."

"Where are they at?"

"Middle area."

Praying that she's right, I focus on all that's left of the upper floor and lift it with my mind. It's a lot, and I'm not used to moving such weight with my power. I have to be careful and keep it steady to not drop it all and crush anyone who might still be alive. When the debris hits the ground safely nearby, I stumble as my head suddenly *throbs*.

Fuck.

"Help me," I say as I rush into what's left of the building. She hesitates before following me and we work together, clearing a path to the main broadcasting room, where I see a body lying on the ground. She rushes for it, but when she flips the person over, she pulls back as she looks down at the mangled body.

"I don't know who that is," she says. "Did he do it?"

"I don't know," I say. "August!"

"They should be in here!" she says before she's attacked by a coughing fit.

The fire is starting to thicken, and the smoke is making it hard to breathe.

I pull my cape up to my face, thankful for it for the first time. "Go outside. I'll keep looking."

She hesitates before backing away as a standing wall crumbles. I quickly grab onto it with my mind just before it crushes her.

"Go. Carefully, go!" I say.

"Thank you!" she says before disappearing in the smoke.

I stand amongst the wreckage. Smoke stings my eyes, and the fire's hot enough it feels like it's burning me even from this distance. I feel like I'm choking as I look around. Even if this place wasn't just a pile of debris, I don't know the layout. I don't know where I'm going. I keep moving piles and piles of stuff, but the pounding in my head worsens with each one. I've never pushed my gift to this limit.

"August!" I shout as something drips down. It takes me a moment to realize it's blood coming from my nose.

That's when my phone rings, and praying that it's August, I snatch it up. When I see that it's Nolan, I hesitate before answering.

"What the fuck are you doing?" he asks. "Do you want to die?"

"I have to find August."

"Shit... Just... you're not invincible, Landon. I don't want to see you die over him."

"I need to find him."

"Okay, okay. Um... I hear... something. I need fucking silence and these sirens and people are fucking loud... okay. Let me listen."

He falls silent as I look around me and realize that Nolan is trying to locate them by hearing their thoughts.

"Okay! I hear their thoughts. I can't tell how many, and I can't tell if August is there. They're just... chaos. I think... someone's thinking about a stairwell. They're hiding under a stairwell. Do you see stairs anywhere?"

"I don't know... it's so smoky," I say as my eyes water.

"It sounds like they're closer when I walk toward the middle. Maybe middle left?"

I look around, but I'm turned around at this point. "I don't know,

Nolan... I need to find him." That's when I see a sign for the stairs. "I see a sign!" I say as I run for it, and that's the moment something explodes.

It throws me off my feet and I slam into the ground, my ears ringing. Pain eats into my arm and side as I look around me. The stupid cape is on fire, so I try to pull my jacket off but it makes my arms scream since the fabric has been burned into my skin, and I nearly pass out from the pain. I tear my cape off instead and push myself to my feet. The explosion has made everything even smokier, so I just pull at the debris and the rocks until I finally see it.

The stairwell.

The roof has caved in, closing off the space underneath the stairs. I rush for it and press my hands against the slab. "August?" I shout.

"Landon? What are you doing in here? Find help! I keep pushing against it, but it's stuck on something. I can't budge it."

I look up and realize the slab that's crushing the stairs is jammed against a part of the wall that has fallen in. I hold my hand out and grab onto the wall and lift, but it barely budges.

"Fuck..."

"Landon, what are you doing here?" August asks.

"I'm sorry," I say, feeling so desperate. "I'm so sorry."

I take a deep breath and force the piece up, lifting it away from the roof and pushing it over. I have never felt this exhausted in my life. I could curl up and sleep right at this moment and barely anything could stop me from it.

"August, keep talking to me. I need you to keep me focused."

"Why are you still here? You need to get out! You'll get hurt!" he calls.

"I'm not leaving without you... I can get you out. I just..."

I stumble and fall into a slab of something. "Just please tell me you won't hate me. Please tell me that. It's okay if you never want to see me again and never want to talk to me again. Just please know that I loved every moment with you because you're the only one who cares about just me. I never lied to you... I never meant for it to go this far. I gave it all up. I'd give it up for you."

"What are you talking about?" he asks as I fight against the slab, but the moment I grab onto my power, my head screams and nausea nearly doubles me over.

"August, I need help. Push. Please, push against it. Have everyone help you."

I grab onto it with my mind and pull as hard as I possibly can. I pull and pull but only when August starts pushing does it finally begin to move. It teeters for a moment before falling and crashing into a standing wall. August catches my eyes and his entire body stills.

The look on his face kills me and I have never felt worse. The look he's giving me hurts worse than the burns on my body. I turn from him, unable to hold his eyes any longer. "We have to get out. We have to…"

"But that's Leviathan! He's probably lying to you!" someone says.

"I don't want to die," a woman cries.

I ignore them and keep moving forward, and when I reach the area where the explosion had knocked me down, I see that new debris has filled the path. August rushes forward, but I don't want him to burn his hands and it's small enough that I can push it to the side with a wave of my hand. On the other side are firemen who rush forward to assist the people as I stand there, confused about what I should do. Obviously, I should get out of the building, but then what? Run? I'm not even sure I could walk much farther. I feel like I can't breathe, my arms and side ache and my head is pounding so hard. And on top of all of that, I can't stop thinking about August who is helping the others.

I step out and someone immediately shouts, "It's Leviathan! He bombed the building!"

And then everything turns silent. The sirens stop. The world pauses as people stop moving and the fire stops flickering around us. There's a tug on my wrist and I look up at August as he pulls me away from the people stopped in time. Obviously, I've heard about this, but I've never seen it happen, since it's not exactly something to see. I didn't even know I could be conscious during it.

He pulls me past the people, down the street, and into an alleyway as my legs feel like they've forgotten how to work and my mind races and throbs. He's silent as he reaches up and pulls my mask down. I swallow a lump in my throat as my eyes start to water. I hurt so fucking much, but nothing hurts worse than the look August gave me when he first saw me.

The look he's still giving me.

I shake my head as I reach for him, but he shrugs out of my reach. "I'm not a bad person. Please—"

There's so much devastation in his expression. "You lied to me. Were you just wanting to get close to me? Find my weakness? Well, congratulations. You found it. It was you."

"August! Please! No—"

Suddenly, he's gone. Almost like he disappeared, but I know he didn't. He must have frozen time again but this time, he left me frozen with it.

My legs are weak, and I can barely hold myself up. I take a step forward and drop to my knees. I want to run after him, even if I end up arrested. Even if they drag me off. I want him to understand that I don't want this. I don't want any of this. I would get rid of all of this power if I could just be with him. With the only one who sees me as a person. But the pain is too much and the throbbing in my head too severe.

I see the shadow of someone as I collapse in the alleyway.

"Landon, what have you gotten yourself into?"

CHAPTER TEN

I wake coated in pain. My mouth feels dry as I open my eyes and look around to find my parents and brothers sitting in chairs around my bed. At first, I'm confused about why I'm here and how that happened. All I know is that I immediately feel annoyed about them being here.

My mom is the first to respond.

"Landon!" she says and everyone else turns to me.

Everything hits me at once. The pain throbbing in my head, Mom's betrayal, but most of all, August. Have I ruined everything by saving his life?

"Hey, baby," Mom says.

"Why are you even here?" I snap.

She looks surprised and confused. "What do you mean? Do you mean why are you here? You were hurt."

I just want her to go away. At this moment, I don't even care if I never see her again. "No, I just want to know why you're even here? You only want something to do with me when you're using my powers. All of you! Get out!"

She hesitates like she doesn't understand what I mean. "But, honey..."

"Tell me the last time any of you wanted me for something other than your bullshit? Nolan's the only one who even cares about me."

The door opens and a nurse walks in. She smiles at me until she reads the tension in the room.

"Nurse, can you escort those three out?" I ask, deciding that Nolan could stay.

She hesitates then nods. "Of course. Why don't we give him some room for now?"

"Landon, we..." Dad starts, but Mom nods and motions for him to leave. The nurse walks with them to the door and shuts it behind them, leaving Nolan, the nurse, and me in the room.

When she returns, she walks over to me. "Hey, Landon, I'm Tonya, and I'll be your nurse this evening."

"Can I go home?"

"You just woke up," she says. "Let's see how you're doing first."

"How long was I out for?"

"About an hour or two," Nolan says.

"Oh..."

"Tonya and the doctor are people I know. They're keeping your presence quiet, so it's not tracked back to the broadcasting station," Nolan explains. "I'm sure they're looking for someone with burns so they can trace it back to you and figure out your true identity."

"Oh... can I go home?" I ask.

The nurse smiles down at me. "Just hold tight. We will discharge you earlier than normal because... you're not actually supposed to be here and my shift ends in a few hours," she says.

"Good."

"How are you feeling?"

My head throbs. It hurts horribly bad. My leg aches as well but not as bad as my head and my arm. But I know that if I tell her it hurts and she ups the pain medication, she might not let me go home.

"Fine."

"Good, good. You have second-degree burns on your arm and first- and second-degree burns on your leg." She fusses over me some and then tells me she wants to monitor me for a little longer, before leaving.

"That was stupid," Nolan says once we're alone.

"That seems to be how I live my life," I say sourly. "Please, not you too. I'm so fucking sick of everyone. August was the only one who cared about who I was because he didn't know my other identity or what I could do. He cared about *me*. He wanted to be with *me*. Mom fucking lied to me to get me to meet with you guys. Fed me some... tale about going out to dinner as a family. And I thought we were doing something... something as a family but no, they just wanted my power *again*."

"Why do you hate your power so much?" Nolan asks as he sets his hand on my unhurt one. "I think... the issue is that you have this ability. This crazy powerful ability. I mean... you picked up a fucking building today, Landon. A *building*. Things that most people couldn't dream of doing. But you never use it... so I think people get a little jealous of what you can do. And no, they're not going about it the right way, but..." He takes a deep breath. "But why did you do it for August?"

"I was saving a life instead of stealing something. And August cares. He cares so much more than anyone but you."

Nolan looks away as he walks over to the window. "You could have died. It would have been so easy for you to have died."

"I know."

"It's a fucking good thing I could sense you or who knows who would have found you in the alleyway. August left you there."

"He didn't know how hurt I was."

And why would he care after what I did to him?

I'm thankful when the doctor finally lets me leave. The nurse insists on wheeling me out and Nolan helps me into his car. It hurts to sit, but it's tolerable.

"Do you want to stay with me tonight since I'm sure Mom's going to be hovering around your place?"

"Yes... but I need Zacia."

"I'll stop and get her. You make me a list, and I'll grab what I can," he says.

"Thank you," I say as he starts to drive. Every time he hits a bump, my head feels like it's going to explode, but I want it to hurt. I feel like I should be punished for all of the shit I've done. All the mistakes I've made. And for how much I hurt August. I should be in pain. I should feel worse than this. How many lives have I made miserable with my bullshit ways?

He swings by my house, since it's on the way, and rushes inside for Zacia and the few things I need. When he comes back, he sets her on his seat and she jumps on my lap. The light weight of her paws hitting the burn on my leg is excruciating, but I can't push her away. Instead, I pull her into my arms as tears begin to fall.

I hate myself. I hate this power. I hate the path I'm walking on.

I just want to be normal.

I've never wanted to be normal more than I do at this moment.

Why?

Why can't I be normal?

It's been two days since the bomb went off. I haven't looked into any information or heard anything else about it since I've asked Nolan to not speak of it. Instead, I've lain in bed and read or cuddled with Zacia.

There's a light knock on the door before it swings open and Nolan looks in at me.

"How are you feeling?"

"Fine."

"You can't just... live in bed and not eat or do anything. Does your head still hurt that much?"

My head is better, but the burns still ache, especially when I roll over or Zacia walks on them. She seems very upset and refuses to leave the bedroom without me.

"Come down to the kitchen. A little walk will be good for you," he says. "I have something to show you."

"I don't want to."

"No choice. Come on," he says as he pulls the blanket back and grabs me one of his zip-up hoodies since it'll be looser than my clothes. He helps me put it on and then motions for me. "Come on."

I grudgingly get up and follow him over to the door as Zacia trails after me. Nolan leads me into the small kitchen that connects to the living room. At the round table is a small Christmas present with a red bow. Christmas is still nearly four weeks away, and it's unusual for Nolan to get anything ahead of time.

He sets his hand on top of the box, the shiny red paper crinkling beneath his fingers. "You know... how I can read minds."

"Of course."

"It's... really hard for me not to. I have to really focus to not read the minds of my family members or friends. Once I know the person for a while, it gets easier to do. But when someone's in pain or their mind is in turmoil, their inner voice is like... screaming. It's so much louder than anyone else's."

"You're... you've been reading my thoughts," I realize. I'm sure that means he knows everything about August and me. But I at least trust him not to tell anyone.

"I've been trying not to, but it's hard when you're in so much physical and mental pain. But that... that doesn't matter. I was just trying to explain why I know that you hate your power. And how you wish you could get rid of it because you feel like it'll solve your problems."

He squeezes the bow, wrinkling it, before pushing the box toward me.

"This is...?"

"For you."

"You bought me a Christmas present?"

"Well... I don't... yeah, I guess. If you want it."

"You want me to open it now?"

"Sure."

I reach out, but his hand is still on it, so I hesitate. He smiles and pulls his hand back, so I grab onto the ribbon and pull. It falls free as I slide my finger under the wrapping and push it up. I pull the shiny red paper away before revealing a plain wooden box. I undo the hook in the front and push it open before looking in at a gorgeous snow globe.

Slightly confused, I pull it out and hold it in my hands. The stand is a deep red color and inside shows a child and a snowman with a gray cat perched on the snowman's head.

"It reminded me of Zacia," he says.

I smile. "It does." But this is very strange. "I'm..." Why would Nolan get me a snow globe? "Thank you."

"A man sells these... whose power is to grant wishes. Now I don't know if it actually works or not, so don't be upset if it doesn't. But he said that if you shake it while making a wish, that wish will come true."

I snort. "And you believed this?"

"Well... I don't know. But I thought the cat was cute, so how could it hurt?"

"Maybe your wallet? I can't imagine it was cheap."

"I stole Mom's credit card and paid for it."

I grin at him. "Then you should've gotten me two," I say, which makes him laugh.

"But only wish for it if it's truly what you want."

I stare down at the globe, honestly not believing a lick of it. But if I could wish my power away, would I? If I was no longer telekinetic, would August want me? Would my family stop using me? Would I give it all up to be with August?

I think I would. What good has this power ever done for me?

I hold it between both hands and give it two good shakes while wishing I no longer had this power. The "snow" swirls around, wrapping around the cat until it's almost a blanket of white before it begins to fall.

I watch until the last snowflake hits the bottom before looking up at Nolan who is watching me closely. I think about the snow globe rising and it instantly lifts out of my hand as my power holds it about six inches above.

"I don't think it works. But I really like it. Thank you."

He gives me a nod and a soft smile. "It got you out of bed, at least."

"I should have wished for a naked August."

Nolan snorts. "You have some strange wishes."

I smile at him before setting the snow globe down, my eyes searching it as if looking for answers.

When I wake up, my world is dark, but my phone is beeping from a text. I reach over and grab for it, accidentally smacking it off the nightstand when I do so. I hear it hit the ground and use my power to grab onto it.

When my phone doesn't automatically hit my hand, I'm confused before realization settles into me. For a long moment, I lie there, mind racing.

Could my power really be gone? Could I be normal? Could I have no reason for people to want to use me?

I quickly turn the light on, needing to know. I hold my hand out, aiming it toward the phone, and will it to me. Usually, it takes barely a thought and the phone would be there. This time the phone begins to shudder on the floor, but it doesn't lift more than an inch before tumbling down. I dive for it before remembering the pain and calming myself.

"Fuck, fuck," I whine as I wait for the pain to settle down. I pick the phone up and look at who it is. Of course it's Brandon.

> Brandon: For some reason I feel like you're mad at me.

I ignore it and grab some clothes. I carefully pull my sweats on and even more carefully pull a baggy hoodie on over the dressings that go from my hand to nearly my shoulder to help keep things from sticking to the seeping burn.

Nolan is fast asleep, since it's only three in the morning, so I snatch his keys off the table and head to the door. Zacia meows at me until I grab her and take her with me.

I don't even know what I'm doing, my mind is too groggy to be thinking straight, right? If I was, would I be rushing around like this?

I back out of the driveway as everything swirls around me. *Am I being rash? Am I being stupid? Did I really wish away my powers? Will I regret it? But if August forgives me, it'll all be worth it.*

I speed all the way to August's house, the entire drive trying to pick up things with my mind just in case I made a mistake. The most I can pick up is a paperclip off the floor, and even that, I can only lift an inch or two. When I pull into the driveway of August's house, my stomach is a jumble of emotions. I feel sick and excited, sad and elated, but most of all, nervous. I get out of the car on weak legs and Zacia jumps out after me. I feel like a newborn foal as I walk up to the front door, but I can't find the courage that made me drive here to knock on the door. Everything seems to have left me until I'm questioning what I'm doing.

So there I stand on his porch in the dead of night with Zacia rubbing on my leg. What am I doing here? August is too good for me. I don't deserve someone like August. After every wrong I've done, do I really think I should be allowed something like this?

I pick up Zacia as her purrs fill the quiet night air and turn around.

August deserves someone so much better than me.

"You're not even going to knock?"

I jump and turn around to see August standing with the door cracked. He swings it open and steps out onto the porch. "I don't know," I admit.

"Why'd you come if you weren't going to knock?"

It's an excellent question. "Because... I wanted to tell you that I lost my power," I say as I hold my hand over a rock and watch it quiver. "I got rid of it because I want to be the person you thought I was. I'm so sick of this power and of people using me for it. But more than anything, I want to be the person you think I am."

"I think you're a liar, and conniving, and a thief."

I swallow hard as I step back. I want to tell him I'm not, but it'd just be more lies.

He takes a deep breath as he rubs at his face. "At least that's what I thought when I realized who you were. I've had time to think about it... and if I still thought those things, I would have let you go back to your car and hoped you never returned. But instead, I stopped you."

"I don't deserve it. I don't deserve any of this. You're too good for me."

He folds his hands across his chest. "I saw what you did... they have recordings of you... of what you did to get me out. People already love you. An antihero is what they're calling you, and of course, they're wondering why you would save us. They're wondering if there was someone inside that building you cared enough about to risk losing everything for. Funny enough, they don't know it's me, but I do. I also know that you could have died going in there to rescue me. Not only that but everyone in the villain world *knows* that you saved me, a person that many of them have spent years hoping would die. There was a chance I might have died, but you came out and saved us all..." He takes a deep breath. "I was so pissed and upset... because you're a villain. At Superheroes United, we sat at a table and watched videos of your *power*, and my supervisor goes, 'With power like that, why has he never stopped any of us? He could rule the world.' And it's a very good question. Why isn't it you at the top of this city? No. The top of this world?"

Me? What a silly question. "I don't want to be a villain. I'm not sure I want to be a hero either, but I just want to be me. I was raised by villains, so of course I make bad decisions and do things that a villain might do, but I don't want to hurt people. Besides little things like those suckers and candy bars, I haven't stolen anything in years... I haven't done anything like that since you became a hero... because I began to realize how wrong it was and the thought that you would hate me if I was a villain devastated me. So I tried to be good. I used my power just for myself... at least I wanted to. But my family is so big on my power and being bad, and I felt like the only time they *ever* cared about me was when I was doing something wrong, but... I'm tired of it. I'm so tired of it," I whisper. "And then I met you again and you made me feel like there was more to me than this stupid power. So I got rid of it! My brother... knows this person with the power to remove it. I can barely lift a rock!"

"How is that possible?"

"I don't know, but it's gone, and now I can't be bad. I can just be a person. I can just be the same person you knew before. I can be the person you wanted me to be."

"I wanted you to be honest with me."

I bite my lip. "Could you have wanted me if you knew I was a villain? If I was honest from the beginning and told you exactly who I was?"

He opens his mouth before closing it again. And in the light leaking out from the house, I can see all the emotions on his face. "I don't know."

"What about now? You don't have to like me... just know that I'm sorry for all the pain I've caused you. And I'm sorry for deceiving you. Sometimes, when you're raised to believe that deception and lies are good things... it's hard to figure out when something is wrong."

He's quiet for a moment before stepping back toward the house, and my stomach sinks. "Landon... come inside where it's not so cold."

I follow after him as he holds the door open for me, and I set Zacia down the moment we're wrapped in the house's warmth. August shuts the door and turns to me before brushing my hair back, and I lean into his touch.

"You'd give up all the villain stuff? No more bank robberies, no more of that bullshit?"

"All of it," I say in earnest as I lean into the touch of his hand.

"How can I trust you?"

"Look at what I could have done with my power, but I didn't. Am I really a horrible person?"

He shakes his head. "No. It might take me a while before I can fully trust you again... but I want to."

"You're going to make me cry, and I'm not a very good supervillain if I'm crying. Wait... I'm not allowed to call myself a supervillain, am I?"

"Nope. So that means you can cry if you want. Heroes cry all the time."

"I sure as fuck am not one of those."

"That's what people are called when they save lives, Landon. And you saved a lot of lives that day. There are no other heroes in this city who could have freed us before the fires killed us."

He reaches for me, and in my moment of bliss, I forget about the burns and step into him. That is until he hugs me, making me jerk back. "Nope! No hugs! Well... you can hug my left side," I say.

"Did you get hurt?" he asks.

I try to wave him off while looking casual. "Nah, I'm fine."

He cocks his head and narrows his eyes. "You literally just took a pledge to not lie to me and you've broken it in two minutes."

I sigh. "Fine. I got slightly singed."

He pulls away and I curse myself for not putting up with the pain involved with the hug. "Let me see."

"See what?"

"Your slight 'singe.'"

"Uh... there's really nothing left to see," I say as he starts unzipping my hoodie. "Ooh. We've already gotten to the stripping part. This night started horrible and ended amazing."

He ignores me and pulls the hoodie off. I don't have anything on underneath but my burns are covered in dressings, so he can't actually see anything but the spot on my hand that is a first-degree burn and healed enough to not worry about.

"See? Beautiful. I was getting tired of this skin anyway since I'm so pale. I needed a little color."

"That's not how you get color. You get color by going outside and enjoying the sunlight."

"Ew, gross. How do you read outside?"

"Easily. What degree burns are these?"

"Like sunburn degree."

He peeks under the edge of the gauze closest to my wrist and then looks at me. "Landon! What happened? Oh god, and I just dumped you in an *alleyway*. I'm so sorry."

"You're so cute," I say as I pet his head with my left hand like I would my cat. "I'm fine."

"What happened?"

"It's from being around you. You're like the sun."

He glares at me. "Be serious."

"Something exploded when I was walking through the rubble to find you. I'm fine!"

"Did you go to the hospital?"

"My brother took me."

He sets his forehead against mine and takes a deep breath. "I'm so sorry."

"Stop fretting! I'm fine."

He pulls back and gives me a *look*. "What else is hurt? Truthfully."

I sigh. I hate this new truth stuff but I suppose if he's going to trust me, I need to be truthful with him. "I have minor burns on my leg. My face is fine because I was holding my cape up to protect my face from the smoke when it happened. Imagine if I lost this beautiful hair! And I have a raging headache because I've never pushed my gift so far. Like it feels like my brain would like to be crushed then ooze out of my skull but my eyeballs are in the way. Happy? Now, are you hurt?"

"No. I saw the man with the bomb so I immediately froze time.

He was a wannabe villain who thought he was making the world better by killing me. I knew I had less than a minute before time started again, and that it wouldn't be long enough to get everyone out of the building, so I thought that things would be okay if I could at least get them to the stairwell. So I rushed them under there, hoping that getting them behind two heavy surfaces would help. I really didn't have much time to think about any of it," he explains. "Time started up again and the bomb hit as I was dragging two people in. It threw us forward and that's when the roof fell in. Thankfully, my suit is fireproof so the blast didn't hurt me, and my body covered the two I was dragging."

"I want a fireproof supersuit."

"You don't need a supersuit if you're going to be nice and safe reading your book."

"True. I could just use yours when I need to like the last time."

Realization dawns on him. "You're the one who stopped the robber at the gas station!"

"I was. And I stole all of the suckers you suckled on the entire ride home. So now you're my accomplice villain."

"You're not a very good villain, saving people all the time."

"Just when I'm around you."

He kisses my forehead. "Thank you."

"Do you forgive me and want to devote the rest of your life to being my sidekick?"

"Let's... let things settle a couple of days first. I'm still kind of mad."

I pick up Zacia with my left arm and stare at him. I feel like a devastated expression while cuddling the cat works best. "Y-You're still mad?"

"Don't give me that look."

"Oh, the pain! It hurts so much."

"I'm sure it does hurt horribly bad, but I'm still slightly mad. Why aren't you lying down? You should be resting."

"I had to see you. But... I'll head home and be sad if that's really what you want."

"You could... sleep here if you want. But I still don't totally forgive you."

"Ooh, where's your bed?" I ask as I wander off. "Zacia, I got you a new daddy."

He sighs but doesn't correct me.

"And if he tries to run away, we'll tie him up and take him to my secret evil lair."

Zacia and I *both* like that idea. August sighs again, but he reaches back and holds his right hand out to me. I put Zacia on the ground and slide my fingers between his as he leads me after him. I follow him upstairs and into his bedroom where he pulls the sheets back for me.

"Do you need anything?"

"No, I'm fine. Really, it's all good until I have to change the dressings. That's hell, but it's getting better," I say as I carefully crawl into the bed. He climbs in next to me and shuts the light off.

"I'm really sorry that you got hurt. This is my fault."

"It was my choice to go in there," I say as I carefully move forward until I'm pressed against him, cautious to keep my right arm and leg away as I lie on my left side.

"I don't want to hurt you," he says as I press my bare chest against his.

"You're fine," I say as he slowly reaches out and presses his hand against my chest. I hug it to me with my left hand as I close my eyes. "Thank you for not giving up on me. Thank you for giving me a second chance."

"Thank you for saving my life."

As I lie there, pressed against August, his hand against my chest, I have to fight back the happiness I feel. I don't want to wake in the morning and find that he's decided that I'm not worth the work, but I can't help but let it all wash over me. Even the aching in my arm and head isn't enough to push it all away.

CHAPTER ELEVEN

I wake when my phone starts buzzing. I reach for it and pull it over to me, checking to see who it is. When I notice that it's Nolan, I almost ignore it before remembering that I might have stolen his car.

"Hello?" I grumble.

"Where's my car?"

"Hmm... somewhere."

"I need it to go to work."

"Huh. But I don't want to leave."

"I do because I don't want to be fired."

I sigh and feel August shift. I want to snuggle up against him, but any movement makes the burns feel tight and achy. "Fine, will you drop me off at home so I can get my car?"

"Sure."

"Thank you. I'll be back in twenty minutes."

"Make it ten if you need me to drop you off at your house."

I sigh and hang up on him since supervillains never say "bye." Then I slowly turn to August. "I have to get my brother his car." I tuck myself up against him, planning on forgetting about my brother. I feel like someone should have to drag me from this bed to get me to leave because life is much better where I'm currently at.

"Do you want me to take it to him?" he asks, because he's so sweet that I don't deserve to be in his heavenly presence.

The thought of August going to my supervillain brother doesn't sound good, so I shake my head. "I got it."

"You should rest. Will you come back here? I have the day off."

"I can?" I ask in excitement.

"Yes… but bring a litter box or something for your cat so she doesn't shit in my shoes."

"If Zacia wants to shit in your shoes, she can shit in your shoes. She's a villain cat, after all."

He raises an eyebrow. "Oh my god. Is that what she is? That's a thing for villains, isn't it?"

"Yep. Isn't she cute?" I ask as I slowly sit up. I always hurt the most in the morning. The skin feels tight and those first few movements are horrible.

"You're clearly in pain, let me take the car to your brother."

"My supervillain brother? Yeah, I'm not sure that's a wonderful idea. I'll be back and then I'm going to lie on the couch and pretend it doesn't feel like the skin on my arm and leg is trying to leave my body."

"I really think you should stay here. I'm fine meeting your brother."

Yeah, well, he doesn't know Nolan is part of The Rebellion.

"No, watch my cat."

"I'll go with you."

"Uh…" I have two sides battling inside me. The side that never wants to leave August, and the intelligent side that knows that I shouldn't take him to my brother. "Did you forget about the whole supervillain family thing?"

"Eh, I'm actually more used to dealing with supervillains than the family of the guy I like, so I call it a win."

I grin at him. "You like me?"

"Not as much as I did before you crushed my hopes and dreams."

I look over at him, but thankfully, he doesn't look mad. "Aw. I didn't crush them, I added a fun new layer to them! We're like Romeo and Juliet."

"We're both going to die?" he asks in alarm.

"Smart Romeo and Juliet."

"You're going to kill my cousin?" He seems less alarmed about this.

"I take it you don't like your cousin?"

"He's a bit of an asshole, if I'm being honest."

"I'm glad you've embraced being Juliet. You're just *such* a Juliet. Look how pretty you are, even when you wake up. You're like the women in the movies who wake up with their hair done and their makeup perfect. Now, I don't wear makeup, but if I did, that shit'd be all over everything."

"Especially your cat because I don't think you go an hour without mauling it."

"Are you jealous?" I ask as I walk over to my zip-up hoodie, since it's the only thing I brought. "Aw, how cute. Did you hear that, Balzac? He's jealous of you." Zacia is pretending we don't exist by continuing to sleep on the bed.

"If I was that ugly, would you like me more?" he asks as he gets dressed, like he thinks he's still going.

"If you looked like a ball sac? I don't know. I kind of like more than fuzz on my men," I say.

"Oh, so the only thing that'd be stopping our love is the amount of hair on my head?"

I snicker. "Maybe? And you're not going to my brother's. He probably doesn't want you to know where he lives anyway."

"He lives on Conner Drive."

I look at him in surprise. "Wait... how'd you know that?"

"We heroes know more than we let on."

"Seriously?"

"No, I just looked you up, and then I knew you had two brothers and the address for them was right in front of me."

"I thought you said you didn't look me up."

"That was before you jumped out of a pile of flaming ash and shouted, 'Surprise! I'm a badass motherfucking supervillain!'"

"But did it make me look hot?"

He snorts. "I think you need your brain checked. Did you get a concussion too?"

"If I did, it got forgotten about while my brain was shredded through a grater. And the skin on my body burned off."

"Is it any better this morning?"

"A little. Gosh, you're so sweet. Too sweet. Suspiciously sweet."

"I can see how someone who was raised believing that bank robberies and stealing were normal would think that."

"We also do these really stupid things," I say as I watch him find a shirt. I kind of prefer him without a shirt, but I suppose my brother might like the shirt on. "Like if we were on a bus as a child, my mom would make us each take a seat and then refuse to let anyone sit near us."

"That's awful."

"There'd be these little old crippled ladies staggering on and we'd have to glare at them and tell them to fuck off and find their own seat," I say. "I was like six."

"I don't know why that sounds so much worse than robbing a bank."

"But see, I was smart. I'd tell them that if they gave me something, I'd share. Most would just tell me to scoot over and whack me with a bag when I didn't move fast enough."

"I'm starting to see why you don't want me to meet your parents."

"Yeah, they're a bit strange."

"A bit?"

"Yep."

He laughs as he disappears into the connecting bathroom. We both get ready and head out to the car which he drives for me. I text Nolan to let him know that August is coming with me and that he already knew Nolan's address and to not lose his shit. And also ask him to grab a few of my things. And when he bitches about how late I am and how he doesn't have time to gather up my stuff, I ignore him.

When we pull up, Nolan is eagerly waiting outside and jumps in without a care in the world like August isn't inside.

"Do you know how long ten minutes is?" he asks.

"We rushed the whole way here." Besides the time where we just talked about Romeo and Juliet, but that was *important*.

"*Ten* minutes. Do you know how long that is?"

"Yep, that's the longest you've ever kept a girlfriend, right?"

He grumbles before looking at August who is still driving. "I remember you from middle school. Landon was always, 'Oh he's so cute! I can't go in there! *August* is in there and my heart can't take it.'"

I reach back and smack him before quickly regretting it since it tugs on my burns. "Dammit! You made me hurt myself!"

"Good! You shouldn't smack me when I'm being truthful! And then one time we saw you at a grocery store, and I was like, 'Just go say hi to him.' And when he wouldn't, I started to, so he took his power and slammed me into the wall while crying, 'I didn't brush my hair!'"

"I hate everything about you," I decide. "From your face, to your attitude, to your horribly accurate memory."

August just laughs and laughs. "That's alright. I did some strange things when I was young too."

Nolan snorts. "Oh no, that last one was like two months ago," he says.

"Don't listen to him. I'm cool and awesome and would've totally just strutted up if I'd ever seen you and been like, 'Want me to lick your banana?' and your heart would have exploded or maybe something else, and then we'd have probably gotten married right on the spot."

August looks slightly alarmed when he looks at me. "Wow... a lot would have happened if you'd have just brushed your hair that morning."

"I know, right? But now that you like me to the point where you've forgiven me for being a *villain*, this," I say as I wave to my body covered in sweatpants I've worn for days out of depression, a hoodie two sizes too big for me, and hair that hasn't been brushed since the accident, "is as good as it's going to get."

August smiles at me. "You're perfect in every way besides that supervillain lair of yours."

"Did you hear that, Nolan? He thinks I'm perfect."

Nolan leans forward like he needs to get a better assessment of August. "Clearly, both of you have had far too much brain damage."

"On our second date, I rammed his head into the dashboard so hard that he passed out," I explain.

"Why do you sound proud?" Nolan asks.

"Because! When's the last time *you* took a girl on a date and smashed her head into the dashboard?" I ask.

"Yeah, I would be arrested for assault."

"Maybe that's August's kink or something because he promptly asked me out again," I say. "He even asked if I would like a gander at his tush."

"Yep," August nonchalantly says. "Nothing gets me off more."

Nolan and I both start laughing as August pulls into the driveway of my house.

"All I can say is the sex must be really good for him to even want to stick around," Nolan says.

"We haven't even had sex yet!" I say.

"You really *are* a villain!" Nolan says.

I start laughing. "Maybe," I say as I get out with August. August takes my bag of stuff from Nolan before Nolan gets back inside the car and waves bye as he rushes off to work.

"Would it be more comfortable for you if we just stayed here?" he asks.

"Eh. My parents will probably bother us if we're here, so let's just grab some stuff," I say as I head inside.

The moment I step in, my parents and Brandon leap out from behind the couch and shout, "Welcome home!"

I just stare at them as August jumps into some type of defensive position in front of me, which is super cute. It's like he's planning on fucking up my family for me, while I'm so used to their shit I'm not even fazed.

I wave at them. "Here are my parents who have decided that the best way to greet an injured man is by scaring him. There's my mom, Patricia, and my father, Mark. The thing next to them is my brother Brandon. They were all dropped on their heads excessively as children. Brandon doesn't have an excuse because he's invulnerable, so no amount of dropping has damaged him, surprisingly enough."

Mom points at August while giving me "the look," like I haven't noticed the gorgeously hot man in front of me, and was instead introducing everyone to Zacia, who is trotting off for her food bowl. "Yes, Mom, I'm aware of the hot guy. I know, it's hard to believe I've hooked someone whose favorite pastime isn't switching the ketchup at local restaurants with hot sauce."

"Wait..." Brandon looks between us. "Is *that* what we were supposed to be doing? I was taking out the Heinz ketchup and putting the Walmart ketchup in its place," Brandon realizes. "No wonder why no one seemed to care!"

"Nolan and I took all the intelligent genes and what was left went into making Brandon," I say, even though he's older than me.

"Ah... it's nice to meet all of you," August says with a smile.

Everyone's still just staring at him. Until my mom says, "My special little boy finally found someone who can tolerate him!"

"We thought it'd never happen!" Dad says.

"Even I found love before him!" Brandon inputs, and I suddenly regret losing my power because I want to grab them all and send them flying out the front door.

"Wait... that girl you were going on that date with actually likes you?" I ask in disbelief.

He looks offended. "Of course! We started dating almost immediately!"

"Don't trust any of them," I warn August. "Don't let them get close, touch you, or feed you. The last part is because my mom doesn't know how to cook."

"I know how to cook!" Mom says. "Honey, how are you feeling? Do you still hate us?"

"Maybe a little more now that you guys broke into my house after I had the locks changed."

"I just melted the door handle," Dad explains.

"And you're going to also replace the door handle, *right*?" I ask.

"Nooo*yes*?" He doesn't seem too convinced.

"All of you are horrible people," I decide.

"He is injured, you need to fix it," Mom says to Dad.

Dad sighs like the thought of fixing *my* door that *he* broke is bothersome. "Fine, but you're paying for the doorknob since you never paid me back for the cat."

"You stole the cat!" I say.

"The guy was an asshole and kicked it!" he says.

"Why would you pay for a cat your father stole?" August asks.

"Because my father is money hungry. Why would he melt my doorknob? No one knows. Alright, you guys can leave. Thanks for... nothing, I guess."

"I brought you some stuff and put it on the counter," Mom says.

"Let me guess... a new villain suit, something stolen, or something that'll cause bodily harm?"

"You're such a kidder. Now get feeling better," she says as she walks up to me and gives me an air hug. "So I don't hurt you."

"Thanks."

She jabs August in the chest with a finger. "You break his heart, I'll sic the entire SAVCGEM team on you," she threatens.

"That is...?" August asks.

Mom looks mortified that the superhero in charge of real crimes knows nothing about their weird little make-believe villain club. "Super Awesome Villains Combined for the Greater Evil of Mankind, of course!"

"Of course!" August says. "How could I have forgotten about SAVA... SAC...uh... that thing that's so heinous I can't even say it out loud without shuddering!"

"That's right," Mom says. "We're watching you."

"It's wonderful to meet you," he says with a smile.

She instantly smiles back. "You too. You were the cutest little kid back in middle school when Landon was fawning all over you. Then when you became a superhero, Landon made me buy him all the posters of you. He told me it was so he could throw darts at them, but instead of darts, there were tissues lying *everywhere*."

"Oh. My. God. Kill me now," I groan.

"Even when you went through that ugly little gangly stage where your limbs looked like they were too big for your body, Landon was all into it," she says.

"August, stop time, please! End my misery!"

"Is that what he was doing up there all the time?" Dad asks. "He made me buy him your dolls. You know, like those action figure dolls that look like Barbies? He told me it was to practice popping your head off, but who *knows* what he did with those things."

"I hate all of you," I say. "With a passion."

"You two have fun now, but not too much fun," Mom says. "You don't want to get some seed or something in those burns. Actually... I know nothing about burns. So maybe it's good for it."

"Seed?" August asks with raised eyebrows.

I just walk away, feeling that drowning in the sink would be better than these last few moments.

"My girlfriend says it makes her skin feel soft," Brandon supplies, and I hurry off as August follows me.

I can never look at him again.

"Hey, it's okay," August says as I slam my bedroom door behind us. "Everyone's parents are a little embarrassing."

I turn to him with extremely wide eyes and open my mouth, before realizing that no words can fix any of this.

"All I want to know is if you're part of the Super Awesome Villain group, and did you change the ketchup to hot sauce?"

"I just... yeah... I am. I feel like lying gets me nowhere at this point. My parents made me an honorary member, and why didn't you freeze time and just leave during any part of that?"

"I was taught in hero school to *never* be rude. Smile, wave, and the biggest thing of all, never get a boner."

"Oh, that's nice."

"Yep. No face tattoos either."

"Ah, makes sense," I say as I walk over to my bed and climb into it before curling up under the covers where I can hide from him.

The bed dips a bit as he climbs in and gently presses his front against my back. "Hey, I think your family's kind of funny," he says, voice soft in my ear.

"You can never let them know that or they'll get horribly worse," I say as I look back at him. "You seem strangely okay with all of this. Like it's just any day that the guy you kind of like turns out to be surrounded by super-stupid supervillains."

"Maybe that just shows you how much I like you."

I roll onto my back so I can look at him without craning my neck. "Why?"

"If we ignore the childhood crush thing... I guess the first thing that stood out to me was that you didn't care who I am. You can't even imagine the number of people who treat me differently because of who I am. I could get them fame, or money, or... I don't know. You... clearly don't seem to care about any of that. If you did, you wouldn't have been jerking off to posters of me as a fifteen-year-old."

109

"Oh my god. I was not! Just leave and let me never leave this house or this bed again."

He snickers as I glare at him. "Alright, alright. I'll stop."

"You better."

He watches me for a moment. "Can you still not use your power?"

"No," I say as I hold my hand out and aim it for a book. The pages flutter, but that's it.

"How?"

"I don't know. My brother knows this superperson who supposedly can grant wishes. I really don't know. Sounds suspicious as fuck, but I was depressed, and it was in the shape of a snow globe, so I immediately wanted to shake it."

"A... snow globe? You don't find any of this suspicious?"

"Don't care."

He watches me for a moment. "You don't care that your power is gone?"

"No. I... used to love my power but more and more I began to associate it with negative things, and I began to hate it. I just felt used all the time for it. I felt like my family only cared about *it*. I was really tired of it and then this stuff with you happened. If I still had that power, could we easily be together? I mean, it's not like I could have ever used it being with you. If *anyone* saw it, they'd automatically figure out who I am after that last incident and that would make your life so much harder."

"I just... don't want you giving up a piece of yourself for me, Landon."

It makes me overwhelmingly happy how much he cares. "I didn't do it just for you. I did it for myself. I did it to make myself happier. I am, after all, lazy. And I can be even lazier now that I don't have to help anyone."

"But you'll have to get out of your chair to turn the light on and stuff."

"That's why I have you," I say.

He smiles at me before kissing my forehead. "True. Are you hungry? I'll go make you breakfast."

"I can make it."

"You need to rest."

"I don't like being seen as weak. Just lazy."

"Then be the laziest you can be while you rest, and I'll make breakfast."

"Make sure my parents are gone and they didn't set up a trap or anything for you first. If they did, just shout your safe word."

"Which is?"

"Bubble berry ball sac."

"Oh. Okay. Glad I asked."

"I'll come slowly shuffling to you if I hear it."

"Good to know."

He gives me a smile before leaving the room and I realize that even after he's long gone, I'm still smiling even though it feels like my skin is dying. What did I do to deserve something as wonderful as this? All but the skin dying thing.

After breakfast, August leaves for a little bit, and I'm afraid he's not coming back. I'm like a dog at the window waiting for him. The moment he pulls into the driveway, I rush off to act like I haven't been obsessed.

As soon as he comes inside, he finds me in the living room and walks over to me before kneeling down. "So... I might have nabbed this from Superheroes United's medical facility. It's not made public yet because they're still trying it out, but basically it's an ointment that a superhero with healing powers made. He's found that his power adds to things like this to create a salve that will help people heal faster. So I thought you could try it on your burns."

"You stole this... for me?" I ask, eyes wide.

"I did. My manager would skin me alive knowing I'm giving this precious stuff to a villain," he says with a grin.

"Thank you."

His smile turns soft. "I just want you to get better. It's not magical. It won't clear it up instantly, but it should heal it about twice as fast."

"That means a lot to me."

"You saving all those people meant a lot to me."

I lean into him, glad he's semi-forgiven me.

CHAPTER TWELVE

I'm living in bliss. Absolute, undying bliss because August *likes* me. He really likes me. ME! The nerdy kid who only ever read books has hooked the hot kid who was nice to everyone and loved by all.

"What's wrong with you?" I ask as I sit at the table with a fork in one hand and a knife in the other. It's been over twenty-four hours since I forced myself back into his life. He had to work today, but after work, he came straight over to my house and declared that he would make me supper.

"What do you mean?" he asks as he looks up from where he's frying chicken in a pan on the stove. I realize that I look a little food deprived with my fork and knife at the ready, so I set them down. What I really want to do is eat him up—or have him eat me up—but I still hurt too much for anything of the sort.

"Like... you're handsome, sweet, caring, and funny, and for some reason, you picked me."

"You mean because you're a supervillain? Ex-supervillain. You do realize you're all of those things too?"

I cringe back, thoroughly disgusted. "No! Take back those heinous words. I am evil and conniving—"

"And sweet, and caring, and funny, and definitely handsome."

I scowl at him. Villains don't like such disgusting words. "Why *did* you forgive me so easily?"

"I haven't forgiven you."

"Liar. If you hadn't, you wouldn't have rushed over. You even said you didn't get off work until five, yet there you were at four. And then you just start making me supper? Gosh, you're so cute it hurts my tiny little villainous heart."

"You're not a villain, remember?"

"Oh. But I kind of like being a villain. Are you controlling me? Are you telling me what I can and can't be? That doesn't sound very hero-like. Only a manipulator controls someone like that."

He turns to me, opens his mouth, closes his mouth, and narrows his eyes. "You're conniving, aren't you?"

Why's he so cute? "Thank you."

"It's not a compliment."

I grin at him. "Is to me."

"Do you need help changing that dressing on your arm? You refused to let me help yesterday, and it looks like a two-year-old put it on."

"I've actually decided I'll never change it again. It's a non-stick dressing, but it feels like you're ripping your skin off when you take it off. It's really fun."

"Sounds fun," he says as he comes over and scoops some chicken, onions, and peppers onto my plate before putting some on his.

Why he isn't butt-naked wearing an apron, I'll never know. Maybe because I don't have an apron, but he could be butt-naked. "Looks good. Gosh, you're so cute. I should have brainwashed you sooner... I mean... wooed you."

He narrows his eyes. "Did you snow globe me too?"

"I rubbed that ball real good while wishing you were naked. While maybe you were naked at the time, I was highly disappointed when you didn't poof right in front of me, balls flopping and dick a swinging."

"Huh... I can't imagine why that didn't work."

"I'd have rubbed your globe if you needed me to," I say.

He snorts. "How about you get better first."

"That," I say as I point a fork at him, "sounds like a good idea.

Today is the first day where my brain isn't complete mush. Today it's more of a cottage cheese consistency."

"Sounds just as bad."

"Nah! It's good. Especially with you here."

He smiles at me. "I'm glad."

I pick up my fork and stick a piece of the chicken into my mouth while beaming at him. The moment it touches my tongue I realize why August has never found true love. He's poisoned them all.

"Is it alright?" he asks with a beaming smile.

I'm not sure if I can even open my mouth. Can I trust myself not to cough or gag? Spewing chewed-up chunks of chicken does not sound sexy or even villainous, just downright nasty. So instead, I try to make a positive grunt like an "uh-huh" or even a "hmm," but it comes out a little strangulated and reads much more like "I'm dying. Tell my family that they're assholes."

"Did I put in too much salt?" he asks as he takes a bite and instantly chokes, and I suddenly feel really good about myself that I can keep something like this in my mouth without gagging.

I swallow it, give him a smile, and go, "Yum!"

He looks at me in disbelief. "Oh my god, you're such a liar."

"I was born and raised to lie! It's like a family trait. When the hot guy makes you supper that tastes like it came from the depths of hell, you grin and bear it, all in the name of love or lust or like. Or whatever I feel for you at the moment. It changes depending on whether you're wearing your glasses."

"Wait, what? You really do have a glasses fetish, don't you?"

"All I'm saying is that maybe if you had your glasses on, you wouldn't have dumped half of the spice cabinet into the frying pan. And even if glasses couldn't have saved you, you'd have at least looked hot doing it."

He shrugs, like he's just giving in at this point. "True! Try the baked potato. All I did was wash it—"

"Ooh! And then?"

He starts grinning at me. "I wrapped it in Saran Wrap."

"Oh!" I moan. "And then what? Tell me! Please! Please!"

"Stuck it in the microwave."

"You know how to get me hot and bothered."

He snickers. "You're welcome."

I take another bite of the chicken, causing him to look alarmed. "You don't need to eat that! It's awful!"

"But you made it for me, and no one's ever made me food before besides like my mom and that was just so I didn't starve to death. I think it's... really, really nice even if it makes me feel like death is breathing down my neck."

"That started off nice and just went to shit after that. But please, please don't eat this."

"I see now why you made me toast for breakfast yesterday."

"I'm good at toast."

"It was delicious."

He smiles. "Thank you."

"I have an idea. Now hear me out," I say as I go to the fridge and grab some ranch dressing. I pour some on my plate then dunk the chicken in it. It's *almost* enough that I can't taste the chicken. "Much better."

"Gimme."

While we eat, August tells me about his day, and I love hearing every moment of it. Especially because he sounds like such a badass and it's so hot. I might have a fetish for August's action. My day consists of reading, so I don't have as much to talk about, but he acts like every moment of it is interesting.

When we finish eating, I grab my plate, but he waves me off. "Don't you have to soak that dressing to get it off? Isn't that what you did yesterday?"

"Yeah. It's fine. I decided I'm going to let the arm rot off."

He raises an eyebrow. "I'll clean up supper. Go get a bath or whatever, and I'll come in and help you."

"Ooh, while I'm naked?"

"However you want me to help you."

"I want you to come in wearing your supersuit and shout, 'I'm Penetratorman!'"

"Ah yes, Penetratorman will be coming to rescue you."

"Coming." I snicker.

He snorts. "Go take a bath."

"Fine! I suppose I'll worry about what I smell like *just* because you're here. If you weren't here, I'd probably still be wearing the sweats I've worn for days."

"Call me when you're done."

I hesitate before looking at him as he dutifully washes the plates off in the sink. "I actually can't take a bath alone. I need help."

He drops the plate he's holding, and it hits the sink with a loud clatter. I think we're both surprised it doesn't break.

"Like..." He slowly turns to look at me. "Help... washing?"

"And undressing. My clothes are really hard to get off. And *then* washing."

"You were fine this morning."

I narrow my eyes and he snickers.

"I'll help you."

"Good," I say as I reach over and take his hand, pulling him away from the dishes and after me into the bathroom. Inside, I let go so I can turn the water on before turning to him. I thought he'd be hesitant since he's never really a go-getter when it comes to this stuff, but he steps up to me and starts undoing the top button of the flannel I'm wearing. As he slides his hand to the second, I can feel the pads of his fingers trail down my chest, making me shiver. He continues down my chest to the next button.

"I still don't understand why you forgave me. Am I really worth that much?" I ask.

He looks up, meeting my eyes. "I'm not sure why you think you're not."

"Because superheroes and villains are never supposed to be together."

"Who says who can and can't be together? We're both human. You've never hurt anyone, *physically* hurt them."

"No, I wouldn't do that. I don't like hurting people. I like fucking with them. That's a lot of fun, but not at the expense of their well-being."

"See? So how are we both so different?" he asks as he slides the flannel off and gently pulls it from my bandaged arm. As he watches me, he runs his fingers down my chest. "We both have skin, a heart, and a brain. We're not so different from each other. I make mistakes. I make bad choices too—it doesn't make me a bad person, just like it doesn't make you a bad person."

"You're too perfect to make mistakes."

He snorts. "I'm not," he says as his hands slide down to my waist. "Pants off?"

I nod. "I kind of wanted you in your supersuit the first time you saw me naked though," I say. "I had this dream about you rushing up while I'm tied up to a bed and you shout one of your superhero lines and rip the headboard off to free me."

He raises an eyebrow. "Is this... another of your fetishes?"

"Maybe... maybe not. You never know."

"I think I have a good idea," he says as he slides my sweats down so I'm only standing in my underwear. His eyes drop to the dressings on my leg. "You lied."

"Shhh, sweet creature. I have a penis that is much more interesting," I say as I push my underwear down.

"You said only your arm was burned and your leg was very lightly 'singed' like a sunburn."

"Huh. That's weird. But you should be so blinded by my penis that you don't even notice."

He stares me right in the eyes.

"Penis?"

He snorts.

I sigh and climb into the tub before sitting down since the only reaction I'm getting out of him is not one I want. He shuts the water off as I lower my bandaged arm into the water to help soak it so it's easier to remove the dressing.

"Is the ointment helping?"

"I really think it is. It feels better, at least, since using it."

"I'm mad at you again," he informs me as he kneels next to the bath.

"You haven't even *seen* my leg. It might be completely fine. Maybe it's wrapped up just because I want you to dote on me."

"You're so difficult," he says as he grabs my face in his hands and pulls my head toward him. He kisses my forehead before gently wrapping his arms around my body in a way so he doesn't touch my arm. "Thank you."

"No thanks needed," I say as I press myself into him. "You just owe me."

"Deal."

"Hee hee... you have no idea what I'm going to request of you."

He reaches down and gently squeezes my left hand. "I don't care. Whatever it is, it'll never make up for what you did for me."

I narrow my eyes. "Shh... don't be all sentimental and stuff."

He pulls back, and I grumble but let him go. He takes the showerhead off and tips my chin back as I grin at him.

"I feel so special," I say.

"You are special."

I grin wider.

"You also look like you're up to something while grinning that maniacally."

"Nope. Completely innocent," I say as he runs the water over my head.

He grabs the shampoo and massages it into my hair. I never knew a head massage would feel so good. Or maybe it's just being pampered by August. He rinses the shampoo out and instead of grabbing a washcloth, he squeezes the soap onto his hand and slides his fingers over my chest. The feeling of his fingers and my desire for something more makes my cock begin to harden. He runs his fingers down my stomach, making me draw in a breath. His hand moves through the water, trailing down my leg as I ache for him to touch me.

He leans in and takes my face in his hand, tipping my chin up as he presses a gentle kiss against my lips. I open my mouth and lean into him, needing more. He pushes back, tongue against mine as his fingers run over my thigh before reaching up and drawing a finger across my lower stomach. Then his hand slides down to my cock, a finger wrapping around the base of it. I moan against his lips as his fingers close around me.

"Have you soaked enough?" he asks.

"Definitely," I say, not caring in the slightest.

He pulls away from me as he reaches over and unplugs the drain. He grabs my towel and dries my hair as he guides me from the tub. I'm getting water everywhere, but the moment his mouth presses against mine, I realize that I don't even care. I'm so drawn into him that I could flood the bathroom at this point and not even bat an eye, *especially* when his mouth presses against mine.

He eases me down until I'm sitting on the edge of the tub and he slides the towel down, running it over my body until it brushes over my cock. I reach around with my left hand and undo his pants. It's hard pushing them down with just the one hand, but I manage to get them down enough that I slip my hand inside and pull out his hardening cock.

I slide my fingers up his thick cock, loving the inhale of breath it causes him. "I'm not a left-hander, so it's not my fault if I squeeze your dick off."

He chuckles. "Just let me handle things. I want to make you feel good," he says as he kneels down, cock pulled away from me. He kisses my lips now that he's level with me and I press into him, wanting all of him. When he pulls from me, he runs his lips down my neck to my chest. I grab onto him as his mouth moves farther and farther down as he takes my cock in his hand. That's when he runs his tongue along the base, making me inhale sharply. His tongue moves over my cock as his mouth wraps around the head, and I moan. I slide my good arm around him, gripping tightly onto him as his free hand wraps around his own cock.

His tongue swirls around the head before sliding down and sucking. The moment he looks up at me, I nearly lose it. Just seeing him kneeling before me, my cock in his mouth, is driving me crazy. I ball up his shirt in my hand, gripping tightly to keep myself from falling off my thin, wet perch.

He sinks down my cock, making pleasure rush through me. I grab tighter onto him so I don't slide off the slippery seat and plummet back into the tub while gagging the man of my dreams with my penis. I look down at where he's stroking himself and slide my hand down his back. His head bobs on my cock until I can't take much more. I can feel his moans, the vibrations making my cock ache.

"I'm going to come," I say, but he doesn't pull away. He takes me in deeper and I groan as my balls tighten.

I grip tightly onto him as I come in his mouth and watch his cheeks hollow and his throat move as he swallows it. I don't know why it's so damn hot, but it's all I can think about. He slowly presses into me as he comes. I draw him up to me so I can kiss him and touch him. I want more of him, but I know I'm being too reckless when I grab on with my right arm and bump my burns into his arm.

"You alright?" he asks as he pulls back. He must have noticed my grimace.

"I'm fine. I just smacked my arm. I'm good. Very good. Too good," I say as I pull him in and kiss him again.

Breathless, he pulls back and smiles at me. "Let's get you dried off for real and actually do what we came in to do."

"I don't know about you, but this was a much better thing to do."

He snickers as he grabs my towel. "I agree. Do you need to soak your arm again?"

"No, it's still wet enough. I've gotten water everywhere."

"That might've been my fault," he says.

He dries me the rest of the way off and helps me into my underwear. Then he sets to work unwrapping the gauze from around my arm.

"I can do it."

"I know you can, but you wrapped it so badly earlier that it was already falling off."

"No. I'm better than that."

"Eh."

I cock my head. "What's that mean?"

He gives me an innocent look. "I can't imagine!"

"Don't sass me, boy. I'll spank your ass so damn hard."

"Oh? You're acting awfully tough when I can stop time *and* I'm stronger than you."

"Ooh, what are you planning to do when you stop time?"

"Maybe find someone to help me come to my senses?"

"That sounds like an awful idea," I say as he assesses the dressing on my arm.

I grab it and start to pull. It's painful, but at least it's more tolerable than it'd been earlier in the week.

He looks really upset when he sees what's been hidden beneath the bandage. Honestly, the burns look a lot better. The ointment he'd given me really was healing it quickly. But the look August is giving me tells me that maybe I should have done this alone. "Why have you been running around and pretending you're fine? I'm so sorry."

"Shush your beautiful lips. It was my choice to run in there for you, not anyone else's. No more complaining. Got it?"

"Fine," he says as he kisses my forehead.

He runs his fingers down my face, then sets to work on helping me change the dressing. He's super careful, and I'm secretly glad he's helping so I don't have to do it all myself. I know my parents would help, but sometimes I feel like they're so unreliable that when I need them, it's hard to count on them. Growing up, it never seemed like I had mature parents that I could rely on. Instead, it was like being surrounded by children. It's nice having someone there for me besides Nolan.

CHAPTER THIRTEEN

"How much do you like me?" I ask August as he sits beside me on the couch. He'd been reading a book that I forced on him while I read the third book in the series.

"Like on a scale of one to ten?"

"Yeah, that works."

"Eh... I don't know... sometimes a ten, sometimes a one."

"When would it be a one?" I exclaim.

He grins at me. "Depends. I already told you that."

I poke him in the side.

He waves the book he's holding. "Like right now, the dog just died in this book. I'm *pissed* and you recommended it, so it's taken our relationship down to a one."

"Ooh, just wait until her entire family dies." I make my eyes go wide. "Oops. That was a spoiler."

"You liar."

I just grin at him as his eyes slowly narrow.

"Are you lying?"

My grin widens even farther. I have to look manic at this point. "I don't know. *Am* I?"

He slams the book shut. He's so dramatic. "You're like a demon wrapped up in a sweet exterior."

"Ooh, keep talking dirty to me," I say.

He just shakes his head. "So what were you needing?"

"Needing?"

"I was thinking you needed something."

"Oh. *That*. I was already trying to block it from my memory. But... I need to talk to my family and it's going to be an absolute disaster, so I was hoping..."

"I'd stop time so you could escape if it gets bad?" he guesses.

I give him a huge smile. "Yes! You're very smart, and it's so hot."

"Aw, thanks, babe. If you want me to go with you, I can."

"I do and if anyone says anything stupid, punch them."

"Generally, if I punch someone, it really hurts them."

"Sounds perfect."

"Oh... well... okay."

"But I want it to look like I punched them, so like, I'll wind my arm up, you freeze time, punch them, then when time starts up again, they'll think I did it."

"Deal."

"My brother is invulnerable, so full strength. It won't hurt him any more, but it'll make me happier."

"Got it."

I grin at him as he shakes his head. "We're a match made in heaven, you know that, right?"

"Somehow, I believe you're right."

Since we're already at my house, I decide that we need to just get it over with. It's like ripping off a Band-Aid but attached to the Band-Aid are three infectious viruses that should, really, be put out of their misery. I pull up a group text that my family uses to harass and irritate me.

> Me: Will you guys come over? We need to have a talk.

> Mom: We were already heading over. Your father is driving. Don't ask him about the bandage on his hand. He'll go into this long spiel about hurting himself while battling off a superhero.

> Brandon: That was AWESOME!!!!! I can't b leave he popped a bitch u no?

> Me: Brandon, what have I said about you not texting with your stupid slang that makes no sense?

The front door slams open and August leaps into the air. "Holy shit, that was fast!" August says as my father drops the doorknob he just replaced. It's a melted slab of metal now and falls to the ground with a clatter.

"The door was unlocked!" I yell.

"I told you to check, Mark!" Mom shouts as she smacks Dad.

"Were they just... hovering outside the door?" August asks as he stares at them like they're alien beings.

I'm pretty sure they are. "I don't even question them anymore."

Dad holds his bandaged hand out before him, flipping it this way and that. Clearly, he wants me to ask what happened to it, but I refuse. Mostly because I don't give a shit. August doesn't understand the protocol yet and says, "What happened to your hand?"

Dad instantly perks up, and I can tell he suddenly likes August a whole lot more. "Oh! Let me tell *you*. So here I am, minding my own business and this superhero comes up and just starts *attacking* me. And we began to fight with—"

"He cut his hand while opening a pickle jar," Mom interrupts.

Dad turns on her. "Dammit, woman! You promised not to repeat that!"

She shrugs. "Shouldn't have been annoying me then."

He stares at her in disbelief. "How did I annoy you?"

"Just looking at you annoys me."

"Yes, yes, such a lovely display of affection, can we talk?" I ask.

"Of course, hon. What are you wanting to talk about?" Mom asks.

Dad comes over and pats me on the back. "Aw, the last time we had a talk, he came out to us!"

"Came out about what?" Brandon asks.

"That he's gay."

Brandon cocks his head. "You're gay?"

I look over at August, who I'm practically sitting on as he holds me to him, then to my brother. "Oh... that's right. He was in jail when I came out, and I forgot to tell him later. Brandon, you've seen me with guys! How have you not figured this out yourself?"

"I just thought you were really close friends!"

"Do you usually kiss your close friends?" I ask.

"I have! How long ago did you tell Mom and Dad?" he asks.

"Probably about ten or twelve years at this point," Dad says.

Brandon looks shocked. "What?" Poor simple Brandon.

Mom doesn't seem too concerned about her middle child. "Guess if you were better at staying out of jail, we wouldn't keep secrets from you."

"What other secrets are you keeping?" Brandon asks.

She shrugs. "Too many to remember, honestly."

His eyes go wide. "But Landon knows?"

"Landon knows just about everything," Mom says, which shatters Brandon a bit more.

"Just because my skin is invulnerable, it doesn't mean my heart is," he whispers.

I feel slightly bad at this point, but then within seconds, it's gone. My level of care is very brief when dealing with Brandon.

"So what did you want to talk about?" Mom asks me.

"Have a seat," I say.

Dad pushes the loveseat so it faces us and sinks into it. Mom sits next to him and Brandon looks around for a place to sit, so I point at Zacia's cat bed that she is far too prestigious and precious to use. The only place she's happy with is my lap or August's.

Brandon sinks down on it, engulfing it with his body.

"What's going on?" Mom presses.

"I want to have a serious talk," I say. "I'm tired of all of this shit. I'm tired of this family. I feel like you guys *only* care about my power. You only want to do something with me if you're using me. I just want you guys to be my family. I want to be able to rely on you or have you there for me when I need you, but you never are. None of you are ever there for me."

"Oh, honey, of course that's not what we think!" Mom says.

"Mom, you lied to me when I thought you finally were wanting to do something as a family. I was so excited to do something with you guys, and *again* it was just to use my power. Do you all not even care about me? Do you only care about this villain bullshit and powers? I'm so sick of it. Do you know how disappointed I was?" I ask.

Mom quiets down. She opens her mouth, clearly thinking about defending herself, but the look I give her makes her think twice.

"Try to prove me wrong. Try to give me a single time that you guys have wanted to do something with me that hasn't involved using me."

"But honey... I thought you enjoyed it!" Mom says.

I stare at her in disbelief. "At what point have I *ever* acted like I enjoyed anything? Why would you think any of this would be *enjoyment?*" I ask. "Do you want to know why I would join you guys or agree to help? Do you want to know why I did anything? Because I felt like my power is the only reason you care about me or the only time you want to be with me. So I would just suck it up and do what you wanted because I was afraid that if I didn't, you guys wouldn't want me."

Mom leans forward. "Honey, you know that's not true!"

"How the fuck would I know that's not true?" I ask. I feel desperate, almost shaky. Like I don't know how to handle this. Maybe I'm as big of an idiot as they are. I always fall into their ways. I give in to them every time just because I want something more from them. Something I can never seem to find.

August reaches over and takes my hand, squeezing my fingers gently. And it fills me with so many emotions. It makes me remember that I'm not alone. There's someone beside me who cares about what I feel and what I'm going through.

I take a deep breath and look over at him as he gives me an encouraging look. I don't know how it gives me so much strength, but it does.

"I got rid of my power," I say as I look at them.

There's disbelief written across all of their faces. "You did what?" Dad asks.

"My power is gone," I say as I hold out my hand to demonstrate. "I can't lift anything. Sometimes I can make light things shake, but most of it is gone."

"Why would you do that?" Mom asks.

Brandon is staring at me in shock. "You were so powerful. Why would you get rid of that? Why?"

I don't want to have to explain myself. "Because it's done nothing but cause me issues."

Mom looks at me with wide eyes. "But your power is—"

"My power is what? What is there to my power? What do you like more, me or this goddamn power? Well guess what? It's gone. I got rid of it, so what are you going to do about it?" I squeeze August's hand, needing his power to get me through this. Not the power that makes him different, but just the power of him caring, him being there for me, him wanting me for who I am. "Decide at this moment what you want. If you are going to stay with me and care about me, then there will be no more talk about my power. You will stay here just for me. But if you're going to judge me for my decision, then I want you to leave."

They sit in silence for a moment as they process what I've said. I'm waiting for them to complain. I've prepared myself to fight them. To not sit still and let them go on and on about what I've chosen to do and why I would do it.

"I'm sorry," Mom says quietly.

"But you know we're just having fun," Brandon starts.

She holds up a hand to stop him. "No... I think Landon is right. Sometimes, we get too caught up in ourselves," Mom says as she stands up and walks over to me. She kneels down and sets her hand on my knee. "I'm sorry. I guess when I saw how disappointed you were the day of the bombing... and I was scared when you went inside that building. I was scared you weren't going to come back, and they wouldn't let me go in. I sent Nolan as close as he could to help you. I was terrified you were hurt or worse and... then when Nolan found you... I realized how serious it was, and I regretted not doing what I promised you. You'd been so excited, and I realized what I did wrong... I'm really sorry."

For a moment, I'm confused. She's *actually* apologizing for what she did?

"Really? Like... it's not a joke this time?" I ask. "You're not... this isn't..." I don't even know what to say about it. I don't even know how to take her apology. I'm pretty sure she's never apologized in her life, so why would she apologize now?

127

She squeezes my leg before quickly pulling back. "Oh, did I hurt you?"

"No, that leg is fine. I'm fine..."

"I'm really sorry that we've made you feel this way. We've just..." Mom looks back at Dad.

Dad looks between us before nodding. "You have so much power. Power that... all of us would love to have. And here you have it and you want nothing to do with it. So I guess... we kind of just... used you because of that."

"I know. I know I have all of this power but what do I *do* with it, you know? I don't want to be bad. I don't mind these stupid little things you guys do but... if the Rebellion knew about this... can you imagine what they'd do? I don't even know if any of you understand what I can do. But now, I don't have to worry about it. And August doesn't care what I do or what I have, and I love it so much."

"I'm sorry that we've made you feel this way," Mom says.

"I understand," Dad says. "I get what you're saying, and I'm sorry for being so close-minded."

"What's wrong with you guys? Is one of you dying? Am I dying? Why are you being so compliant?" I ask, suspicious of them. Someone has clearly replaced my family.

Mom squeezes my leg again. "Because when you weren't coming out of that building and Nolan couldn't find your mind, everything hit me. I was terrified something happened to you. And so relieved when you finally got out. And then talking to you today made me... rethink some things," she says softly. "Your father and I talked about it as well. Okay?"

I nod.

"I'm sorry you felt like you had to get rid of your power to be accepted," she says. "We never meant to make you feel like that."

"Okay."

"I'm sorry it took so much to get us to understand."

"It's okay... I'm just glad you understand."

"Do you want me to make you supper? Will that make you feel better?" she asks.

I look at her in horror. "No, I would prefer to not be poisoned if it's up to me," I say, which I feel is the gentlest way possible to explain that her food is borderline toxic.

"I've been getting better!" Mom says.

Dad is quickly shaking his head, telling me that she hasn't.

"Nah, August already fed me," I lie. August isn't allowed to feed me anything. He's just as bad as her. I guess he can't be perfect.

After they annoy me for an hour or so, they eventually leave. Brandon tells me the cat bed is more comfortable than the blow-up mattress he's been sleeping on and asks if he can have it. Since my cat wouldn't get caught sleeping in something as lowly as a cat bed, I let him have it. I feel like it makes up for never telling him I'm gay.

CHAPTER FOURTEEN

"Get that sweet ass into the outfit I laid out on the bed for you, we're going on a date!" I announce.

August warily looks up from where he's been reading the blurb on the back of my book. "I'm all for the date, but you're dressing me?"

"I am! Now snap to it," I say.

He shrugs and sets the book down before heading toward his bedroom and I follow after him. He walks over to the bed where my old supervillain suit sits. He picks it up and stares at it before looking at me.

"What... is this?"

I grin at him, overly excited about the upcoming events. "My mom bought me a new one. This is my previous one from before the fire, so it might be a little tight on you, but put it on anyway."

"If we're trying to go somewhere where you don't want my face seen... I can wear like glasses and a hoodie or something."

Ah, what a fool! Like he'll get out of this that easily! "Put it on," I urge as I hurry into the bathroom. Once in there, I open the bag of "necessities" my mother caringly got me. Which includes a new super-suit. There's nothing inside the bag to help me heal or even like a can of chicken noodle soup so I don't have to cook for myself. Nope. Just a new supersuit.

They're such idiots.

But I kind of love them.

And even though I'm complaining, I did just put on the suit they got me. The top is ridiculously tight since my mom always thinks I look best when my clothes look like a second skin. She told me that's how I could "Get the boys." So I carry it into the bedroom where August has already pulled the other skintight pants and shirt on. The outfit he's wearing is older, so the colors are different. The pants are lime green and the shirt a very bright yellow, like I would *ever* wear either of those colors. When I told my mom that a suit should help me blend in if I ever have to get away, she looked flabbergasted.

But now that it's on August, I realize that it was all worth it. He's about six inches taller than me so the pants are highwaters on him, sucking so tightly onto his skin I can see the outline of... everything. The shirt shows a thin line of stomach that makes me grin manically since I never imagined August in a belly shirt.

"Is this a joke?" he asks as he raises an eyebrow and gives me a grin.

"Oh gosh, I wish I could make a joke this funny, but no, it's not. Can you help me into my shirt?"

"What are you up to?"

"It's a secret!" I say as he steps up to me with a super suspicious look on his face.

But he's clearly naive or love blind because he holds the shirt out and helps me slide my bandaged arm through. It's been a little over a week since the accident, so it won't be long before I can get rid of the dressings. It's still hard to get this tight outfit on over them without his help if I don't want to risk ripping them off, and I have to work the sleeve up so it's not putting pressure on the wounds.

"Who came up with these outfits?" he asks.

"My mother. She makes supervillain outfits. Nice, huh?"

"Um..." He's trying to think of something nice to say. He's so cute. "Colorful," he decides on. "Why do you get the dark blue one?"

"Because you're the sucker who tugged the neon one onto your body." I walk up to him and set the mask on the top of his head and pull it down. It's a half-face mask, so it covers everything above the lips, including his hair, which will keep people from recognizing him.

"Are you ready?" I ask.

He sure doesn't look ready. "For what?"

"To go."

"Go where?" he asks.

"On a date."

His eyes get even wider. "Wearing... these?" he asks as he waves to his orgasmic outfit. It's beautiful, so I pull out my phone and snap a picture of him.

"Turn around."

"Right now?"

"Yeah," I say as he willingly turns because he's gullible and easily distracted.

And I was right. His ass looks *fine* in those tight pants.

"Put your hands on the bed and look over your shoulder at me. Then rawr like a wild cat."

He set his hands on the bed, making his ass pop as he looks over at me. "This good?" he asks.

"Yes," I jokingly moan as I lift my phone. The moment I go to snap the picture, he screws his face up into this ugly expression and he makes his legs bow-legged. "Dammit, August! Be sexy! I want to sell these online and get a lot of money. This is masturbation material for August fanatics! And me."

"Snap the picture," he urges.

"No, it'll give me nightmares," I cry. "I am *wounded*. Now give me that sexy ass."

He sighs, but he must feel guilty because he gets right back into position, allowing me to snap a picture. Then I see Zacia and scoop her up before turning August around and putting her in his arms.

"Pose again!"

"You're so needy," he says as he takes the cat, but the moment I go to snap a picture he pretends to bite her ear.

I start laughing. "Don't eat my Balzac! Fine! Let's get going since you're so difficult," I say as I head out while he carries my cat. He follows me out to the car where I start driving.

"I'm very concerned about where we're going," he reminds me, in case I'd forgotten.

"Good. Just keep your mask on and everything might be alright," I say.

"That sounded like a threat."

I chuckle. "Maybe it was. Did it turn you on?"

"A little bit."

I'm loving this so much and I don't even know why. "Good. You'll have fun. I promise. If anyone asks your name, it's Sue."

"Oh."

"Do you not like it?"

"Oh, no no! I love it."

"Good! I'm glad," I say as I drive. We talk some, but it's mostly filled with August expressing his worry and confusion about me abducting him. There's also some wedgie picking that he tries to stay on top of that is quite distracting.

I pull into a parking spot and get out while August stays in the car. When he's still not out, I go around to his side and watch as he locks the door.

"I'm scared," he calls out.

I start laughing as I pull my keys out and unlock the door. "Don't be frightened."

He acts like he's reaching for the lock before jerking his hand back. "I'm scared."

"Shh, my sweet angel. Don't fret," I say as I pull open the door. "Don't you want to take a walk on the evil side?"

He shakes his head. "No."

"Of course you do," I say as I take his hand and I pull him out. He cuddles Zacia to him, like that'll protect him, while letting me lead him. I take him through the front door of the building and down the hall to an open room filled with about ten or so people.

Everyone turns to look. Most are confused, especially my parents as I direct August into a seat. But no one is more confused than August.

"What... are we doing?" he whispers.

"It's a date," I say. "I promise, you'll be entertained."

"Uh... huh." I can't *fathom* why he sounds suspicious.

My father walks up to the front of the room before clapping his hands together once. "It looks like we... have a new member! Newest member, welcome to SAVCGEM!"

August quickly turns to me. "Oh my god. Am I in a villain meeting?" he whispers.

I can't help but grin. "You are!"

"Are you crazy?"

"A little, but you like me anyway, right?" I ask.

"I do. But still!"

"Let's bring our newest member to the front of the room to introduce himself!" Dad calls.

"Yay!" Ravengirl shouts.

"Fresh meat!" the elderly man, Baker, declares. "Don't worry, I don't bite... hard!"

Everyone laughs. Literally everyone. Full belly laughs as August looks over at me.

"What is happening?" he asks.

"Come on, he wants you to introduce yourself," I say as I pull him after me to the front of the room. "Hey, evil people! This is my friend, and he's really *really* eager to see what we do here at Super Awesome Villains Combined for the Greater Evil of Mankind. So I thought, what better way to show him than to bring him?"

"If you try to leave, we'll give you the raisin cookies!" Buzz shouts and they all snicker like it's a good threat. I suppose that if my mom made them, it would be an excellent threat.

"What's your villain name?" Baker asks.

While it probably wouldn't be a super huge deal if everyone figured out it's August, I think it'd be best to keep him hidden at the moment. No one here, besides my parents, know that we're dating. And everyone always wears villain suits anyway.

"Uh..." August looks over at me.

"It's Moistman," I announce. "He'll get you wet with just a look."

"Oh my god, what are you doing?" August whispers.

"Hi, Moistman!" Buzz calls out.

"Moistman! Moistman!" the rest begin to chant. It sounds satanic, but I'm *loving* it. I need August to feast his eyes upon the insanity that is my life so he can truly understand my pain.

My father turns to him. "Moistman, since you are an honorary member of SAVCGEM, we would love for you to pick our evil deed for the week!"

Poor August looks very concerned. "Uh..."

And there he is, the city's hero with all eyes on him, completely at a loss for words. He looks over at me and raises an eyebrow as I grin at him.

"It can be anything!" Ravengirl says. "My choice was two weeks ago, and we all went over to my college and popped the tires of my professor's car because he's a dick and kept looking at my chest when talking to me."

"Anything," I urge.

"Uh... why don't you choose for me?" he suggests.

"Nope. This is your day to shine."

"I... want to..." He looks around at the eager faces. "TP someone's house?"

"Ooh! Good choice!" Mom says as she claps her hands. I can't tell if she knows it's August and doesn't care, or if she thinks I was actually able to make another friend, but she's all in. "Do you have a house in mind?"

"I do!"

"Ooh! Let's go!"

"But what about the cookies that I made?" Darling, a lady in her late thirties who is currently having an identity crisis, asks.

"No one likes your cookies, Darling. They taste like an old crusty dish rag," Baker croaks out as he grabs his cane. "Let's go!"

August turns to me, eyes unbelievably wide. "What are we doing?"

I grin as everyone rushes toward the door, and when I see that no one is looking, I lean in and kiss him. "Enjoying life. Letting loose. Embracing the crazy. Just one night. They're stupid as fuck, they claim they're villains, but they're basically harmless. Come on. Let's go TP someone's house."

He grins. "It sounds strangely fun... letting go a bit. Doing something a little wrong."

"Right?"

"Yeah! Let's TP my manager's house."

"Ooh, naughty. You're such a bad boy."

"What are you going to do about it?" he asks with a grin.

"Spank that sexy ass," I say as I give him a light smack on the ass. With the tight bodysuit on, it makes a very nice noise. "I don't think I spanked you hard enough."

"No!"

"I could play the drums on that ass. Be a one-man band."

"Or a pervert."

"I like that too," I admit as I lead him through the door and out to where everyone is having a super-secret meeting.

"Let's hit up Walmart on State Street with our powers combined!" my father says as everyone puts their hands in like we're in a children's TV show that runs during the hours where no one watches it.

"Get in here, Moistman and Leviathan!" Ravengirl says, so we squeeze in and put our hands in. Usually, I'm so annoyed by their antics, I just ignore them, but what the hell? I guess I can be a little crazy every now and then as well.

"On the count of three!" Dad shouts.

"Three!" Mom adds in.

"Two! Brandon says.

"One!" Dad shouts.

I shout, "Penis!" as everyone else shouts "Super Awesome Villains Combined for the Greater Evil of Mankind."

August just mumbles.

Mine is clearly superior.

Instead of taking separate vehicles, my mom insists we go together because breaking the law is the cat's pajamas in her eyes. So we all head over to her SUV. I pull open the back and wave August inside as he looks at me in amusement. Baker pushes August out of the way and crawls in next before patting his lap.

"You can sit on my lap, kiddo," he says. "I promise not to poke you."

August stares at the elderly man in horror.

"He's talking about his knife collection. I know he sounds like a huge pervert because he informed all of us last week that he's found a drug called Vagra, which I'm assuming is Viagra."

"Ooh, I have, and my wife can barely walk when I'm done with her," he says proudly.

"That's because your wife is as old as dirt," I say as I push August in before crawling onto his lap. I'm probably crushing his leg, but I don't even care because nothing sounds better than being as close as possible to him.

"Isn't this horribly illegal?" August asks as all of us cram into the tiny vehicle.

"That's the point, kiddo," Baker says. "I take it you haven't been a villain for long?"

"Just... doing a trial," August says as I sit happily on his lap while cradling Zacia. I lean into him because he smells ridiculously good as I wrap my unhurt arm around him.

"I'll sit on your lap!" Brandon says to Baker as he climbs into the back.

"Brandon, you'll crush his lap!" I say.

"But... Where should I sit then?" Brandon asks as he looks at the already packed vehicle.

"Just hang on to the bumper. If you're still there when we get to Walmart, then I guess you can go with us," I say as I try to reach for the hatch with my mind before I remember that I can't do it. I *really* wanted to close Brandon outside it. Being mean to my brother might be the only thing I miss from having my power.

Brandon reaches in, picks up Baker, and crawls in while holding Baker like an infant. "I fit!" he says as he pulls the hatch shut and slams it on Baker's head.

"Holy cock cakes!" Baker yells as he grabs for his head.

"What happened?" Brandon asks as he reaches for the hatch again.

I would just let him keep at it, but I kind of like Baker and it looks like Brandon is preparing to bash his head in again. "You slammed it into his head, you idiot!"

"Ooh. Yeah. I was wondering why it wouldn't close!" he says.

"What's a cock cake?" August whispers.

"I don't know. He tries taking a dirty word and a normal word and combining them because he thinks it makes him look villainous," I explain.

August nods. "Taint toaster, that makes sense."

I snicker as I squeeze him tighter to me and snuff his hair, since he smells so good.

"You're holding me tightly and breathing heavy. You alright?" August asks.

"Yes! Thank you for asking," I say as I loudly sniff him which makes him laugh.

He squirms a little, so I lock my legs over his. "I'm starting to wonder if this is really a date or a hostage situation."

"What makes you think that?" I ask as I stuff my nose against his neck again.

He shakes his head and says, "I can't escape!"

"Good! You're mine now!"

"Wait... this is a date?" Baker asks. "If my wife took me on a date like this, I'd marry her on the spot!"

"Aren't you already married?" Brandon asks.

"I'd marry her again."

"Are you marrying me on the spot?" I ask August.

"Hmm..." He looks thoughtful. "There are red flags everywhere, but it's a possibility."

I start laughing then. "I know, right? My entire life is filled with red flags, yet you haven't run off yet."

"True love," Baker says. "That's what does it to you. I was planning on becoming a priest, ya know? But my wife was in a gang and could do no wrong! Love at first sight!"

"Wow... I don't even know what to say to that," August says.

"I want to be a priest, with all those sexy nuns everywhere," Brandon decides. "I'd take them to heaven every night in my bed."

I stare at my brother in disbelief. "Baker, did you ever learn how to exorcise people? I'd love to have my brother exorcised, and if you can't, just disposed of. That'd be fine with me. No joke." Hey, I can't simply go from being a villain to a normal person overnight, right?

"Wait... you want to exercise with me?" Brandon asks Baker. "I mean, that's cool, man. I start off with a four-mile jog every morning."

"Not unless you're planning on carrying me," Baker says. "When I'm done fiddling with the wife, I don't have much energy left for anything else, ya know?"

"Oh, I know," Brandon says.

"That's not what your girlfriend said. She actually asked if there was something wrong with your little penis," I say.

His eyes get really wide and then he pulls the front of his pants down. "Baker, is my penis little?"

Baker looks down and assesses Brandon's penis for a strangely long period of time. Even August shifts uncomfortably. Then Baker pats Brandon on the shoulder. "I'm sorry for your loss."

"W-What?" Brandon asks as Baker cackles.

"It all depends on how you wield it, ya know? Ask your brother. He likes the peen."

"Oh my god," I groan.

"Even *you* knew he was gay?" Brandon asks in shock. "Why'd everyone know but me?"

"I've known for *years*," Baker brags.

Brandon turns to me. "Brother."

I turn to August and try to pretend that I'm not so close to my brother that we're playing footsies.

"Brother."

I try to become one with August. I try to mold myself into him.

But Brandon isn't deterred. "Brother."

"What?" I ask warily.

"What are your thoughts on penises?" he asks.

"They're good for aiming while peeing," I say.

He nods, clearly agreeing. "But like... slightly less than average penises. Thoughts."

"I already told you!" Baker says, still on Brandon's lap, but at least Brandon's buttoned his pants. "Depends on how you wield it."

"Is that true?" Brandon asks me.

I look at August. "Save me," I whisper.

August's grinning too much to be of help. "Why? I'm enjoying this chat you're having."

I decide that we've been leaving August out of this conversation and he needs to be involved. "Ask Moistman."

"Oh... yeah, that's probably better than asking you. Moistman, what are your thoughts on averagely small penises?" Brandon asks.

"Depends on how you wield it," he says, making me laugh and Baker nod.

"Told you!" Baker says.

"Your father has a wee penis!" Mom shouts from the front.

I burrow my face against August's neck. Not because I want to snuggle with him, but because I would like to end this life and start again with a new and normal family. "I'm so sorry. Please don't hate me."

August laughs as he wraps his arms around me. "Your family is funny."

"He was able to knock me up three times!" Mom says. "Because he knows how to wield it."

Brandon pulls out his phone. "I'll just ask Esme." As it rings, Baker hits the speaker button so we can all hear. Literally *everyone* in the vehicle quiets down to listen.

"Hello?" she asks.

"Babe, it's me. Do I know how to wield my penis?"

Silence. Dead fucking silence.

"Babe?" Brandon sounds worried.

"You have other amazing qualities. Like your muscles! Oh, those are enough for me, babe."

"Aw! I love you, snugglemuffin."

"I love you too."

He hangs up with her and proudly looks at all of us. "She says I'm amazing in bed. Best she's ever had."

"I love how optimistic your brother is," August whispers.

I snicker. If Brandon is anything, it is optimistic.

Mom pulls into the Walmart parking lot as an elderly woman crosses from the front of the store to the parking lot. Instead of kindly waiting for her to cross, my mom lays on the horn.

"Oh my god," August breathes. "Is she honking at an elderly woman?"

Mom rolls down the window. "Get out of the road, hag!"

I reach over and plug August's ears. "Shhh... it'll all be over soon."

He starts laughing, which isn't the reaction I thought he'd have. "Get that lady out of the road, we got shit to TP!" August says, which nearly kills me.

"What have I done to you?" I ask.

He's laughing harder now, almost deliriously so. "Oh my god. I don't even know what is happening, but I love it. This is amazing. Why is this so amazing?"

"I don't know," I say as Mom's SUV's wheels squeal as she takes off and pulls into a parking spot. The doors open and people just fall out into the parking lot.

We're all in our supervillain outfits as we make our way up to the front door. The greeter warily stares at us, but people dress up in supersuits all the time and she can't stop everyone who passes through wearing one.

"To the toilet paper!" Dad shouts, and all twelve of us charge the toilet paper aisle.

"I think one pack for everyone will be enough. Like a twenty-four pack, maybe," Mom says. "That would be enough, right? I'm not good at math. Someone help me."

"That would be almost three hundred rolls of paper, I don't think we need that much," August says.

"Sounds perfect!" Mom says as she grabs her pack.

August looks at me as my father stuffs a pack under his arm. "Are we stealing these?" August asks.

"I honestly don't know," I say as the twelve of us walk up to the front before everyone gets into this compact circle while holding their pack of toilet paper. It looks like we're summoning a toilet demon with our toilet paper.

"Mark, why don't you distract them, and we'll sneak the toilet paper out," Mom says.

Dad nods. "Okay!" He walks toward the door as we watch and the security guard *instantly* sees him.

"Sir, you must pay for that," the man says.

"You can't stop me!" he yells as he runs through the front of the store. Mom just laughs as the security guard runs two feet and catches Dad.

"God, I love it when he gets caught. Alright, everyone to the self-checkout!" Mom orders.

"Did your mother just send him through to laugh at him?" August asks in disbelief.

"She did," I say as I see a bin filled with Santa hats. Our town *does* love dressing up for Christmas. Lights were out by Thanksgiving and the town square's Christmas tree was up and shining brightly. I grab a hat and take it over to the register where I pay for it, my toilet paper, and August's. Then I put the Santa hat on his head and smile at him.

"You look so cute in everything."

"You're not worried about your dad?" he asks as I watch Dad get dragged off by the security guard.

"Not in the slightest," I admit.

And just like that, the SAVCGEM became eleven as we leave Dad behind and continue with our operation.

With our newly purchased toilet paper, we all crowd into the slightly more spacious SUV and head off using August's directions.

When we pull up to the nice house just outside the city center, we all get out.

"I can't believe we're doing this," he says. "Should we not?"

"It's just toilet paper," I remind him.

"Yeah, but it's two hundred and eighty-eight rolls of toilet paper."

"Nope, two hundred and sixty-four now that my dad's gone," I say.

He grins at me as he nods. "True. I suppose since it's only two hundred and sixty-four, it'll be alright."

"Alright, Moistman," Mom announces as she tears open her pack and hands him a roll. "Do the honors of the first throw."

"I don't even know how," August says.

Mom prepares it for him before handing it back over.

"Moistman, Moistman," Baker begins to chant.

August flings the roll toward the nice two-story house and watches it soar over the roof.

Everyone cheers, clearly forgetting that we're supposed to be stealthy. Instead, we all tear into our packs and start flinging toilet paper all over the house. August is laughing as he picks up the next roll and flings it. It makes me laugh and enjoy this so much. There's something about seeing August just let loose, forget the stress from his job, and have fun.

That's when a light turns on in the house.

"Oh no," August says.

"Hey!" someone shouts as the door opens and a dog comes flying out.

"Run!" Mom yells.

We drop the rolls and scatter, running in different directions. Brandon turns and rushes back, scooping up packs of toilet paper.

"Run, you idiot!" I yell as the dog goes for Brandon.

"But toilet paper is expensive!"

I can't run fast because of the burns, and I quickly realize that I need to slow down. "I can't run," I realize.

"Do you want me to carry you?" August asks.

"I want to say no, but it's so sexy when you do," I realize. He scoops me up without another word into this bridal carry, and his suit is so tight that I get a beautiful view of his biceps. "You're so sexy."

"I am?" he asks.

"Flex your muscles a little more," I say as I run my finger down his biceps as we turn onto the street Mom parked, only to find the SUV speeding off without us.

"Oh my god, she left us!" August says in disbelief. Clearly, he's still not getting the whole "villain" part of my family.

"Of course they did, the hero thing would be to wait, the villain thing is to leave anyone too slow behind."

He starts laughing as I look behind his shoulder and see someone chasing us with a bat.

"Not to worry you, but we're being chased by a mad person," I say.

"What?" he asks in alarm. He turns to look and then, suddenly, time is frozen. It's so strange that everything just suddenly stops as he keeps running.

"You're wasting your freezing time!" I say.

"It's worth it! Can you *imagine* if she realized it was me? She'd murder me!"

I laugh as he turns the corner and slows down as time starts up again. "You can put me down," I say, and he does, even though I wouldn't mind being a princess for him. We're close to the town center, so I point at the city's Christmas tree burning bright.

"Walk with me to the tree?" I ask.

"You feel good enough?"

"I feel fine," I assure him. "It was just the running that was hard."

He switches to my left side so he can take my hand, and I can't stop beaming at him. He's just so thoughtful and considerate all the time. To him, it's always me first.

"What?" he asks.

"I can't just stare at you?"

He gives me a crooked grin that makes me push up onto the balls of my feet and kiss his cheek. "Is it the outfit? Are you digging the highwaters or the pants up my buttcrack?" he asks.

I lean back so I can take a peek and see that it wasn't even a joke, they've worked their way right up his ass crack. "Ooh, man, beautiful."

"Thank you," he says as he pulls it out of his crack. "Normally, I try to hide when I pick wedgies, but with you, I feel like I don't have to hide *anything* because nothing I do can top anything in your life."

I grin at him as I take my mask off since it doesn't really matter who sees me now. He reaches over with his free hand and fluffs my hair, since my hair is stuck down from the mask.

"I needed this... so fucking bad," he says.

"What? TPing houses?"

He gives me a huge smile. "Just... this. My work is stressful, and with you, I just do things I would never do, and it's so freeing. I don't hate my work, but that's all I do."

"I'm glad my crazy family could entertain you," I say.

"It's not your family. It's you. Although, I'm a little worried about your dad, but clearly, no one else is."

"Eh, he'll be fine," I say as we walk toward the fake Christmas tree.

There are couples and families crowded around it as it reaches for the sky. The lights are blue and white with silver ornaments. Underneath it are fake presents.

"We stole all the presents under that tree one year," I tell him.

"Did you really?"

I nod.

"I love that, and I don't even know why."

And I love every moment of this. But I do know why.

We walk hand in hand, August still wearing his Santa hat. And I've never been happier.

CHAPTER FIFTEEN

A ringing phone wakes me. Thankfully, it's not mine, so I just roll over and curl up against August as he reaches for the phone.

"Hello?"

I lean forward so I can hear who he's talking to because I'm nosy and clearly don't respect his personal space. It's a woman, but I don't know who it is.

"Where are you? You have a press release at nine, and it's already seven-thirty."

"I'll get there in time," he grumbles.

"And who is this guy you've been seen frolicking with?" she asks. "You *know* you're supposed to have us vet *anyone* you're planning on being around. Are you two dating?"

August looks over at me. "Are we dating?"

"Sure," I mumble, still half asleep but secretly ecstatic. It's like love birds are singing praises inside my head and I grab onto him even tighter.

"Yes," he says to her.

I'm trying not to scare him off with my grinning.

"Are you *sleeping* with him? Oh my god, August! Your *image*! At least he's cute. Do you know how much harder this would be if he were ugly? Your fans would riot."

"She's crazy," I decide.

"Is that him? I can hear him. Oh hell. You just stress me out, August. Did you know that someone *TP'd* my house yesterday! Can you believe that?"

August instantly starts laughing.

"Shush," I whisper. He's clearly not very good at this villain stuff.

"I swear to heaven and hell if you know who did this, I'm going to..."

"Did what?" August asks. "Landon tickled me, and I giggled a little."

I snicker as August grins and pulls me to him.

"Bring him."

"To the press release? Isn't the mayor just blabbing about boring stuff?"

"Yes, and then you're going to introduce him and state that you are in a good and healthy monogamous relationship with the intent to marry," she says.

"That's moving a little fast, dontcha think?" he asks.

"Your fans are hungry, August. They will *eat him alive.*"

August squeezes my arm. "I'm positive Landon can hold his own."

"They'll *eat* him," she says.

"I'll fuck them up," I tell her.

"Oh my god." She sounds horrified when I'd think she'd be pleased with my ability to not let people walk all over me. "We need to put him through some classes, don't we? Bring him in now! Let me meet him. I'll write him a list of things he can and cannot say."

August glances at me with a grin. "I'm sure he'll be fine."

I lean into the phone so she can hear me. "I'm very fine, thank you."

"Get in here!"

"We're coming!" August assures her.

He finishes up with her and instead of getting up, grabs me and pulls me into his arms. He guides me on top of him and I sink down, resting my head on his chest. "This is going to be a disaster."

I can't help but grin. "Me? You think I'm going to make things a disaster?"

"No, Valerie. She's going to make it a disaster."

"I can't wait," I say as I grudgingly get up. We get dressed, eat breakfast, and head out to the main building of Superheroes United. Zacia is on my lap dressed in her superhero outfit.

August glances over at me. "Are you okay showing your face? I mean, don't some of the supervillains know who you are?"

"Only the ones from SAVCGEM," I say. "And I honestly don't think they're going to care. They'll probably think I'm infiltrating the place or something. As for real villains, I've always worn my mask around them and never given them my name. So I don't think they know who I am."

"Good. I don't want to cause issues for you. You are... prepared for how people will react to you?"

I'm more than positive that I can deal with them. "I'll bring some mace if I need to."

"No! Don't mace my fans."

"No, for this manager lady."

August looks even more concerned. "This is going to be a disaster."

"I didn't know you had the power to predict the future."

This seems to amuse him. "I do now."

I just smugly grin which seems to worry him further. He's so cute when he's concerned that I'm going to eat his manager alive.

He parks in this special parking spot that says, "Reserved for the Hero of the City."

I snort.

"You don't like my sign?" he asks with a grin.

"I'm actually jealous of it."

"I would complain about it, but it means I don't have to park half a mile away."

"You could also park in the handicap spots, like my mom does."

He looks at me in horror. "Imagine if I did that. They'd let me too because *everyone* loves me."

"Do I need to be concerned about this? I'll fight them for you. I always carry a book with me and they fucking hurt when you get smashed in the face with one."

He shuts the car off and we both get out. "You know this from experience?"

"No, just by the sound my victims make."

147

"*Victims?*" a woman asks, and I turn to see a lady in her early forties. I've seen her before, plenty of times actually. She's always hovering around when I want to stare at August flaunting his supersuit.

"Yeah, you know, the people I keep locked up in my basement," I tell her. "Hi! I'm Landon!"

She ignores me and turns to August with wide eyes. "If you want a boyfriend, we can find you one. What about Tony? He's so sweet and he's tried so hard to get your attention and he knows how to say all the right things."

I scoff. "Ew, Tony sounds like a nark. And does Tony have a hairless cat?" I ask.

The woman looks at my cat and cringes away. I realize that I hate her even though I may or may not have done the exact same thing when I saw Zacia. "God, it's disgusting, but the people will love it."

"Can't you get a new manager?" I ask. "What if I become your manager? I'd love to boss you around and tell you that you've been a bad boy."

This sounds like a delightful idea, but August looks a little concerned by it. "Valerie is a little... much, but she's... um... got good intentions."

I raise an eyebrow because I'm not convinced. "That's basically the definition of a nark. But I'll keep an open mind," I say as I walk up to her and smile. "I've heard about you."

She takes a full minute to run her eyes over my body. "Oh sweetheart, we need to do something about your wardrobe. What are you wearing?"

I look down at my black pants and dark blue shirt under my dark gray coat. "Excuse me? You're going to... dress me?" I ask.

"How about a nice khaki? Khakis are welcoming. Not too formal but not too casual. A very light gray would work as well."

"August, I think this strange lady wants to see me in my underwear, and I feel *very* uncomfortable about that. Does she make you show her your willy?"

August looks disappointed as he shakes his head. "She hasn't yet. She must like you more."

I try not to laugh. "No, I don't want to show her my willy."

"I don't want to see your... penis," she says before giving an exasperated sigh. "Just let's get inside before anyone... sees you."

"I think we hit it off well, what do you think?" I ask August as I bump into his hip.

"I think you're doing an amazing job getting to know each other," he says as he walks with me into the building. I've never been in the Superheroes United building, but the first thing I'm greeted with is a metal detector.

August turns to the right but Valerie stops him. "He needs to go through security."

"You think my boyfriend is toting a machete?" August asks in disbelief. "He's fine."

"Through security."

He sighs but walks with me over to the security station.

The man running it says, "Take off all metal. Is this a service animal?"

"Yes."

"Papers?"

"Yes."

"Can I see them?"

"August, this man is abusing me," I loudly announce.

The man looks alarmed.

"He doesn't need papers for his cat," August says and the man nods.

August could be like "This man here is a chicken" and everyone would instantly be like "Ah yes, I can see it."

I pull the harness off Zacia and toss all other electronics and metal into the bin. Then I send it through before walking with Zacia in my arms as naked as the day she was born. When I get to the other side, Valerie is waiting with a grimace as she stares at my cat.

"I see why you cover it up."

"She's not an 'it.'"

She sighs. "What's her name?"

"Balzac."

She waves her arm. "Security, please escort this man home and make sure he can't come within one hundred miles of this facility."

She reaches for me, probably planning on guiding me to the nearest security guard, and I jerk back. "Oh my god, she's trying to touch my Balzac!" I yell and *everyone* turns to look at us.

"Valerie, don't you just love him?" August asks as security hovers around, unsure of what to do about me and the cat.

"If I'm being honest, it's going to be a no. Tony is so much more your type," she insists.

"Who is this Tony guy that I clearly need to display my dominance over?" I ask.

"I'll point him out," August assures me as he heads for the elevator.

When no one comes to arrest me, Valerie grudgingly follows as August and I get into the elevator. And then I do the evilest thing I have ever done. Just as Valerie is getting near, I press the "close door" button and watch the doors shut in her face.

August starts laughing. "You did not!"

"I was looking her in the eyes when I did it." I'm very proud of myself.

"She's going to murder you."

"Good."

"You're so refreshing."

I snicker as the elevator goes up and lets us out on the seventh floor. We have to wait patiently for Valerie who is *fuming* by the time the doors open.

"You will *not* date this man," she decides.

August waves her off. "He's fine. You're making him act like this with all of your rules and regulations and complaints. First, you tell him that he's dressed wrong, then you tell him he should be replaced with Tony, and then you make sure he knows his cat is ugly. And you expect him to just sit there and take it? Landon isn't like that, and that's exactly what I like about him."

She stares at him for a moment before sighing. "Fine. And I'm *only* allowing this because you've been happier these past few weeks than you've been in a long time. He'd better not mess it up."

"He won't."

I'm left waiting as they take August away to dress him up and do his hair and makeup, like he can't do it himself. Valerie hovers around me with a pair of khakis and a nice button-up that would make me look like I'm in my Sunday best *and* a complete loser. So I put my hood up and drop my pants real low so they hang around my thighs and show my underwear. She eventually gives up and storms off.

At least I thought she did, but she returns with a sheet of paper that she passes to me. "August will introduce you and I'll escort you to the front. Once there, these are the lines you are allowed to say. You may not say anything else."

I read it out loud to try it out. "'Hi! I'm Landon! It's a pleasure to meet you on this very fine morning! I am here to support and love Chrono!'" I look up at her. "Why are there so many exclamation marks?"

"To sound happy, enthusiastic, and sweet!"

I return to the script. "'This is my cat, Sprinkles! She loves snuggling!'" I raise an eyebrow. "Her name is Balzac."

"You will not ever repeat that name ever again."

I sigh and remember there's more. "'I look forward to being a part of this loving and fun community! Please love me'... Please *love me?*"

"I don't know. We need *something*. So I thought making you sound like a needy little bitch will help," Valerie says.

"I can be a needy little bitch, if you want. Oh, August! Spank me, August! I need you so bad right now. Oh!"

She clamps a hand over my mouth. "Shut your pretty little mouth. I'm going to tell them you're deaf and mute and can't speak. We'll have a translator for you."

"Awesome!" I say dryly.

August peeks out of the dressing room. "I heard you call me?"

"No biggie. Just to spank me when you get a chance."

"Oh... okay. Let me finish up here," he says before disappearing.

"This is a disaster," she decides. "Let's work on the cat. Can it do tricks?"

"She killed a mouse the other day and left it on August's pillow."

That's clearly not the kind of trick she was hoping for because she grumbles as she hurries off.

August comes out to be with me and smiles. "How's it going?"

"I think she stormed off... so amazingly well!"

He laughs. "Don't stress about it. Just say 'Hey, I'm Landon. This is my cat,' and they'll love you."

"Okay. I can do that."

He reaches down and grabs a strand of my hair between his fingers before giving it a gentle tug. "Sorry about all of this nonsense. It's probably a lot to deal with."

"It's fine, honestly. I'm just happy to be with you."

"See, why aren't you that cute in front of others?" Valerie asks, making her reappearance. "Let's head down."

The three of us go down to the first floor. She has me stay with her as August goes off to meet up with the mayor. When it gets close to the time for the press conference, Valerie and I head inside and take a seat in the back of this room filled with chairs and a podium at the front. After a few minutes, August comes out and then the mayor does. August sits to the side as the mayor begins to talk. The moment the first word comes out of his mouth, I nearly fall asleep. He should clearly let me write his speeches or take a part-time job helping insomniacs sleep.

That is until he says, "We are going to disband Superheroes United. It's time for a new world and that means cleansing the old one."

At first, I think it's just a new marketing strategy until Valerie stands up and says, "What the fuck?" quiet enough that only those around us hear.

"Superheroes like Chronobender are making this world a worse place. Our police now sit back and just *wait*, instead of reacting to calls. People are dying who don't need to die because we have put all our faith into a twenty-something boy. But this reign is over now. We are starting a new era," he says as two men step up behind him.

One I instantly recognize, even in his supersuit.

And my stomach sinks.

Nolan.

How could you?

CHAPTER SIXTEEN

What is Nolan doing?

I look at the other person standing next to the mayor and realize that it's Racer, the man from The Rebellion who had harassed me about leaving.

"Our first order of business is to kill Chrono," the mayor says.

And *everyone* turns to August. Not in horror over the mayor's words. Or in shock. But in compliance. The security guards here to protect August and the mayor turn toward him. At first, I'm confused. Could all of these people be against August? Could this be planned? But when I look at Nolan, I see that look of concentration on his face. The look he uses when he's using his gift. But his gift is just to read minds. Is he here to read someone's mind?

And that's when I see what's in his hand.

The snow globe.

I don't even have time to think about it as the security guards rush at August. He's confused, not expecting his own people to go against him. When the first guard brings a baton down hard, August barely has time to block it, and even then, he doesn't react. I'm sure these are people he knows; of course he's not going to start attacking them.

Setting Zacia to the side, I lunge to my feet and hold my hand out in an attempt to help, but my gift is gone. I can't protect him. I can't save him.

"Freeze time and get out!" I yell at August.

Nolan turns to August and reaches a hand out, making August stop moving. Instead, he just stares at Nolan as a security guard bashes his baton into the side of August's head. He doesn't even act like he noticed the horrible blow.

"Stop!" I scream at my brother as I run for August, but everyone is rushing for the man that, just moments ago, they respected and loved. It's like they're all driven to kill him, and August is just standing there letting them do it. "Please! Stop!" I don't even know if my voice can reach my brother, but he has to know what this is doing to me. He *knows* how much I care about August.

Someone pushes me out of the way as Nolan's eyes shift to me. They lock with mine and I stare at him in disbelief. My brother is really going to kill the man I want more than anything? He's going to ruin the only good thing that has happened to me recently?

"How could you do this?" I scream. "Let him go!"

His expression shifts before quickly turning back to August. I grab onto the man in front of me and yank him back, but people are pushing and shoving to get to August, and I can't get through them. Hell, most of them are taller than me.

"August!" I yell as I see him driven to the ground.

How could my brother do this? If it was something the others came up with and he knew they'd do this, then he could have told me. I could have pulled August away.

I push and shove, terrified and desperate to reach him, but so is everyone else. They want to kill him, tear him apart, destroy him. Even Valerie is in on it. It's like they've been driven insane. The crowd shifts just enough that I see August lying there doing nothing to protect himself as panic wells up inside me. That's the moment something snaps inside me.

"Stop this!" I yell and suddenly a splitting pain tears into my mind as everyone and everything in the room lifts straight up into the air. Some slam into the ceiling as others float above me. I wave my hand, willing them away because I know that this is because of my power. I can *feel* it, but I can't control it. Nothing moves as I ask; instead, a chair whips by me, smashing into the wall as I realize that I can't hold on to the power. But the crowd is gone, all lifted into the air, so I run for August who is still lying on the ground.

I grab him and yank him toward me. The moment my hands touch his face, he turns to me, like I have snapped him out of the trance with just a touch. "Freeze time."

He freezes it as he rolls onto his side with a groan. I quickly turn to the podium where Nolan had stood, but he's gone and so is Racer. I drag August to his feet but everything else stays frozen around me. He seems confused and disoriented. I'm not sure if it has to do with whatever Nolan did to him or the beating that has left his face bloody. "August, what do I do?" I ask.

"Elevator," he says. "What the fuck is going on?"

After grabbing a frozen Zacia, I pull him after me and look around, terrified my brother is lying in wait before remembering that time is still frozen. I push him into the hallway and over to the elevator. Someone had been passing through the open door when time was frozen, so I push August through and he starts time again. He reaches over to a keypad and presses a finger against it. The elevator starts descending, but I'm not sure staying in this building is a good idea.

"Shouldn't we leave?"

August seems disoriented, but he shakes his head. "It's a safe area... why did they attack me? All of them?"

I wrap my arms around August and tuck my head against his chest. "I'm so sorry. I'm so sorry," I whisper.

His hand is shaking as he reaches out and wraps his arm around me, pulling me to him. "What happened? Do you know what happened?"

"That was my brother... that was Nolan," I admit. "I don't know... he can't... he can't control minds but..." I can't even figure out what to say. It's like *my* mind was the one taken over and I've forgotten the function of words. "I'm sorry. I'm so sorry."

He squeezes me against him. "It's okay. You didn't know, right?"

I feel like I have to tell him. He has to know. "He... he had the snow globe, August," I whisper.

He looks startled. "The... the one that took your power? Wait. You used your power, right?" he asks as the door opens and he guides me out. "You pulled them away."

"I don't know... Yes, I used it, but I couldn't control it."

I hold my hand out, trying to pull something toward me, but my hand just shakes and my head pounds. "Are you okay in this building? What if they keep trying to attack you? What if it's not over?"

"This is a safe area; only specific people can enter."

"Yes, so some of the people who were trying to kill you. They could let Nolan in if he asked them to. Fuck."

"It'll be okay," he urges as he hurries me down the hallway.

"I'm so stupid, why did I give him my power? Why did I trust him?"

"Hey, babe, it's okay. He's your *brother,* of course you'd trust him. He's family. He's never given you reason not to."

The elevator door opens behind us and we both turn. August pulls me back, behind him, like he's ready to protect me. It's Valerie and behind her is a big burly man.

She rushes for August, but it just makes him pull me back more. "August, get away from him! Don't take him any farther! He's Leviathan. There's only one person with that much power in the area."

"He protected me," August says, still pulling me back. "While the rest of you tried killing me, he protected me, so back the fuck off."

"He's a *villain*," she says. "Wyatt, grab him."

"He's not a villain," August says as he wraps me in his arms. "What about at the broadcasting station? Would a villain have gone in and rescued me and those others? He's not a villain."

"Now *everyone* will know who he is. All of that happened on live TV," she says.

I look up at August, and even though I don't want to let go—I want him to hold me and never let me slip away—I say, "I should go."

August's arms tighten as he continues to back away from them. "So what? He was *raised* by villains. It doesn't mean that's who he is. People change."

"He robbed a bank *weeks* ago!" Valerie shouts.

"Did he steal anything or hurt anyone? And he hasn't done it since! He doesn't even have his power anymore."

I've never heard August's voice rise so much, even during the many live broadcasts of him dealing with bad people. I've never had anyone ever want to protect me as much as he wants to.

But Valerie isn't convinced. "We just saw his power!"

And I know she has a right to not trust me.

August squeezes me again. It's putting pressure on the burns, but I love the touch of him so much that I don't care. They're healing quite quickly with the use of the ointment and soon we can squeeze each other all we want. "Just... we'll get to that later. Right now, I think it's more important that we get somewhere safe. Where's the mayor?"

"He went with the supervillains. You're right, get into a safe room," she says as she guides him toward a room at the end of the hallway. The four of us go into it and lock the door. I guide August over to a chair and push him down as I grab his face that's covered in blood. I use my sleeve to gently wipe some of it away.

"August, I'm really sorry about what I did... I couldn't control myself. I'm so glad I couldn't reach you with the amount of people there," she says quietly as she looks down at her hands, like she's not sure if they're her own.

"It's okay. I know you couldn't control it." He turns to me. "Are you okay?" he asks like he isn't the one bleeding.

"I'm fine."

"But you're already hurt."

"I'm fine. I'm healed enough, okay?"

"Yeah, I'm sorry. I really am."

"Shush, you didn't do any of this," I say as I step from him and see a connecting bathroom. I go into it and grab some paper towels, which I wet. When I come back, Valerie and August are in a heated whisper battle that surely has something to do with me.

"You were right up there too," I tell Valerie as I walk by her. "You were prepared to hurt or even kill August. If it weren't for me, would you guys have stopped? Would you have killed him? I pulled him out of that chaos and kept him safe."

She takes a deep breath and rubs at her face. "You're right... I just... you have to understand that people aren't always telling the truth or doing what they're saying they are."

I understand, but I don't want to agree with her. Instead, I quietly clean the blood from August's face. He probably doesn't need stitches since it's mostly shallow cuts, a bloody nose, and bruising. My hands are shaking as August reaches up and takes them.

"Hey, it's okay." His voice is gentle and caring. He's so sweet, even after all of this.

I shake my head because it's not. I sink down to my knees and Zacia rubs against my leg, upset as well. "I'm sorry," I whisper as I bury my head against August's legs.

"It's okay," he says.

"You don't know what he could do with that power. You don't know how far it could go..."

"Can you tell me what happened?" Valerie asks, so August tells her about the snow globe and the loss of my power. When he's done explaining, she looks confused. "What's this have to do with what happened?"

I look over at her and find her watching me. "I think he's using my power. My brother can read minds. He can't do... whatever that was he did today."

"How do you know it was him doing it?" she asks.

"The feeling... the way he stood. I don't know, it's hard to explain. Maybe it was because it was my power assisting his that I knew he was the one doing it."

"How can someone use the power of another?" Valerie asks.

I shake my head as August's fingers trail through my hair. "I honestly don't know," I admit.

"So whose power was it that put yours into the globe and allowed all of this?" the burly man asks.

"This is Wyatt, he's another superhero, but he usually hangs around here for protection," August explains.

I nod at him and he does the same to me. "I don't know. Maybe the leader of the Rebellion?"

We talk some and then Valerie contacts someone from above who will let us know what's going on outside this room. As she does that, I pull out my phone.

> Me: Nolan, I need to see you. Talk to me. Please.

The reply is almost immediate, like he was waiting for me.

> Nolan: Meet me in an hour at your place.

> Me: No. Somewhere with others. I don't want to be alone with you.

> Nolan: City center. Under the tree.

I slip the phone into my pocket and look over at August who is staring at the spot where my phone had been.

He leans into me, tucking his face near my ear. "I don't want you to go."

I don't want to go either, but I have to. "I have to talk to him."

"It could be a trap."

"What more could they want from me?" I ask.

"They know you're with me... you're my weakness, Landon."

At this moment, that means a lot to me, but I still can't sit here and wait. "I trust him. Please, let me do this. He won't hurt me. He's my brother. He won't." Do I even know this Nolan, though? The person up there next to the mayor... was that really my brother?

He bites his lip. "Landon..."

I lean into him and press my forehead against his as I close my eyes. "Please. Let me try to fix this. I'm not weak and useless without my power."

He doesn't want to let me go, but I have to, so I kiss him and stand up.

"Just... wait, please?" August asks as I pick up Zacia and put her in his lap.

"I'll be back," I say as I push through the door and rush into the hallway. I run toward the elevator and call it to me before anyone can stop me. When I slip into it, I find myself hoping I haven't made a mistake, but Nolan is my brother. He wouldn't hurt me, right?

As soon as the door opens, I see people milling around everywhere. But that also means they see me. And now they know what my face looks like. My secret identity has been blown.

"It's Leviathan!"

I turn from them and keep moving, but they begin to block my path. "He's working with them! Didn't you see him with them?" a woman yells.

"He's trying to get away!"

"We must stop him!"

No, no! I can't deal with this shit right now. I need to get to Nolan, but the crowd is getting unruly around me.

"This way," a woman says as she walks up to me with a security team. "I was told to escort you to August's car."

"Thank you."

Her team creates a horseshoe around me, forcing the crowd to part as I'm taken down to the parking garage. Once I'm in the car, she doesn't disperse. "Do you want us to go with you?"

"No, but thank you."

"Okay," she says as I rummage around the back seat until I find a mask, which I pull on. I drive to the city center as everything races through my mind. My mom, dad, and Brandon call me multiple times, but I can't answer. Through texts and calls, August pleads with me to come back, but I can't, not yet.

When I park the car, my stomach feels like a jumble of nerves. But I make sure I look confident as I walk across the city center, toward the towering Christmas tree that I was just at with August.

Nolan is waiting there without his mask when I walk up. He's watching me as I consider if this really could be a trick. Nolan was the one person in my family that I trusted more than the others. But now? Can I trust him?

It hurts to think that I can't.

"How could you do this?" I ask as I walk toward him. The pain of the question shows through in my words. "I *trusted* you. You're my *brother*."

"This city needs to change," he says, expression blank.

"At what cost?" I ask. I feel like my mind is spinning. My world is crashing around me. "You could've told me! I could've tried to get August to leave or something!"

"You made your choice when you decided to be with him. I have made my choice," he says, like it's as simple as picking a color.

"Goddammit, Nolan! You're not talking about something little.

You're talking about *killing* people! Killing the one I care about, the person who I'm with."

He shrugs because it's clearly none of his concern. "You made that decision," he says.

"And if I try to stop you, what are you going to do? Kill me too?"

"I hope you're not that stupid. You're the smart brother, aren't you?"

I just can't even believe him. I can't understand why he would do this. How could he? "You... stole my power."

He shrugs and I'm not able to comprehend what is happening. It's like he doesn't care about any of it. Like none of it even *fazes* him. "You didn't want it."

"That didn't mean it was right for you to take it!" I yell. "I *trusted* you. You made me think you were helping me! Instead, you were..." I wave my hand around wildly because I don't even have words for what he was doing. "Nolan... how could you do this?"

"It's not my fault you don't comprehend this. I was trying to show you the light, but instead, you're too blind. A *boy* is more important? Than family? Than fixing this world?"

"You're not fixing it. You lied to me, stole my power to use for yourself, and tried killing August. I don't even *know* you. Are you even my brother?"

"Oh poor, poor, Landon. You always had such a big brain but were too fucking simple to understand anything. How can you not see how jealous everyone is of this power you possess? And you just sit on your ass and read *books* all day? You play the victim, when you're better than everyone! The *control* you have over your power is ridiculous."

"I'm not better than everyone! And what the fuck would I do with it? There's no way you guys would let me use it for good, so what the fuck would I do with it?"

"Rule the goddamn world if you wanted to!" he says, voice rising for the first time. "Do *something*!"

"I don't want to rule the fucking world! The world is fine how it is!"

"And that, my naive brother, is your problem."

My shock of everything is turning to rage. "Give me my power back. Give me the snow globe."

He has calmed back down, his expression unreadable again. "I don't have it."

"Of course you fucking have it. I just saw it in your hands."

"I gave it to Marauder. It is his, after all."

I look at him in disbelief. "You... you gave my power to someone else?"

He shrugs. "You don't need it anymore."

What I have done... what I have caused begins to sink in. The destruction of this city will be my fault because I had a fucking tantrum about my power. "Why'd you come?" I whisper. "Why are you even here?"

"You asked me to talk to you."

I hold his gaze, even though it's hard for me to do so when those eyes generally watch me with kindness. "Do you care? Is that why you're here? You care that you're ruining everyone's lives?"

He looks away. "Not in the slightest."

"Do you care for me?"

He still avoids my glance. "Stay away, Landon. Go read your fucking book and pet your ugly fucking cat and stay out of it. If you try to protect August again, he might not be the only one who ends up dead," Nolan says as he turns from me and walks away.

My chest aches and my stomach tightens as I watch him leave. And when he's finally out of sight, I sink to my knees and cover my face with my hands.

I feel like a piece of me has been torn away. A piece bigger than my powers. A piece that Nolan had sat in for most of my life as the brother I looked up to and the brother I relied on.

And it hurts.

CHAPTER SEVENTEEN

I drive back to the parking garage, but I don't know what to do now that I'm here. I feel like I can't even comprehend what has happened. I feel betrayed. I feel alone. Yes, I care for August. Yes, he has made me happier than I've been in a long time, but he hasn't been with me my entire life like Nolan has. Being here makes me feel like I'm betraying Nolan.

I hug the steering wheel as my mind races. I want to go back in time and ask my brother why he'd do this until he answers in a way I'd understand.

The door opens and I jump before looking over at August.

He looks very concerned as he reaches for me and sets a hand on my thigh. "Hey, how long have you been sitting out here for? I've been calling you and was worried sick. I finally convinced Valerie to let me go find you, and it was only after I froze time and ran away that she had no option but to allow it. Allowing is... stretching the truth, but it's what I'm sticking with."

I'm relieved he's here even if I still feel upset. "I don't know. I didn't even know that my brother was planning on taking over the city. I mean... stupid, right? He's a supervillain, why wouldn't I expect this?"

He reaches in and unbuckles my seat belt. Instead of pulling me from the car, he pushes me up and slides into the driver's seat before guiding me onto his lap. We don't exactly fit, but I don't mind being crammed in a small space with him when he makes me feel good and forget all the bad shit that has happened.

"He's your family." His voice is gentle and soft. He understands and he cares. *Why* he cares about what I think of my supervillain brother, I'm not sure, but it's clear he cares. "Of course you never expected him to do this. You can't blame yourself for any of this. And we know nothing at this point. Maybe we can talk them down. You don't know."

"They're not going to be talked down," I say as I pick at my pants. He pulls my hand away and cups it tightly. "And on top of all of that, it'll be *my* power that does it."

"If we get the snow globe back, maybe you'll get all of your power back."

"I don't know. I don't understand how any of it works. I thought it was a *joke*."

"I know," he says as he kisses my forehead. "We'll figure it out. We'll get everything figured out."

"I don't want my brother to die, and I don't want you to die."

"Then it's our job to keep either of those things from happening, alright?" he says.

"Yeah... my job to do what? I'm useless now." I feel so stupid now that I realize that Nolan wasn't helping me, he only wanted my power.

"That is the last thing you are. We can do this together as a team. I need you and you need me. So please, let's stop this before anything worse happens."

He squeezes me tightly and I feel like I can finally breathe. He's right. I need to stop focusing on what I could've done and shift my attention to what we can do. At this moment, my brother hasn't killed anyone. Yes, it's illegal to use his power the way he has, but if I can stop him from doing something much worse, he might get away with it. There's no proof that he kidnapped the mayor. To everyone else, it looks like the mayor willingly went with him. I can't even tell if the mayor wanted to go.

I nod, choosing to believe him. "Okay... you're right. What do we do now... or maybe I don't have a choice because Valerie is going to kill me."

"She might try, but I won't let her. You're way too cute to let her get a hold of you."

I give him a half-hearted smile because I know he's just trying to make me feel better. "Hmm... okay. Where's Zacia?"

"Valerie has her."

"Ew, gross. Let's go... let's go and figure this shit out."

"Got it," he says as he kisses my cheek.

He pushes the car door open and gets out with me by his side. He takes my hand firmly in his and I hesitate before looking up at him. "I'm sure by now the public knows who I am. They know I'm a villain."

"They know you *as* a villain. That doesn't mean that's who you are."

"Yeah... and you think holding my hand will change their minds? They're going to think I'm stealing you away and tainting you or something."

He grins at me. "I'd like you to taint me."

I snort, which makes him laugh. "Tainting your taint will have to wait," I say.

"Sounds good," he says as he leads me back into the Superheroes United building. Reporters who had been there to see the mayor are instantly on August with questions but hesitate when they see me holding his hand.

"Chrono, they're saying your boyfriend is Leviathan, a villain, is this true?" a reporter asks.

Valerie comes barreling through the hallway like her ass is on fire. "Why are these reporters still here?" she barks at no one and everyone.

"Let me deal with them," August says. "This is Leviathan and we are dating. I know about his past; I've known about it since the bombing of the broadcasting station. But I also know that he is not a bad person. He has saved my life twice now. Once at the broadcasting station where he saved me and all the others, and here when he saved my life while you guys were trying to kill me. Someone's past doesn't always define who they are or who they'll be. Growing up, my family had nothing. We were dirt poor and there were times when we had to go to the extreme to survive. I remember stealing food a time or two when I was a child because we had nothing. Does that make me a bad person? Does that make my parents bad people? No, of course not. Yes, Landon has made some mistakes. Yes, I've made some mistakes.

I'm sure you all have, but does that mean you're a bad person? No. Landon is with me whether you guys like it or not. He's not working with them, and he's going to help me stop them and keep the city safe."

Someone shoves a microphone into my face. "And what are your thoughts?"

"I think that your microphone is too close to my face," I say in irritation. I have no idea how August can deal with these pests with a smile on his face.

She shoves it closer until it brushes against my lips. "Leviathan, what are your thoughts on what happened today?"

"Thank you for doing exactly as I've asked. You actually went above and beyond. Should I deep throat this now? Is that why you're shoving it in my mouth?"

August lets out a noise before quickly covering his mouth, but it's clear he's amused. Who is not amused is Valerie who runs at me with my cat in outstretched arms.

"Look at his cat. Look at its little outfit! How cute," she says as she shoves Zacia in my arms.

"Aw!" someone says and then all attention turns to my cat, like we weren't concerned about supervillains taking over the city.

"What's your cat's name?"

"How old is your cat?"

"Is it a she or he?"

I take a deep breath and contemplate my decisions. I could be a good boy and tell them her nickname. *Or* I could make Valerie hate my guts.

"Her name is..." I start and silence falls upon the world around me. They wait with bated breath. I catch Valerie's eyes which are growing wider by the moment. My grin is widening in response. But then I look at August who is watching me with such sweetness in his eyes. He's so cute and trustworthy. "Zacia."

I look at Valerie. She's proud of me. She even gives me a thumbs up.

"How old is she?"

"I don't know, my dad stole her from some neighbor who is a complete dick if I've ever seen one," I say. "He stinks too. Wait... what was the question? I'm not very good at this interview stuff. You wanted to know what color my underwear is?"

Valerie's thumbs up quickly flips to a thumbs down and a scowl takes over her face.

"Did you rob the bank?" a man asks.

"I did, but I didn't want to. I just really wanted to catch August's attention, and I thought that if I robbed it, I might get to see him," I admit.

"That's so romantic," someone says.

"Thanks! I thought so! It seemed to work! So if you want the attention of anyone, rob something while they're around. Maybe they'll put you in handcuffs and—"

"That's enough questions!" Valerie clearly doesn't get the joke because she grabs me and throws a coat over my head before rushing me off like it'll help. "You're an embarrassment."

"Was it my deep throating comment?" I ask.

I can hear August laughing.

"And you! Don't encourage him!" she growls as she leads me blindly. For all I know, she's leading me to a drop-off and preparing to push me over.

"I'm not!"

She takes us into an empty room and shuts the door. "We're clearing everyone out of the building. We need to figure out how the villains got into the building and we're going on lockdown. No one in or out without permission. This is now a safe place so that no humans can be influenced by someone's power and willingly let one of the villains in. While that happens, we're going to try and get a location on the mayor, talk to the city council, and get some more supers in here."

"What do you want us doing?" August asks as I try to pull the coat off, seeing as I'm positive she's planning on smothering me at this point since she can't find a drop-off when we're on the main floor.

"Go down to your room here and get some rest. It's been a long few hours. We're going to need you to be refreshed and ready. Landon, we have a different room for you."

August waves her off. "He can stay in my room."

"I will not allow it. We need to keep up a good public image. You may not stay with each other until you're married," she says. "Which I pray to God will never happen."

"Really? I really can't smack this fine ass until we're *married?*" I ask as I smack August right on the ass.

Valerie literally runs for me and grabs me, pinning my arms at my side. It's sadly easy for her to do because she's a giant compared to me. Then she starts dragging me off.

"August! An old hag has taken me hostage! Save me!"

"I'm not even old enough to be your *mother*," she growls.

"Huh, must be all the scowling that's created all those *wrinkles* then."

"Valerie, please let me have him," August says.

"Yes, Valerie! I'm going to show him how I was going to deep throat that microphone," I say.

I didn't *know* how strong that woman is until I say that. She literally picks me up and starts leaving the room with me. Clearly, she has some type of power that gives her the strength to crush my body and carry me off.

"August, she's taking me off to violate me! Save me! I don't want to see her boobs!"

"Will you shut up?" she hisses as she looks around for who might hear.

"They do feel kind of squishy against my head, though. Little fluff pillows," I say as I lean my head back and look up at Valerie with a grin. "I can't wait until my next interview where I tell everyone that you dragged me off to your room and made my head touch your breasts as I cried for you to let me go. Ooh, that made your grip turn rib-crushing. You have so much strength."

"She has a small amount of power that gives her extra strength," August explains.

"Ah," I say as I tilt my head back again to look Valerie in the eyes. "Choke me, Mommy."

She instantly lets go of me and I rush over to August before latching myself onto him.

"Save me. She was being really creepy to me and made me touch her boobs. They were really squishy and kind of soft, but I was really scared. She also tried crushing me with her feminine power. I was a little into that and it made me slightly horny, but it was a confused type of horny."

He starts laughing. "I think... you've traumatized her."

"A little traumatizing does everyone some good," I joke.

August hurries off before Valerie can get her claws into me again. August takes me down a hallway deeper into the building, as far from Valerie as we can go.

"So, when this building goes on lockdown, as they're trying to do right now, no one is allowed in the building besides those of us that are permitted to be. All rooms become locked down and will only open with fingerprint permission. That way supers with mind powers can't affect anyone if there are no humans outside the building."

"Interesting."

"So I need to get your fingerprints recognized before we go up or you won't be allowed in my room."

"You have a bedroom here?"

"It's the room they try to make me stay in, but I refuse and insist on my own home. During times like this, it's probably a good plan to stay here."

He takes me down to the security team who run my fingerprints, get permission from Valerie to submit them—which she shockingly allows—and then send us on our way. We go back into the elevator and go down instead of up.

"Just in case something happens to the building, my room and all other important rooms are below ground."

"You guys have this shit figured out," I say.

"I'm making some of it up to impress you."

I can't tell if he's joking or not, but I laugh. "You have me so damn impressed. It makes me horny."

"Like real horny? Or how Valerie was making you horny?"

I wink at him. "Guess you'll have to figure it out." He has a soft grin on his lips as I let my eyes run down his tight suit that hugs him perfectly in all the right places. It makes me want to see him with it completely off. While he's seen me totally naked, the most I've seen of him is with his shirt off, and his cock out the time in the bathroom.

Thinking back on that time makes me ache to feel him again. To feel *all* of him, instead of the brief moment I was able to touch him.

The elevator door opens, snapping me out of my perversions, and he leads me down a hall to a door that requires both of our fingerprints. We step inside and I look at the living room. It's set up very casually, completely different from the businesslike look the rest of the place has. It looks just like a house, if a house didn't have windows. Where the windows should be are glass aquariums where fish swim around.

He notices me looking at them before I set Zacia down and take her harness off.

"You like fish?" I ask.

"I complained about having no windows and how I wanted a house outside, so they tried compensating for the lack of windows with fish. They're pretty, though, and I like them. It's just not the same."

"Too much work for me." But there is a different type of work that I'd prefer to be doing, if he would ever get to it. Especially because I want something to distract me from the day's events and he is exactly that thing. I want to feel all of him and connect to him because I know he's there for me. He will fight to keep me by his side and it's one of the things that makes me care very deeply about him.

"Yeah, I don't have to clean the tank or take care of anything like that here," he says as he looks around.

"Are you feeling alright?" I ask. It's clear he's not getting to it without a little push from me, but maybe he's feeling sore and tired from earlier. Or maybe he's not the type to lead. I never have balked when it comes to taking charge and getting what I want and right now, I want him.

"Yeah, I'm fine."

"Good," I say as I walk up to him as he stands there still in his superhero outfit, looking unbelievably sexy. I drape my arms over his shoulders and lean in. "Because I want you to fuck me."

His eyebrows shoot up and he gets this half-grin on his face. "Right now?"

"Is there a problem with that?" I ask as I push up and gently kiss his lips. It's more of a brush than a peck, but I want him to need more. *Ache* for more.

"Can't imagine there would be," he says with a grin as his hands wrap around my waist. "But are you healed enough?"

"I'm fine. Just don't go slamming my right side into anything, and it'll be perfect."

"Perfect, eh? I have a lot to live up to."

"I'm pretty sure I'll come just from seeing you naked with your glasses on."

"You and your glasses fetish!"

I snicker as I start pulling him back toward the bedroom.

"That's the kitchen, but if you wanna fuck on the table, I can figure it out," he jokes.

"Huh... and where might the bed be? Or is Valerie already waiting in it to make sure I don't taint you?" I ask as I let him push me in the right direction. He presses the front of himself against my back so I can feel his cock against my ass.

"If she is, that table is always an option."

"I'm good with anywhere," I say as he kisses my throat. I lean back into him as one hand slides under my shirt, fingers running up my stomach as his other hand dips down, slipping under the band of my pants, but not far enough to touch my cock that is aching for attention. He pulls his hands free and turns me around to face him.

"Want to see a magic trick?" he asks.

I grin because I would watch just about anything he asked me to. "I do."

He snaps his fingers and suddenly he's *completely* naked. It may be the greatest thing I've ever seen in my life.

I instantly start laughing. "That was amazing. I don't know what I was expecting, but that definitely exceeded *all* expectations. I would watch a *whole* lot more magic if all tricks were like that," I say, although I know he just froze time and stripped.

He starts laughing with me, doubling over so it makes it hard for me to fully appreciate his gorgeous body.

"Do me! Make me instantly naked!"

"It's much harder to do you," he says. "You don't bend as easily when you're frozen in time."

"Boo. Fine. Rip my clothes off with your muscles."

"You have no other clothes to wear."

"Just the shirt then. And I'll wear your clothes."

He takes one step up to me, grabs the front of my shirt in his hands and just tears it right down the middle.

"I nearly jizzed in my pants," I inform him as he gently takes it off my arms.

He snorts as he grabs onto me. "Shush."

"I nearly jizzed so hard."

He shakes his head. "You know Valerie wanted us up here to relax so if we need to use our powers later, we're not drained."

"Yeah, of course. I'm reinvigorating you with the power of my penis."

"Ah, makes sense."

He shuts me up with a kiss as he works my pants down. He at least tries to before realizing that he's struggling to get anywhere with my pants and the desire the denim has to stay on my body. "Why are your pants so tight?"

"Because my leg finally feels good enough that I can wear them! You don't like them?"

"They make your ass look very sexy, but they're unbelievably hard to get off," he says as he gently pushes me down on the bed. Then he works my pants off and removes my underwear with them so we're both naked. I pull him onto the bed then flip him onto his butt before straddling his lap as he sits up.

I thrust my hips forward, pushing my cock against his as he reaches behind me and grabs my ass.

"What kind of superpowers do you have in the bedroom?" I ask as he squeezes and rubs my ass cheeks.

"I can disappear in the blink of an eye if the sex isn't good."

I start laughing. "Wow, not what I was hoping for."

He grins as a finger dips between my ass cheeks. "Thought I'd tell ya, just in case."

"Thanks. Now how about you do something with that finger other than flutter it around on my ass?"

"You're so *bossy*." But the grin he wears tells me that he's enjoying it.

I slide my hand up the back of his neck and into his hair before yanking his head back as I rise up on my knees and look down at him. "I like bossing you around," I say as I lean down and nip his lip. "I'd be even bossier and rougher if your face wasn't bruised. Now where do you keep the goods?"

"Drawer," he says as he points. I push him down and he drops to the bed as I swing my leg over him, giving him a very nice view of my balls and cock as they probably graze his nose, which I find hilarious.

I yank open the drawer and pull out what I need. He grabs my waist and drags me back before climbing onto me.

"I don't know how much time we'll have before Valerie comes hammering at that door," he says.

"I'll just invite her in if she does. Who knows, she might like it."

"But I won't."

I grin at him as he takes the lubricant from me. His mouth runs down my throat to my chest as a hand slips between my legs to my ass. His finger slides between my cheeks as my own hand reaches for his hard cock. I grasp it and feel his murmur of approval against my neck.

I slide my fingers around the base of his cock, gently tightening, before drawing my hand down to the tip. That's when his finger rubs around my hole before pushing inside me. I moan against his lips as I pull him down until his cock is against mine and then rub them together as he adds a second finger. He stretches me as he moves in and out, making me ache for more. I want him inside me now, but I know that would be rushing things.

He must be just as eager because he reaches for the condom and tears it open. I still his hand, taking it from him and sliding it down his cock before coating him in lubricant.

"Are you ready?" he asks.

I nod. "Yes, I want to feel all of you."

He pushes a pillow under me before settling between my legs. I watch him closely as he presses the head of his cock against my hole. Excitement and anticipation fill me as he pushes until I feel myself opening up to him. It's been a while since I've had sex, so it feels tight, but he's slow and gentle as he pushes into me. I wrap my arms around him as he settles inside and kisses me gently.

"Are you good?"

"I'd be even better if you started moving," I say teasingly.

He grins at me and kisses me again. "Ah, that makes me want to move even *slower*," he says as he pulls out just a fraction and pushes back in just as achingly slow.

"Don't torture me," I say as I grab him and yank him into me.

He begins to pick up the pace, thrusting and moving inside me as pleasure takes over. I stop aching for him to move fast and instead just sink into the bliss of it. My body relaxes into him as his hand finds my cock. He strokes me as I draw my hands all over his body, wanting to feel all of him as he moves.

That's when he hits that spot inside me that makes my entire body tense up as I dig my fingers into him. "There," I moan, and when he does it again, I feel like I can't take much more. His hand tightens, understanding the need I have for him to guide me over the edge. His moans spur me on until my balls tighten. Pleasure washes through me as I come, but he doesn't stop and I feel like the pleasure is too much, though I don't want it to end. His movements quicken and I feel his cock pulse inside me as my body tightens around him. He groans as he comes inside me.

We're both panting as he covers me in soft, gentle kisses and I hold on to him without ever wanting to let go. I'd spend the rest of the day like this if he asked. Instead, he slowly pulls out of me, but he doesn't leave yet. He continues to kiss me and run his fingers down my body like he can't get enough of me, and I'm not sure I'll ever get enough of him.

And then Valerie ruins it all by hammering on the door and shouting, "Answer your goddamn phone, August!"

"Shit," he says as he jumps up.

"At least we won't have to invite her for a threesome."

He snorts. "Definitely not."

"I'm jumping in the shower. Get me if you need me."

"Alright, hopefully I'll join you in a moment."

CHAPTER EIGHTEEN

When I get out of the shower, I see that there are clothes waiting for me on the sink. I smile, thinking about August slipping in without me noticing. That is until I pick it up and see that it's a superhero suit that looks like bright, happy colors vomited all over it. I toss it onto the floor before yanking open the door to see August standing with Valerie.

August snickers and Valerie looks shocked, but how was I supposed to know she was on the other side? Even if I knew, I still might have yanked open the door.

"You let that crazy woman peep on me?" I ask in disbelief.

August shrugs. "We're currently discussing that. Did she touch your willy?"

Valerie looks disgusted. "I didn't *peep*. I just set the clothes on the counter."

"You call those clothes? And you actually expect me to wear them? I'm not wearing that."

She sighs. "What would you like to wear?"

"My clothes," I say as I head over to August's dresser and grab some underwear.

I pull them on as Valerie stares at me like the perv she is. Maybe it's been so long since she's seen a naked man that she's deprived.

"Are you enjoying the show?" I ask.

"I am," August inputs.

She doesn't bat an eye. "No."

August pulls a t-shirt out of his drawer and hands it to me. "She's gay, otherwise I'm sure she would be."

"I'm sure I *wouldn't*."

I give her a wicked smile. "Oh. Any unlucky ladies in your life, Valerie?"

"*Un*lucky?" she asks.

"Yes, because they'd have to be to be with you," I say as I pull on the T-shirt August hands me.

August claps his hands together in front of him. "I can tell you guys are just going to get along *smashingly*. It's weird remembering that you guys have only met this morning and are already the best of friends."

"I bet she'd carry our children if we asked," I say.

She shudders as I turn to find my pants. Before I can escape her radiating wrath, she grabs my wrist and pulls me around to face her.

"What?" I ask, before realizing she's looking at my burns. "Did this happen when you saved August?"

"It's nothing. It's fine."

She refuses to let me go and continues to scrutinize me. "These must have been pretty severe if they're still not healed."

"They're fine," I say.

She reaches out and sets a hand on my shoulder. "Thank you for saving him."

"I kind of like him and would prefer he's not burned to a crisp," I say.

"Me too."

"I like myself too!" August says as he walks over and wraps us both up in his arms. "I'm glad you guys like each other."

I grunt. She grunts.

Neither of us are really into that statement, but we'll put up with it for August.

"You better not be trying to steal my man," I warn her.

She snorts. It's no wonder why she can't find a lady. "Don't fret."

I give her a wide-eyed look. "Oh? Were you trying to steal me? I'm flattered, but really, *really* not looking for a cougar at this point."

She decides that she'd like to hug me as well, which turns more into a chokehold.

"August, she's killing me!" I cry.

"I might if you hadn't sacrificed yourself for August," she threatens before letting go of me and heading toward the door. "What color do you want your suit?"

"Black."

"Blue? Red?"

"Black."

She scowls.

"I'll just wear the one my mom made me. It's in August's car."

"No, we're getting you an outfit with protection," she says.

"It has built-in condoms?" I ask like I'm confused.

She slams the bedroom door before shouting. "Meeting room in ten!"

"She loves me," I tell August.

"I think she at least tolerates you."

"Love."

He shakes his head and yet somehow sort of nods it at the same time. But of course he can, he's Chrono and Chrono can do everything. "Yep. Love."

"Pure, nasty, sweat-filled love."

"A little gross, but okay."

I grin. "You've got ten minutes if you're taking a shower."

"Ah, right," he says as he heads into the bathroom, leaving me to flip through his clothes until I find the hoodie he was wearing when he saw me at the pet store that day. As I pull it on, my smile falls and my mind wanders away from happy thoughts. No matter how much I joke around, I still have to face what my brother has done.

I sink down on the bed as thoughts of my brother come rushing back. My phone is filled with calls and texts from the rest of the family, and I know I have to deal with them, but I'm not sure how to even face my own issues first.

"Hey," August says gently.

I hadn't even heard him come in. I had planned on being up, functioning, doing something before he got out so he didn't see me wallowing around like this.

"Just… taking a nap," I lie.

He kneels on the bed, making it dip. Then he covers me with his body and wraps me up tightly. "You don't need to keep the truth from me. You know that, right? If I woke up one day and my sister did something like that, I'd be upset too. You can't just pretend like nothing has happened. It's okay to be upset."

"Thank you," I say as I wrap my arms around him and squeeze him to me. "Thank you. Now let's go… do whatever ridiculous thing Valerie has planned."

I grab Zacia and put her harness on as we head down the hallway and ride the elevator up one floor. We step through the door and into a room that is already filled with five people. The room is clearly decorated for something that has to do with the holiday season because there are garlands hanging from the ceiling and a table centerpiece filled with holiday cheer. It kind of looks gaudy, so I bet Valerie did it.

Valerie is there with Wyatt, as well as three supers who sit at the table. Two are females and one is a male who is grinning at August. He winks at August and wiggles his fingers at him, and I cock my head as I assess his dark brown hair and almond-brown eyes.

He might look lithe and is very attractive, but I will win the fight for August.

"Hey!" August says with a huge smile as he rushes over and hugs the man. I'm fine with all of this until the man gives August's tight ass a nice smack. Only *I* am allowed to smack that ass.

"I've missed you!" the man says as he pulls back and kisses August's cheek. Then he turns to me and gives me a mischievous grin. "And who is this? I just want to eat you up!"

He grabs me into a hug like I know him—I suppose I know him from TV, but he doesn't know me—and I just awkwardly stand there as this strange man who smells like lavender hugs me.

"This is Landon," August says.

"Landon, it's a pleasure to meet you. You can call me by my superhero name, Schlongferno."

"Nope! His name is not that. We have talked about this," Valerie snaps as she grabs him and tears him off me. "Your name is Inferno. *In*ferno. Nothing else to it."

He sighs and sits down. "Just *Inferno*."

The young woman to his right leans over and says, "You realize that's Leviathan?"

Inferno's eyes get ridiculously wide. "Ooh. I do love meself a bad boy."

"This is mine," August says as he directs me away from Inferno.

"Oh, but do you have what it takes to satisfy him?" he practically purrs.

And suddenly, I'm loving this interaction. I've always wanted August to fight for me and now my fantasy has come true. *Fight, August, fight.*

"Why do you look so smug?" August asks as he pulls out a seat for me.

I feel like a little bit of truth is needed every now and then. "I want to see you guys fight."

"Oh lord," he says. "Sit down."

"Getting bossy now, are ya? I like it. What are you going to do if I don't sit?"

"I'll spank him for you," Inferno says as he leans forward.

"My life has turned to hell," Valerie says.

"Aw, did you look in the mirror?" I ask.

Inferno's eyes pop from his head. "Oh *damn*, he stands up to Valerie? Even I can't do that. I asked for a flamingo-pink supersuit. Does it look like I got my wish?" He dramatically waves to his dark purple suit.

"She brought me a gaudy suit and I refused to wear it," I say.

"Ooh... and she didn't murder you?" Inferno asks.

Valerie smacks the table. "I'm going to murder all of you if you don't sit your asses down and shut your mouths. Introductions are starting now. This is Landon. Landon, this is Inferno, real name Alexander."

"Lex," he interrupts. "She refuses to call me Lex because she's *evil*."

She ignores him. "Then this is Cinder, real name Amelia, and Joy, who doesn't have a hero name yet."

Joy looks like she's going to murder me with a look, her red-lined lips pursed. "He's a villain."

"Moving on," Valerie says.

I know of Lex, he's a hero from a bordering city. While he can start fires, as his name suggests, he doesn't seem to use his power too often. Through the villain grapevine, I was told it's because he can't control his fire. Supposedly, when he was a child, he burned down the foster home he was living in and nearly killed everyone inside it by accident. As for the other two, I don't know Joy at all, but if she doesn't have a hero name, maybe she's new. Amelia, on the other hand, I've heard some about, though she's generally not front and center because she's inexperienced, but her ability deals with manipulating earth.

Joyless folds her arms across her chest. For being named after a blissful emotion, she looks like she hates life. Or maybe just me. "You asked for my help, but you didn't tell me I'd be assisting a *villain*."

"I understand your concerns but at this moment, we have no reason not to trust him," Valerie says.

"What about his brother?" KillJoy asks as she stares at me with ice in her eyes.

"We have things figured out," Valerie says. "Landon, have you met the people in the Rebellion before?"

"I have. They actually accepted me into it when I didn't ask. Don't worry, someone else signed me up for it, I'm *far* too lazy to have signed myself up. When I told them I wasn't interested, they tried forcing me to stay. I got up and left though Racer tried stopping me, but I smashed him into the wall and told him I'd murder him if he touched me or my cat again. Then I walked home."

Valerie sighs loudly like she's disappointed in me. "Of course you joined the supervillains."

"I said I quit!"

"Do you at least know the location of their meeting place?"

"Um... I can give you the general direction," I say as I take her notebook and slide it over before jotting down my version of the directions. She snaps a picture of it with her phone and sends it off before her attention returns to me.

"Tell us everything you know about all of the members."

So I talk. A part of me feels like I'm betraying my brother, so I save him until last. Honestly, I don't know much about the others, but I give them everything I can in hopes of never getting to Nolan. The others had been wearing their suits and masks, like I was, but I describe them as well as I can.

"And then your brother," Valerie asks.

I hesitate. It feels so fucking traitorous talking about him. I'm honestly not sure I can even do it.

August reaches over and takes my hand as I pull in a breath. It feels like the first breath I've taken since I started talking about the members of the Rebellion.

"See?" Unjoyful Hag says.

"Joy, you have to look at it from his side. What if your sister suddenly did what his brother did? Would you want to immediately throw her to the wolves?" August asks.

She opens her mouth, then sinks in her chair. "Fine."

Further convincing me that August can talk anyone into anything. Well... besides Valerie.

"My brother can read minds, but that is the extent of his power," I say.

"Yet he was able to control people," Valerie says.

"Because... I gave him my power."

"Gave him?"

So I explain the snow globe, my powers, and Nolan. Not everything about Nolan, but enough for them to know how to avoid being hurt by him.

When I'm finished, Valerie nods and gives me a soft smile. "Good. Now at this point, we know very little. The mayor is with them, so we're going to the mayor's house to talk to his wife and see if she's noticed anything unusual. We're also going to check out this meeting place and bug it if we can, in case they go back to it."

"What do you want us to do?" I ask.

"August, Landon, and Lex, we'll send you three to the mayor's house. If there is any type of confrontation, call us immediately. Joy and Amelia, the two of you will go with me to check out the location and see if there's anything we can do to bug it. Wyatt will stay here and keep things under control. Landon, until we get you something in your size, wear August's spare suit. It's fireproof *and* bulletproof."

"Can I put on the one he's currently wearing? I want to smell like him," I say and Valerie glares daggers at me. "I want to wear his skin."

Lex, who'd been picking at the black nail polish on his nails, starts laughing. "I could help you make little mittens, if you want."

I nod, like I actually agree with any of this. "Ooh, his butt hair would be perfect for keeping my fingers warm."

Valerie walks over and glowers down at me. "You will not taint my others," she warns.

"I'm gonna taint them so hard," I assure her.

She wrinkles her nose and waves me off, like shooing me will save everyone from being tainted.

August pulls up to the mayor's home as I busy myself with picking my underwear out of my ass crack.

"How do you wear these pants? They go right up the crack," I say to August.

"That's why I don't wear that suit."

"Give me your suit, Lex."

"Not unless it means I get to see you N-A—"

August turns in his seat to face Lex. "Unless you're spelling napkin, you're going to shut up," August threatens, and it's unbelievably hot.

"Oh no, August! Lex is trying to rip my clothes off, what are you going to do?" I make sure all of this is said very dramatically and with a lot of emphasis. It comes out a little fake.

August ignores me and gets out. I look back at Lex who is grinning. "Aw, did you fail at getting August jealous? I'll fight for you if that's what turns you on."

"It does. Go fight August," I urge.

"I'll have to fight him with my brain, not my body because I don't want to chip a nail... *and get my ass kicked.*" He says the last part really fast and quiet, but it makes me laugh.

I get out of the car and look up at the house, gasping out of horror. "It's hideous," I cry.

"August? I know. I'm so much better than him," Lex says.

"No, their house."

Clearly, the mayor and his family get into the Christmas spirit if the blinding Christmas lights that coat every square inch of the borderline mansion have anything to do with it. There are fake reindeer scattered across the yard.

"I think it looks nice!" August says.

"I will never let you decorate our house like this," I warn him. "It's clear now what happened to the mayor! He was driven insane by the amount of gaudy lights. Case closed."

"Just because you hate brightness and cheer, doesn't mean everyone else does," August says.

"The only reason I would be into *any* of this is if you were wound up in Christmas lights, riding that fake reindeer naked."

"Ooh," Lex helpfully adds.

"With a Santa hat on your penis."

"Like a regular hat? Or my penis has a little penis-sized hat?" August inquires.

This is important. "Penis-sized, so basically it's the same size as a regular hat."

"Aww! You're so cute," August says.

"And I just vomited in my mouth. Romance is dead, boys. Don't try to bring it back."

August rings the doorbell and we wait and listen.

And wait.

"I don't think anyone's here," August says.

"We could break inside to make sure," I say as I start to reach for the doorknob.

The other two look aghast that I would ever think of breaking into a guy's house who is either bad or who is being brainwashed into thinking he's bad. Heroes.

"We're not allowed to go into a house without a warrant," August explains.

"They shouldn't be allowed to decorate the house like this without a warrant."

The day turns up nothing. From the mayor's house to the meeting location, everything is fairly uneventful, which I'm not at all sad about. I could take a heavy dose of normal for a while.

CHAPTER NINETEEN

"Landon!"

The world swirls around me, endless colors that make up everything and nothing all at once. I can't even understand what is happening, but I know that it's mine. It's all mine. Everything that surrounds me, every part that's inside me, it's all mine. But then I see a spot where the colors change and shift and dull.

I can't reach it, and I begin to panic.

Why can't I? Why can't I feel it?

"Landon!"

I look around myself, panicked now that it's gone. It was so close, but what happened to it? Where could it possibly have gone?

"Landon!"

I snap awake and look up before realizing that I'm still in a dream. Everything around me has risen into the air as light flickers up high from a tableside lamp floating above me.

"Landon!" August shouts and I turn to look at him as everything in the room turns with me. And then it's like an explosion happens. The dresser smashes into the wall as the lamp flies past me and shatters, immersing the room in darkness.

"What the fuck," I cry as August grabs me and a light comes on.

"Hey, hey, it's okay," he says as I look around at the massacred bedroom. The bedside table is punched halfway through the wall, into the next room. The dresser appears to have exploded and clothes are littered everywhere. My head is throbbing and my hands are shaking.

"What happened?" I ask. "Who did this?"

He squeezes me to him, but I don't understand why he's not getting up or doing something about the explosion that just took place in his room. "I think... you did this."

"I... did this?" I ask in disbelief, but now that the drowsiness is melting off me, it makes sense. It's the same thing that happened when they were attacking August.

That's when I hear hammering on the door and hurried feet. Clearly, they didn't wait long to let themselves in. The door slams into a chunk of the dresser that now blocks it.

"August, open the door! What happened?" Valerie yells.

"We're fine," August says as he gets out of the bed and rushes to the door. I slowly get out and look around me, turning to assess the damage I've caused. Besides the spot I'd lain, the entire room has been destroyed. It looks like a bomb went off, yet August and I are completely unharmed.

Valerie rushes in and grabs onto August, looking him over before stilling as she stares at the room. "What the hell happened?"

"I don't know, we were asleep when I heard something," August says as he walks over to me. "When I woke up and turned the light on, the dresser was shaking. Then everything just shot up into the air. It stayed elevated as I tried to wake Landon, and when he finally woke up, it all just went nuts." August gently pulls me to face him. "Are you okay?"

I nod, slowly, but I'm not sure if I really am.

I hold my hand out, over the top of a book. The book shakes on the ground. I fixate on it, watching it, fighting with it. It's like I'm slamming up against an impenetrable wall. My power is something that I've always been able to grasp onto almost immediately. I could lift cars with barely a thought, but once I lost it, I thought it was gone for good. But do I want it back now? Even if my brother wasn't wanting it for evil, would I want it back?

Maybe I would.

Suddenly, the book slowly lifts up into my hand.

"You're getting your powers back, right?" August asks.

"I... don't know. It's hard to grab it, but it's there. But why this?" I ask as I wave my hand around the room. "Why did it just... destroy everything? I'm really sorry." I ruined everything in his room. "I'm so sorry. I didn't mean to do this."

"Hey, it's okay," he says as his fingers gently move over my bare back. "You didn't do this on purpose."

There's more hammering on the front door, so Valerie slips out to talk to whoever has been alarmed by the horrible noise I caused.

"Come on, let's step out of here," he says as he guides me over to the bedroom door. When we pass through, Valerie is shutting the front door. August grabs me a blanket and drapes it over my bare shoulders. Thankfully, we'd worn underwear, or we'd be giving Valerie quite the view.

"I'm really sorry," I say again.

"It's okay," August urges. "Honestly. If anything is ruined, it can be replaced."

"I don't like this. I don't like not being in control..."

Valerie walks back to us and I realize that I should be as truthful as I can.

"What if this happens and I hurt someone?" I ask earnestly.

"You didn't hurt me either time. Both times you were able to keep me safe."

"I don't think you guys realize how powerful I am," I say.

"I saw you pick up a building, I'm aware."

"But I can do little things too. Like... I could think about your heart and crush it with just a thought," I whisper. "I don't have to kill someone by hitting them or hurting them. I can kill them just by thinking about it. What if I accidentally kill someone when this... thing happens? What if I can't stop it?"

August squeezes me gently, making me lean into him. "You've never hurt anyone. The last time you picked people up too, but no one was hurt," August assures me.

Valerie is quiet, but when I look at her, she meets my eyes. She opens her mouth, but before she can speak, her phone starts ringing. When she sees who it is, she backs up and quickly answers it.

"It'll be okay," August promises. "I trust you."

"But I can't control it."

"Subconsciously, you have to be. If you weren't, you would have hurt someone."

I'm not convinced, but I still my racing thoughts because Valerie looks upset about something.

"Okay, I'll get my team there immediately," she says as she waves for us. August goes back into his room to fetch his suit, but I remain standing there as Valerie hangs up.

"The villains have been sighted at the East River bridge," she announces.

"What are they doing there?" August asks as he comes out with his outfit and mine. He shakes a few wood shards off them and pushes mine into my hands.

Valerie shakes her head. "I'm not sure yet, but I fear they're planning on destroying the bridge to keep help from coming or anyone from leaving. I'm going to call the others. Meet me upstairs."

"I'm not sure I should go. I have no way to help," I say.

"We need you, Landon. Now excuse me," she says as she rushes out the door.

I look over at August, who gives me an encouraging smile, and put the suit on. Dressed, I follow him up to the first floor where Joy is already waiting. She's nervously pacing before looking to August who is very calm and collected. I haven't seen Joy at all through the media, so she might not have any experience out in the world. Lex has definitely been around for quite a while, but he's stationed in a nearby city. What I've been told about Lex is that since he has a hard time controlling his fire, they keep him on little jobs, just in case he incinerates the city.

But he's cute and the girls love him, so they flaunt him because he's personable. I've pretty much ignored his media existence since August is all I have, and have ever had, eyes for.

Valerie comes rushing up with Amelia, who is quite new, and I also know very little about.

"Everyone ready?" Valerie asks, and I'm not sure if it matters because she's pushing us out the door.

We step into the parking garage where a large SUV waits. It's heavy-duty and makes me wonder if it's bulletproof to protect us.

Valerie gets into the front passenger seat and the five of us file into the two back seats.

"You alright?" August asks.

"Yeah. I have a little headache, but I'm fine."

"When this is all over with, do you want to come to Christmas at my house? I'm assuming you guys don't celebrate it," August asks, and I wonder if he's talking about this to distract me from what happened earlier in the bedroom.

I force my mind away from what happened. "Aw, and not get the chance to break into a store and steal stuff?"

He laughs, then it seems to dawn on him that I'm not joking. "Oh... you're... serious. That's what you guys do?"

"Yep."

"Oh..."

Lex turns around in his seat to face us. "I'll break in anywhere and steal you," he tells me with a wink.

"Back off," August says, and I can't help but grin maniacally.

I reach over and squeeze August's hand. "I want to. And I want to cheat at board games again and make your family love me. I also want you to kiss me under the mistletoe. I want you dressed as Santa Claus and then you'll tear your clothes off and go 'Ho, ho, ho, suck my cock.'"

That makes Joy and Amelia turn around.

August just looks amused. "Sure, babe."

"He's been brainwashed," Joy decides.

"I'm... going to have to agree," Amelia says. "I used to think he was the normal one of the group. A little happier than the average guy, but still normal."

"He likes the brainwashing," I assure them. "I can even make him wear his glasses on command."

"You wear *glasses*?" Joy asks. "Why didn't I know this?"

"Because he does it just for me," I say smugly.

"I actually do it whenever my eyes get tired of contacts as well," August adds.

"No, it's just for me."

"Listen up!" Valerie barks in case any of us have lost our hearing in the past ten minutes. "The police have arrived and are trying to create a blockade. There is a ton of traffic from people trying to get out of the city, so the bridge is filled with cars. August and Lex, your priority is stopping the villains. Amelia, Joy, and Landon, you will assist, but you three also need to help keep an eye on the police who are going to be escorting people off the bridge. We need to walk away with *no* casualties. Understand?"

"Do we know who is there yet?" I ask.

"We don't. We're going to have to go in assuming the worst and hoping for the best. Now listen to me, *all* of you. Do not take chances. If you think something might be too risky, then it is. Don't do it. Worry about yourselves and your comrades. We'll do everything we can for everyone else, but you'll be saving *no one* if you wind up dead," she says, and I gain a little respect for her. "Even you, pain in my ass."

Clearly, she can't be talking about me. That's when I realize *who* she's talking about. "Aw, she's talking about you, KillJoy."

"KillJoy!" Lex gleefully says, and even August wraps me up in his arms like he's going to protect me from Joy's wrath.

"If the villain disappears, no one will care, right?" Joy asks as she glares at me.

"I will," August says as he hugs me even tighter. "He's a good guy, I promise. He's just a little prickly."

"I'll *try* to trust him, but I'm keeping a close eye on him," Joy says.

"Is there anything else we need to know?" I ask.

"We'll talk with the police when we arrive," Valerie explains.

Which should be in another minute or two since it's not too far now. I lean forward to look out the window as I see a line of police cars with police hiding behind them. They're facing the mouth of the bridge, a huge six-lane structure that stretches over the river. It's one of the few ways out of the city, since it's cut off by the large river that wraps around it.

The SUV pulls over and we all file out as the police hold a barricaded line.

"One of you really needs to get on top of this flying shit like they do in the movies," I say.

"It'd make our job easier," August says.

"Sergeant Thompson!" Valerie says, but the man doesn't instantly turn. Instead, he stays fixated on whatever is going on in front of them.

The police are trying to escort vehicles off without letting the villains through, so they've created a straight line using their cars for cover.

"Thompson!" Valerie shouts.

And that's when he begins to turn. But when I notice everyone else turning, almost as if by one mind, I throw my hand up to stop them, before remembering that I can't. As their guns aim at us, I shout, "August!" He turns, having not been looking at the police, but at something beyond them.

That's when the guns fire. I grab him, yanking him back as the sound of gunfire lights up the street. But when I'm not instantly turned into swiss cheese, I look up in surprise, only to find Joy holding her hand out. The bullets hit an invisible wall, instantly dropping to the ground as I realize that she's created some type of barrier around us.

"I can't hold it long, get behind the vehicle!" she shouts, and everyone starts rushing for the SUV.

"I can't do anything," I say as August pulls me behind the SUV. "I'm useless."

"You are not useless. You were able to stop Nolan last time. Nolan is obviously here if these people are doing this," he says. "*You* can stop him."

I know he's right. I know I need to stay focused and stop getting down on myself for not doing enough. "Okay. You're right. I can't see anything."

"I can only freeze time for a short period. I'd probably have time to get past the police, but I don't have enough time to disarm them all," he says. "Valerie, what if I take Landon to the other side where we'll see if we can get within range of the villains?"

"Take Lex instead. We need someone who can fight back," she says.

"And when Nolan forces me to stand there while they beat the shit out of me again?" August asks.

I look to August because I see Valerie's side as well. "You can't take both of us?" I'm not quite sure *how* it works.

August shakes his head. "I could, but it shortens how long I can freeze time."

"We need to decide something quickly because they're coming for us."

August takes my hand. "Everyone else, get in the car. Landon and I are going to try and get behind the parked vehicles on the bridge and see if we can figure out where the villains are," August decides.

Valerie looks like she's going to say something, then shoves a gun into my hands. A *gun*. Like I have a freaking idea of how I'm going to just shoot someone with it. I'll probably shoot myself first.

"What do I do with this thing?"

"Shoot them!"

"How?"

"With the gun!" she says.

"Are there bullets in it?"

Her eyes get unbelievably wide. "No. I just gave you a *gun* with *no* bullets in it and said, 'Here, take on some supervillains.'"

I narrow my eyes. "You are the worst villain of all," I growl.

"I'm just *saying*."

"And I'm just *saying* that I don't know how to shoot someone with a gun!"

She pulls out a finger gun, pulls the "trigger" and cocks her head. "There. Guns 101."

"There's a part of me that wants to hate you, but you're so evil that I can't help but like you. Try not to die because I want to be the one to strangle you."

"Your tiny, little arms couldn't strangle a kitten," she says.

That's when my phone starts ringing, and I see that it's Brandon. I'm not sure how much more stupidity I can deal with before realizing that maybe... just maybe, he could be helpful for once in his life.

"Brandon!"

"How do you tell if cheese has gone bad?" he asks.

"I need you at the East River bridge *now*."

"Do you really want to see the cheese that badly? I mean, I can bring it, I guess. I was just hoping you already knew."

"Dammit, Brandon! Nolan's turned into a *villain* villain, and now he's trying to take over the city with that fucked-up crew of his, and if we don't stop him, someone might kill him. Please come help me. When you get here, look for a black SUV and help them."

"Alright! I'll be there in five minutes. Do I bring the cheese or leave it at home?"

"You figure it out," I growl as I hang up.

"Everything good?"

I give August a smile and a nod. "My brother's bringing cheese so I can help him figure out if it's gone bad or not."

August's head cocks. "Oh... That's... interesting."

I sigh. "I'm ready to go."

"Let's move out, then," August says as he moves to the side of the SUV as everyone else gets into it. The cops are moving in and I try to understand how my brother could do this. How he's making people want to *kill* others. It's hard to understand. It's hard to fathom why he'd do this.

But I know I have to stop him.

CHAPTER TWENTY

August grabs my hand, and suddenly the world around me is frozen. He yanks me forward as he starts to run, but he makes a wide berth around the cops.

"Just in case time starts up again, I can't have us getting shot," he explains as we move past them. The moment we are behind them, I see that there's a wide expanse before we can reach the cars that are blocked on the bridge by cement dividers that someone with a lot of strength or some type of power had put there. We slide past the first row of vehicles and time starts again.

We duck down, using the cars for cover as the sounds of the police and bullets fill the dawn. Once we're sure the police haven't noticed our escape, August peeks above the car we're using for cover. He assesses the situation before giving me a nod.

"Okay, as we move forward, we're going to try to push anyone still in their vehicles out to the south end of the bridge. Once Valerie—"

Something *slams* into me with so much force, I'm flung away from August and bash into the guardrail of the bridge. I teeter for a moment, grabbing for anything I can reach but my hand grasps nothing as I begin to slip. At the very last moment, I catch onto the railing as I begin to dip over the edge. My arm strains as I pull myself back to keep from plummeting into the water a hundred feet or so beneath me. I scramble back, falling onto my ass in my panic, and turn around while trying to figure out how I got from one end of the bridge to the other so quickly. I even sailed over the middle barrier at some point.

When I turn, I get my answer as Racer faces August, hand outstretched with the snow globe in it. For a moment, I think August is reaching to destroy it, before I realize that he's got that slack expression on his face that the others wear when Nolan is controlling them.

And August is going to touch the snow globe and give his powers to them. If August lost his powers as well, we would truly be fucked and the villains would have an unbelievable amount of power.

"August, stop!" I scream as I run for him, but I have three lanes to cross before I even *reach* the barrier for the oncoming traffic. There's no way I can reach him in time. "August, listen to me! Please!" I beg. There are so many cars blocking my path that I'm having trouble getting to him, but I keep moving because I have to. I can't let them take August's power as well. They would destroy everything with it.

Suddenly, fire leaps up in front of August, clearly from Lex, who I don't see. While August doesn't even flinch and keeps moving forward, toeing the flames, Racer jerks back, globe toppling from his hand and hitting the ground. It rolls back as I leap the barrier and run for August. I grab him, wrapping my arms around him and tugging him back just at the moment he was planning on walking straight through the flames.

"Landon?" he asks, snapping out of the trance as I pull him away. It seems like there's something about my touch that removes him from Nolan's grasp. "What's going on?"

"Freeze time!" I beg.

"Okay," he says as time freezes and I yank him after me, toward Racer who is frozen as he lifts the globe from the ground.

"I can't hold onto the time," August says, and everything snaps back into place just as I'm reaching for the globe. Racer, seeing me, rushes off, moving faster than my eyes can follow him.

That's when Darknight slips out from behind a car to stop our chase. I pull the gun out that Valerie gave me and aim it at him.

"Back the fuck off," I growl.

He does the exact opposite, while looking quite villainous in his completely black suit that I kind of dig. He moves with silent steps, completely ignoring me like I'm of no concern while he stays fixated on August. He rushes for August, and I pull the trigger.

Nothing happens.

"Dammit, Valerie!" I snap as I remember that guns have safeties, right? So people don't shoot off their nuts when they're sticking it into a holster.

I flip the gun around to examine it while August rushes up to meet Darknight. They begin to fight as I dumbly try to figure out how to switch the safety off.

August throws Darknight back, and finally, here is my chance. I pull the trigger and a bullet flies straight for him until he literally catches it out of the air, looks at it as he holds it between two fingers, and then flicks it at me. The bullet hits me square in the middle of the forehead before tumbling down.

This is why you don't go to a fucking superhero fight with a goddamn gun!

I nearly chuck the stupid thing before remembering that it *might* have another use later down the line. Or maybe it was enough of a distraction because August punches the man right in the face so damn hard the man drops to his knees. A nice roundhouse to the side of the head just adds to Darknight's demise.

"Let's keep moving. Our priority is getting the globe and getting anyone on the bridge off," August says.

"I'm coming!" Lex yells as he rushes for us.

When I hear more feet behind us, I turn to see Valerie as she tails Lex with Amelia and Joy at her heels. "We'll secure Darknight," Valerie assures us.

Lex, August, and I move forward, making our way across the bridge. When Lex sees someone in their car, he rushes to tell them to meet up with Valerie as August and I continue moving forward.

But as I move, my mind is fixated on my brother and the mess he's creating.

"I need to stop Nolan. When he took control of you… they were trying to take your power," I explain as I jog alongside August, keeping low to try and use the cars for cover as we make our way across the bridge in the direction Racer went. There's no way of knowing if the others are with him, but if we get the globe and I get my powers back, I'll be able to do so much more to help. Hopeful for that outcome, we race down the middle, sliding between stopped trucks and cars as carefully as we can. Lex meets up with us as we use another car for cover.

It looks like we'll be able to reach the middle of the bridge before long, and hopefully, we'll be able to see what's going on.

That's when the cars begin to shake.

At first, I fear the bridge is collapsing, but the ground beneath my feet stays steady as a lighter car lifts up and slams into the bridge's support. The sound of crunching metal fills the air as we shy away from debris raining down on us.

"They're trying to bring the bridge down," August says, but my concern is something else.

No one else has the power of telekinesis besides me in this area. Not this powerful, at least. Maybe I'm wrong. Maybe they're not using telekinesis. Maybe they can affect metal or rubber or something.

That must be it.

Please let that be it.

"We have to move. I'm going to try my best to freeze time to get us off the bridge and to the side they're on," August says.

"Lex, the moment time stops, throw fire around us to keep Racer from grabbing one of us like he did with me," I say.

Lex looks worried but nods. "I'll try my hardest. My fire is... hard to control sometimes. Especially if I'm not gentle with it."

"Do your best. We have fireproof suits on and most of the people are off the bridge by now."

He nods as August grabs both of our hands and freezes time just as a car flies into the air. It's frozen there, suspended above us as we run, but we make a wide berth around it to keep from being crushed by it in case time starts again. August's grip tightens and I can tell he's struggling, but he keeps moving forward. When he stumbles, he throws Lex and me forward. The world snaps back into motion as the car slams into another support. Fire erupts before us as August struggles to catch his breath.

"August, we can just run if it's—"

My words are cut off by a car flying toward us. I hold my hand out, *begging* my power to stop it, but August grabs Lex and me, tearing us back. Then he uses his strength to shove the car out of our path.

"We should go back. We're outpowered and outnumbered," Lex says.

"We can stop them," August says, but I'm not sure we can. "I promise. I'll go ahead if you guys don't want to."

"I'm not leaving you," I say when the car that'd been hiding us is lifted up, leaving us in the open and vulnerable. We start running forward as cars shift and the bridge quivers.

As I'm rushing past a semi, it begins to shake before teetering, falling toward me. I rush forward, barely slipping out of the way as it crashes to the ground, making the bridge shake beneath my feet.

Or maybe something else is doing that because support beams snap and fall and the bridge begins to vibrate.

Lex motions ahead of us. "I can see Marauder. We have to stop him."

"Lex, can you send fire that far?" August asks as my eyes settle on Marauder flanked by Nolan and Racer. His hand is firmly on top of the snow globe, using its powers... no... *my* power to destroy everything.

"I can try," he says as he holds his hand out. Fire races toward them as the ground shudders and Lex is thrown forward. The fire goes wild, rushing for a car instead.

August grabs for me, and at first, I think he's pulling me toward him until he retrieves the gun from where it's tucked and aims it toward Marauder. He pulls the trigger and Marauder falls back, hand snapping away from the snow globe.

I will never ever tell Valerie that her dumb little gun might have saved our lives.

Racer pulls Marauder back, leaving the others to follow behind, but Nolan stands there, eyes fixated on mine.

"Dammit, Nolan!" I yell, unsure if my voice will even reach him over the creaking and groaning of the bridge. "Why'd you do this?"

He tears his eyes away from me as August pulls me off the bridge and onto safe ground. But I can't stop watching Nolan. His face shows so much *emotion,* so many overwhelming emotions that it confuses me.

"Nolan!" Marauder shouts and his voice seems to come from everywhere at once, even though I can't see him. "Do it now."

And the emotions are gone. Nolan reaches his hand out and I turn around as the bridge begins to crumble, chunks falling, cars slamming into the railings. That's when I see the police, Valerie, and the others standing on the bridge, faces slack, no intention of leaving as the bridge falls apart around them.

"Valerie!" August yells, but it doesn't even faze her.

"Nolan, you can't do this!" I plead as I turn to face him, but he's gone. August seems to appear five feet in front of me, clearly having tried to stop time again, but his nose is bleeding, telling me that he's already overexerted himself. Then he begins to run for the bridge as it collapses around them.

"August, don't!" I shout as I reach for him.

Suddenly, my power flows into me, swirling around me as the bridge finally gives way and falls into the churning river below, but the single slab that they'd been standing on stays elevated as I fixate on it. I wrap my power around all of them as everything else falls away. Praying I have them all held up with my mind, I allow the ground beneath their feet to fall, lightening my load as I pull them to me. But it's strenuous, dragging them with each tug. It's like physically pulling a semitruck as the power is torn from me, split between the globe that seems to have some connection to me, and the people who are beginning to realize what the circumstances are.

"Just a little farther," August says gently.

"I'm not sure I can do it." My hands are shaking and the people are beginning to drop, but they're still twenty feet from the safety of the edge.

"You can do it. You're the most powerful person I've ever seen," August says as he gently touches me. It's like just the soft touch of his fingers gives me the strength to keep pushing., to find that source of power inside me. It's hard to reach, and it's even harder to hang on to, but I grip onto it and I pull and I tug it with all I've got because I *have* to save them. I *can* save them.

August's attention snaps away and he pulls back, making my power dip and the group of people suspended in the air scream.

"August, come back."

"I'm right here, just stay focused," he says, but the strain in his voice tells me that he's focused on something else.

"August, I'm losing my hold on them," I say as I see the terror in their eyes. Will they die because of me? Because I lack the strength to hold on to them? Because I *gave* my power away?

I reach back and grab August's hand and it feels like power rushes back into me. It floods into my body. I can grasp onto my gift and feel it again so I can pull them toward me until there is ground beneath them. I drop them from five feet up, unable to set them down, and they fall onto the cracked earth, but they're safe.

That's when I see what August had been worried about.

Darknight rushes forward, knife in hand as he drives it right toward me while August pulls me back. Exhausted, he struggles to be as fast as Darknight. He lets go of me to rush for Darknight but slams right into the side of someone.

"Don't you dare touch my brother," Brandon growls and he whaps Darknight in the side of the head with a bag of cheese. The knife is driven against Brandon's chest, but bends and snaps. Brandon grabs him in a chokehold and throws him to the ground. The man struggles and fights, clearly not taking the choking well, but Brandon doesn't let up until Darknight sags in his arms and drops to the ground.

"Whoops." Brandon looks over at me with a huge smile. "Hey, Bro. I saved your life."

I lean against my giant of a brother, exhausted, tired, and relieved. "Oh, my special brother. You never cease to amaze me."

"Is that a good thing?" he asks.

"It's a good thing," I whisper.

"It looks like the others ran off," August says as he assesses his surroundings. "Let's get everyone out of here. I don't have the power to stop them if they come back with another attack." August pats Brandon on the back. "Good job, and thank you for saving us."

Brandon gives August a huge smile. "Does this mean I'm a hero now?"

I look at Brandon in surprise. "I thought you wanted to be a villain!"

"Yeah, but... it's kind of nice being thanked for doing something instead of yelled at about it."

Valerie comes over while looking calm and collected like nothing that has happened to her has been concerning in the slightest. She begins barking orders, sending people here and there, putting Darknight in cuffs.

All the while, August and I stand there, mentally and physically exhausted, using my brother as a support. I feel almost sick and I know it's from pulling my gift back to me when it's wherever the fuck it is. In the snow globe? Who knows. I've given up looking for answers.

"My head is mush," August says.

"I got some cheese. Will that make you feel better?" Brandon asks.

I pat Brandon's arm. "No one wants your moldy cheese."

"Is it okay to eat?" he asks as he holds it out to me.

"I kind of feel nauseous, so if you don't want me to throw up on it, maybe keep it back," I say as I slowly sink to my butt as Brandon stands over me like a guard dog. A cheese-holding guard dog.

He's eating the cheese now. Of course he is.

"Are you alright?" August asks as he kneels next to me, blood smeared across his face from his nose bleeding. We're clearly messes.

"Perfect," I lie. "You?"

"Perfect," he says as he sits down beside me and leans against my shoulder. He grasps onto my hand as we take a moment to let the havoc settle down that our powers have caused.

Valerie walks over to us, eyes my brother, then squats down to face us. "You guys alright?"

"We're good. Just taking a breath," August says. "Need us?"

"No, there are enough people on it. Media is here, and will be harassing you soon," she says. "Do you know what happened to them?"

"I shot Marauder and Racer pulled him away," August says. "I'm assuming the rest just went with him."

She nods before looking at me. "Thank you... for saving our lives." She looks very earnest and it feels strange. "But don't think this will keep you from having to listen to my rules," she jokes.

I smile at her. "I actually tried just catching everyone but you, but somehow you just dug your talons and malice in and clung on."

She shakes her head but gives me a warm look. "You did good."

"Am I allowed to spank August's booty in front of the cameras now?" I ask.

"Absolutely not. If you do, I'll personally hand you over to the villains."

"She likes me," I tell August.

"I think she does."

And that's when a reporter finds us. "Chrono and Leviathan, tell us what happened," the man says as he charges for us.

"Please save the questions for later. The area is still unsafe," Valerie says.

"What's your name? Are you a hero too?" The man shoves his microphone into Brandon's face.

"Ooh. I am! I crushed that man's neck when he tried hurting my brother. If you try hurting my brother, I will also crush your neck."

The man looks worried. "A... villain, then? And I'm not going to hurt your brother."

"Then do you want some cheese?" he asks.

The reporter seems to be trying to figure out if "cheese" is a code-name for something until he sees the literal bag of cheese in his hand. "No... thank you."

"You're welcome."

"You were recently arrested for breaking into a bank; how did you become a hero?"

"Enough questions, this area is unsafe and if you don't choose to move, you will be arrested," Valerie growls.

"You heard the pretty lady," Brandon says.

The man chooses to ignore them both and stuffs his microphone back into Brandon's face. "What happened here today?"

I reach out and squeeze my hand shut. Both the camera and the microphone fly toward me, so I toss them behind me in the rubble as the men cry out and run for their equipment, only for a police officer to stop them.

"Whoops. My hand slipped. I was trying to shove it up your assholes," I growl.

Brandon thinks this is hilarious. Valerie does not, but she doesn't yell at me. I suppose saving her life might make her a bit more lenient.

CHAPTER TWENTY-ONE

I feel like I've barely fallen asleep just to be rudely woken up *again*. We'd spent all day yesterday after the attack dealing with the wreckage. While there were some injured, there were no dead, thankfully.

Still, we had to deal with the wounded and the living. Then we had to go through this big whole thing where we had to give our statements to be "legal" that resulted in everyone hating me because my head hurt and I really didn't feel like retelling the same damn tale fifteen times.

"Why is the phone ringing? Destroy it with your super strength!" I command as I roll toward August and wrap my arms around his bare chest. I snuggle up against him.

August pulls me close with one arm as he picks up his phone and looks at it. "It's just a text."

"From?"

"Valerie, asking us to meet in the meeting room at nine."

"That has to be like fifteen hours from now."

"Twenty minutes, actually."

"How dare she wake us at nine," I grumble as I close my eyes and calculate how many more minutes I can sleep so that I can arrive *just* at nine. At least twenty.

August's fingers gently run over my back, rubbing away all the anger that came with being woken at such a horrible hour. Doesn't she realize that I nearly exploded my brain yesterday for *her*?

Clearly, she doesn't.

Zacia stretches, digging her claws into my side as she does so, then begins kneading my skin like mortally wounding me would be ideal.

"Ready?" August asks.

"To go back to sleep? Sure, I'd love to. Thanks for asking," I say as I close my eyes again and just listen to the beat of his heart. I had strange dreams last night. Dreams of August falling from the bridge, dreams of Nolan begging me to join him. But thankfully, the room didn't explode this morning, so that's one positive start to the day. I did notice that the cleaners removed everything but the bed.

August stops rubbing and squeezes me before giving me a cheek kiss and slithering out from under me.

"Traitor," I growl as he leaves me cold and alone. So I roll over and pull Zacia to me. She's wearing her pajamas, so she's like a little fleece fluffball. Even with the pajamas on, she paws at the blanket until I pull it over her to cover her little naked legs and head. I'm getting her a full bodysuit next time. All that will be seen is her little snout and eyes.

"Have you talked to your parents?" August asks curiously as he folds the covers back, like he's not happy enough ruining his morning, he needs to ruin mine as well. Zacia and I both glare at him. Okay, maybe she can't glare, but if she could, she would be.

"Nope. Don't plan on it."

"I'm sure they want to know what's going on with your brother and everything," he says as he holds out his hand. What he wants to do with it, I'll never know because my hands are now preoccupied with holding Zacia to me to steal her warmth. Her tiny little body is barely adequate.

"I really don't want to talk to them. They'll probably want me to join my brother."

"Or... maybe they'll be like Brandon and just want both of you to be safe."

Oh, poor sweet August, always thinking the best of everyone when they're secretly strange monsters. "Ehhhh..."

"You don't know until you try," he says, pulling a pair of his jeans onto me like he's giving up on me getting out of bed.

I give him my hand and he pulls me up to my feet and works his pants the rest of the way up my legs before buttoning them. Then he uses a belt to help keep them on since they're clearly too big for me.

I grudgingly get dressed while ignoring all ideas about contacting or talking to my family. I can only imagine what Brandon has told them now that he's convinced he's going to become a hero.

We head down to the conference room with one minute to spare.

"I could have slept for one full minute."

"Aw, that's awful. I'm so sorry I deprived you of your minute," August says with a toying smile.

I narrow my eyes. "You better be. Keep doing shit like that and who knows what'll happen to you."

"I'm shaking in my panties," he whispers.

"Good," I say as I step into the conference room where everyone but Lex is waiting.

"Have a seat. If Lex doesn't get here in the next minute, I'm going to hunt him down, pin him to the ground and force him to remove that godforsaken nail polish," Valerie threatens.

Lex pulls open the door, looks at Valerie, then shuts the door while never coming into the room.

"Get your ass in here," she snaps.

"You're so mean!" he cries as he comes in with a pout. "I like my pretty nails. Do you like my pretty nails?" Lex holds his hands out in front of me so I can see the black polish.

"I do," I say. "They're the color of Valerie's heart. Maybe that's why she doesn't like them."

"Oh, come here, sweet child," she says as she walks over to me and grabs me into a hug. "You have a face that makes me want to love you but a personality that makes me want to throw you out."

"Aw, you think I'm cute," I say with a smile. "I think I am too."

She snorts and pushes me toward a chair. "Sit, all of you."

"You *could* just kick him out," KillJoy says.

"Joyless, I think they have a spot for you cleaning toilets," I say. "And my cat's litter box needs cleaning every five minutes."

"I literally think the only way you know how to make friends is by being mean to people," August decides.

"Friends? Ew, gross. Yuck. Will you guys be my friends? All my other friends are villains," I say.

"I'll be more than a friend," Lex purrs as he reaches out and takes my hand.

"Aw, thanks, bud. But I don't really want a butt-fuck friend," I say. "Any other takers? All of you? Awesome. I love you guys too."

Valerie sighs and sits down as the door opens and Wyatt comes in. He gives us a nod and also takes a seat before dutifully listening.

"We've questioned Darknight, but I'm positive we would get more out of a brick wall. He refuses to say anything to the point where I'm not even sure if he even talks. He's currently been completely useless. So I want to compile everything we know about this snow globe," Valerie says.

"It seems to strengthen the power of others who touch it," August says.

"They were trying to use it on August, so I don't understand how it can take some powers or amplify others."

"Maybe it has to do with where they're touching it or how?" Amelia suggests.

Valerie nods. "Good question. That's something we'll have to look into."

"Marauder, who we are assuming made the globe or powered the globe, was able to use my power," I say. "He was using telekinesis on the bridge."

"Landon, would you be able to sit down and talk with our powers specialists? They'll just go over parts of your power so we know what we're up against if Marauder uses it against us," Valerie suggests.

I nod, not seeing any harm in it. "Sure."

"Why attack that bridge?" Lex asks curiously.

"I don't know," Valerie says. "It could be a power statement, to show what they can do and to inflict fear. Or they could have more motives, such as stopping the flow of traffic in and out of the city. There are four main bridges that span over the river surrounding the town. If they were to take all four down, people would panic and try to leave out of fear of being stuck in the city with no way out. But now that we know what's going on, we'll do our best to keep the other bridges under surveillance."

We talk some more, but then Valerie sends me off with a small team and keeps the others. I run through their questions and do all of their little tests. Tests that I would have flown through with barely a thought before take me time and energy now. Thankfully, they don't push me too hard because they want me to be able to do something if we're attacked again. Still, I've been without August for about four hours and even had to eat lunch with these guys.

When I head upstairs, I find August reading a book with his glasses on and decide it's the hottest thing I've ever seen.

"Oh my god," I breathe as I dramatically grab my heart and fall against the door I just shut.

"What's wrong?" he asks as he looks up at me.

"You're so hot."

He snorts. "Valerie said we have the rest of the day off to recoup and relax in order to rejuvenate our powers," he explains as he shuts the book. "So... I thought we could go on a date."

"We're not allowed to leave. Ooh! Are you going to be a bad boy and sneak me out, then Valerie is going to be waiting up for us when we get back and we'll have to distract her with the ol' playing dead trick?"

"Never heard of that trick."

"Or maybe she'll have a whip and spank your perfect ass?"

"Hopefully not, since we'll stick around here. I'm sure we can do something to entertain ourselves."

"Ooh, I like the way you think. Make Valerie's life a living hell."

He grins. "Or like... play a game?"

"Oh, yeah, I like that idea too," I say. Not as much, but I would literally enjoy anything that involves spending time with August. "Let me get dressed for the occasion," I say as I go over to the pile of clothes in the corner of the living room since I can't even be trusted with furniture anymore.

"What is this?" I ask as I flip through them while acting like I can barely touch them.

"What's wrong?"

"Why are they so *colorful*?"

"Well... you could have had one black shirt to wear but you had me tear it off your body, remember?"

I grin at the thought. "I do. It was so sexy. Quick! Tear my clothes off!"

"We can't ruin all of your clothes."

"Ah, shit, you're right. Ew, did Valerie pick out this ugly thing too?" I ask as I hold up a catshit brown sweater.

"No, that's the only shirt that I picked out in that pile."

"Aw, it's so cute! I'm going to wear it, I love it so much," I say as I pull it on. I look like a giant turd, but August picked it out, so it's now my favorite sweater ever and I will never take it off.

"You don't have to wear it if you don't like it."

"Yeah, but you picked it out, which makes it supreme."

He gives me a smile. "You're too cute for me."

"Nah. Now what's our plan?"

"There's an entertainment room down one floor. They built it to try and entertain me, and to keep me from running away. I spent a lot of time shooting hoops by myself."

"Aw, did no one like you?"

"They all loved me so much that I had to get away from them."

"Ew, they sound hideous."

"Thanks, babe."

"I'll keep all those skanky eyes off you, honey bun."

"Aw, and how will you do that?" he asks.

"I'll take them to my lair and throw them in the dungeon where I'll make them do evil deeds for me like clean the house and sew mini kitten clothes for Zacia with their bare hands," I decide.

"Oh, that sounds torturous."

"I know, right?" I ask with a grin as we step out into the hallway and make our way over to the elevators. We ride one down one level and he takes me to a large open room that reminds me of a high school gymnasium. It's nearly empty, so he heads to a closet and pulls it open.

"What do you want to do?" he asks. "There are bowling pins we can set up."

"Bowling? I was thinking something a little more... violent. Like dodgeball and whoever gets hit has to strip an item of clothing off."

"Um... your entire right side is *burned*."

"Guess you better not hit it."

"No! I'm not chancing that!"

207

"It's *fine*. It's been weeks."

"Like two weeks."

"Yeah? So? All good."

"Not good."

"I just ran across a bridge and took on supervillains. I think I can handle some dodgeball."

"Bowling it is. Whoever knocks down the least amount of pins each time has to strip an item off until they're in their underwear. We can't go further than that, seeing as someone is likely to walk in."

I sigh. "You're no fun."

He catches my eyes with a smug look on his handsome face. "Are you bad at bowling? Is that why you're concerned?"

"Of course not. But I want to play dodgeball because I want to bash you so hard with my balls."

He snorts. "How about some other time?"

"Deal," I say as he goes into a closet and comes out with a bag of stuff. He sets the pins up in the corner and hands me a ball that isn't quite as heavy as a normal bowling ball.

"Each turn, the one with the lowest number has to strip," August says.

"Deal," I say, *very* glad some of my power has returned to me.

"No cheating."

"I would *never!*" I say like I'm mortified he'd suggest that. But I'm also aware that I'll do anything to get him as naked as can be. "Ooh! New plan! After we're done with a game, whoever is the most naked has to sing Christmas carols to everyone in the attire *you*, I mean, they are wearing."

"You're going to sing carols to people in your underwear?" he asks with a raised eyebrow.

"Oh, sweet, innocent boy. I will *not* be the one naked." I'll make sure of that.

"I might be a supreme bowler. You just don't know," he says.

I grin at him. "You are pretty perfect in everything you do."

He snickers as he takes the ball from me, walks away, and looks back at me. Then he shimmies his ass as he walks toward the makeshift starting line and rolls the ball. It makes me laugh and nearly makes me miss seeing the almost perfect roll. It goes right down the center and knocks over all but three pins. Instead of getting the ball, he grabs another and rolls it. This time, he knocks down the three remaining pins before turning around and giving me a wink.

"Your turn."

"I already hate this game," I state.

He starts laughing as he sets the pins up and comes back with the balls. I suppose I could have helped him, but I was still busy pouting about his first roll. He hands me the first ball.

"I love it when you hand me your balls," I say.

"I love it when you grab my balls."

We snicker like a couple of immature teenagers, and I turn to the pins. I pull my arm back and swing, letting the ball go. It immediately goes off center, but with my power, I gently nudge it straight into line.

If nudging meant that my power whips it to the left so hard that it slams into the wall, rebounds off the wall, flies across the gymnasium, and punches a hole into the far wall. All the while, the pins stay perfectly unharmed.

I can't even turn to face August.

"Wow, for not using your power, that was quite the throw," he says, like he's impressed.

"I was using my jerking-off arm. It's quite powerful."

"I see that," he says. "Please continue using your left hand when you fondle me."

"I don't know how that happened. I have *no* idea how that could have done that. You must have given me a faulty ball."

"Uh-huh. Sure," he says as he walks over to the far wall and assesses the ball punched into it. "I'm not sure this will come out."

"Of course it will. Use your manly strength. Take your shirt off first."

He grabs onto it, but his hands slip off. "The issue is that there's nothing to grip onto. You punched the finger hole side into the wall. We'll just leave it and hope Valerie doesn't notice."

"Good plan," I say. "I still get two rolls since there was something defective with that ball."

"One roll."

I give him a devastated look. "Seriously?"

He sighs. "Fine. Two."

209

I smile sweetly at him because he's adorable. I roll the new ball and knock down a grand total of one pin.

"I'm just warming up," I assure him.

"That's fine," he says. "I'm sure you'll do great."

And then I finish warming up by knocking down one more pin for a grand total of two pins knocked down.

I turn to him and give him that same sweet smile that got me the second roll. "I think I won."

His sweet look is gone and in its place is the look of a hungry wolf. "Strip, boy, strip!"

I'm aghast. "You... would make me strip?"

He's enjoying this far too much. "Let's see it."

I grumble but pull the ugly sweater off, just because it's hideous.

He whistles, which makes it impossible to not smile while I'm trying to look irritated and annoyed. It's hard to believe how this man can make me so happy. He makes me feel wanted and cared for. He makes me ache for him with the way he always wears a smile and has a kind word. And I love it best when it's only directed toward me. Obviously, August would be kind to anyone, even Brandon who he put in jail after the bank break-in.

"What?" he asks as he looks up from where he placed the pins.

"Just envisioning how naked you're gonna be when I get done with you."

"For some reason, I seem to have my doubts," he says and just like that, the asshole rolls a strike.

"Evil," I hiss.

He snickers as he trots down to the end to set up the pins he's just demolished. He returns with the ball in hand.

"Give me your balls, boy. I'll show you how it's really done."

"You're going to show me how to roll my ball?"

I press into him, the bowling ball the only thing keeping us apart as it remains pinned between us. "I'm going to roll your ball so damn hard."

He gives me a wicked grin as I turn from him, eye the pins, and roll it. The ball makes a wide right, missing all pins and smacking into the far wall.

I slowly turn to look at August who gives me a supportive smile and a thumbs up. What a traitor. "I see you're rubbing it in."

His eyes get wide. "Me?"

"Yes, you."

"All I've done is show you kindness."

I narrow my eyes until they're barely slits but his sweet little smile stays strong. "I don't trust you."

"Strip."

I grumble as I pull my T-shirt off and drop it with my clothes.

"Aw. Look at that pale belly. I'd almost mistake you for a ghost!" He gives my stomach a gentle pat as I glower at him.

"I'm going to pinch your nip so hard when you're forced to strip."

"I'm not worried."

Once everything is set back up, I hold the ball out to him but refuse to let go.

"I hope you fail," I say.

He blows me a kiss and takes the ball. As he throws it, I touch it as lightly as I can with my gift. The ball savagely snaps to the left, bounces off the wall, and hits the pins right in the middle, knocking them all down.

August looks back at me with a smile. "Thanks, babe. I actually slipped on that one and it was going wide. I wouldn't have hit any of them without your help."

"*Why?*" I dramatically cry out.

"I mean, really, you might as well strip now."

"No, I will roll a strike."

I roll a gutter ball.

"Dammit!" I grumble as I unbutton my pants. "Who came up with this stupid bet?"

"You did! And don't forget, you get to sing carols after this!"

I look at him in horror as he stands there bundled in his fuzzy fleece jacket, cute glasses in place—which is really the only reason I'm willing to forgive him for anything—and a sweet smile.

"You'd make a perfect villain. Or maybe you already are," I decide.

"I would never turn evil."

"Even for me?"

"Eh... a little evil now and then wouldn't hurt," he jokes.

I grin at him. "Then you'll strip with me."

"Nah, I like this much more," he says as he eyes the pins and then rolls his ball, knocking down one pin. As we continue our turns, I can't help but realize how many items of clothing I'm losing.

"Ha! Finally, you suck!" I say as I stand there in my underwear and sock pretending like I'm not the worst bowler known to mankind.

"*I* suck?" he asks as he retrieves the ball and then proceeds to knock down all but one pin.

"You're cheating."

"I'm just good at games."

"Cheater," I grumble as I roll the ball and am in pure shock when I miss them all, again.

August is howling with laughter, so I grab him in a chokehold and tickle him with my other hand. He squirms and wiggles, but he can't get away without being choked.

"It's not funny, Augustus."

He grabs my hand, keeping it locked in tight. "It's actually Augustine."

"*What?* How did I not know this? My entire life has been a lie! You've shattered our relationship!"

"I think you're being a bit dramatic."

I pull my hand free and poke him in the side, which makes him squirm away and gives me some satisfaction as I let him go. "Alright, *Augustine*. Watch me make my second roll."

I roll the ball and by some power unknown to mankind, the ball rolls straight down the line, knocking all pins down perfectly.

"Did you see that? Did you see that?" I say as I do a little dance, in case he wasn't already aware of how much of a better bowler I am than him. "Guess you have to take all of your clothes off."

"One item," he says as he takes his hoodie off and sets it on top of my clothes as I stand there nearly naked in my *one* sock and underwear.

I make a surprising comeback toward the end, resulting in both of us in our underwear with one sock. "I'm so much better than you," I tell August.

"You did get strangely better there toward the end. Now we have to sing Christmas carols to Valerie together," he reminds me.

"I would be *really* against this idea, but it sounds like a ton of fun annoying her," I admit. "Let's go."

"We need decorations first," he says as he pulls me into the hallway and down into another room. It's a storage closet that is filled with boxes, but he pulls one out that is labeled "Christmas" and pops it open. He grabs a thing of tinsel and wraps it around my shoulders, making it into a vest that leaves my nipples exposed. I grab the ornaments and reach down, hanging two round balls right from his underwear.

"Beautiful," I say as I fondle them while looking up and giving him a wink.

"I like it when you fondle my bulbs."

"Ooh. You know just how to turn me on," I say as I dive back in for a set of lights that run off a battery pack. I wind them from his neck down until he's glowing brightly.

And that's when August's phone rings.

"Hello?... Right now? I'm a bit busy at the moment—"

The closet door opens and Valerie looks in at us, phone in hand. "What are you two doing?"

"Caroling," I say, like it's obvious.

She narrows her eyes like she doesn't believe us. "Uh-huh. Sing me a Christmas song, then."

"Okay. *On the first day of Christmas, my true love gave to me, a dildo in a—*"

She slams the door in our faces.

"I forgot you don't like the penis, Valerie!" I call as I push open the door and find her glaring at me. "They do make dildos shaped like other things, though. Wanna get fucked by a flower? There's a dildo for that. Or maybe you didn't like that song. I'll sing you a different one. *Jingle bell, jingle bell, jingle bell cock.* Dammit. I made it about penises again. I'm really sorry."

"*Deck the balls...* Landon, you're right. It's hard to make the song not about male genitalia," August helpfully inputs.

She continues to stare at me. "What exactly are you guys doing and where are your clothes?"

I reach over and tickle the ornaments hanging from August's underwear. "Playing with August's balls."

213

"August, please, come with me. I raised you to be better than this. I raised you to be a good, good person," she says.

"You also tried stomping out anything he likes. Although, after seeing what clothes he *prefers*, thank you."

"His taste is disgusting," she concurs.

"It's sad. Black is such a better color." I make a show of shuddering.

"You're making fun of me after I froze time and rolled all of your bowling balls for the second half of the game so you would have strikes and you weren't sad that you were losing," August says.

I whip around to face him. "You... froze *time* to make me win?"

August stares at me. He's not sure if I'm happy or not about this revelation.

"Oh my god, that's the sweetest thing. Take me right here, you sexy reindeer!" I cry as I rush over and jump into his arms. He, of course, catches me right out of the air.

"What have you *done* to him?" she asks. "Are you sure your power isn't manipulating the innocent?"

"Might be," I say as I kiss August's cheek.

"I like being manipulated," August says as he smiles at me.

Valerie shakes her head. "Get out here so we can talk."

August carries me after her but seems to forget that my head is taller than his when I'm in his arms and whacks it on the top of the doorframe.

"Ow!"

"Oh no. I'm so sorry, love," he says as he squeezes me tightly, but the pet name he just gave me erases all of the pain I've ever felt in my entire life.

"This is why you shouldn't carry him around," Valerie the Grump says.

"You're so sweet," I say as I give him a peck.

"He even *slams* your head into a doorframe, and you're happy as can be."

"He's cute, right?" I ask.

"It's not him I'm concerned about."

That's when I notice Lex heading toward us. "What're all the lights for?"

I'm confused about what he's talking about until I realize he's referring to the strand of lights I wound around August's body. "It's because he's the light of my life."

"Aw, that's disgusting," Lex says. "Did you call me out just for this? Because I now have to bleach my eyes."

"Lex is jealous," I say as August puts me down. "Come here, Lex. Do you want a little love?"

"Sure, Tinsel Tits," he says as he walks up to me and holds his arms out. I try picking him up before realizing that I don't want to strain myself or overexert myself in any way.

"I'm sorry, I don't have enough love or energy for you."

"Aw, thanks. That makes me feel good about myself. Although... your brother is kind of cute."

"*Brandon?*" I say in horror. "Ew, gross. Did you see him carrying a package of *cheese* to a supervillain fight?"

"I did... he asked if I wanted some of his cheese and I didn't know if that was like... slang for his penis, so I said yes. Then he pulled out *actual* cheese. And there was no way I was going to eat it. It was warm and disgusting, so I just smiled and carried it around until he finally looked away."

"He's way too dumb for you *and* he's straight as can be."

"And he has a little penis," August inputs. "Which wouldn't be a bad thing, but he doesn't know how to wield it."

Lex starts laughing as Valerie sighs loudly, in case we can't hear it.

"So what was important?" I ask Valerie.

"The chef is making us a big meal and I thought it'd be nice if we all ate together," she says.

"As long as August isn't cooking, I'll be there... I mean... um... August's food is... perfect!" I give him a huge smile to make sure he knows that he's adorable and the best thing ever.

He just smiles back, so I take his hand. "As long as this is the required attire, I'll be there," August says.

"If you insist," Lex says as he unbuttons his pants.

Valerie gives him a look that makes him whip that zipper right back up and we all laugh, even Valerie.

When we finish eating, we head upstairs and make a straight line over to the couch to watch a movie and be lazy, which I'm craving after August has forced me to overexert myself by being all active. He sits down and I sit on his lap as Zacia rushes over to us. Clearly, she missed us. August wraps his arms around my waist and pulls me close to him as Zacia kneads my pants that I put back on after Valerie told me she was tired of looking at my "chicken" legs.

"Am I crushing your leg?" I ask as I lean back so I can look at him.

"A little bit, but it's worth it."

"Why are you so good to me?"

He kisses my cheek. "You're kind of irresistible."

"Strange."

"Maybe, but I know what makes me happy."

"What? Zacia."

He gives me a smile. "She makes me happy too, even if she's so ugly she's cute."

"Thanks."

"But I'm definitely talking about you."

He pulls me down so he's lying on the couch and I'm pressed against him. I love feeling him against me as he holds me and rubs me. His hand slips under my shirt and trails over my stomach to my chest. I close my eyes and just *feel* him. I don't think I'll ever get enough of this.

"August... I'm scared of what's to come," I admit.

"I know."

"Nolan isn't a bad person... when he saw me on that bridge... it didn't look like he wanted to be doing it. Do you believe me?"

He gives me a gentle squeeze. "I do. I trust you. I could have shot him. It would have solved a lot more by shooting him since he can control us, but I shot Marauder instead. Nolan hasn't killed anyone yet, but he's come close. We need to stop him before he does, or I fear that we might not be able to help him. As long as you truly believe that he's still good, then I'll do what I can. But... I can't promise what the others will do if they're faced with a situation where they're forced to stop him."

"I know... I just..." I swallow hard as I'm forced to say what I need to say. "I just don't want to look at you and see the man who killed my brother. I want to see you and only see the man who cares about me and who makes me happy. Even with that said, I do know that you have to do what you need to do. Don't risk your life because of my brother. Do what you need to do. My brother has made his decision."

He kisses my neck. "I will do everything I can to keep you safe. You will be my top priority, but I'll also give your brother a chance to prove that he isn't the man he appears to have become."

"Thank you," I say as I roll over more so my front is flush against his. His hand slips back under my shirt and begins rubbing circles as I grip tightly onto him. And I silently beg that Nolan doesn't make me regret this. I couldn't live with myself if something happened to August and it was because he hesitated after what I said. "It's so hard to know what's right when you want to keep two people safe, but they're so far away from each other it feels impossible to do."

"I know. And I'm sorry."

"Don't be sorry. You have nothing to be sorry for when you've made me as happy as you have." I'm quiet for a moment. "Can I ask you a question?"

"Of course."

"That day that we were on top of that building and looking out on the world... you seemed very unhappy. Do you not want to be a superhero?"

He thinks about it. "It's not that I don't want to be one... it's that the pressure is ridiculous. I feel like everyone relies on me and I'm usually alone. Lex is only here because of what's happening, and Amelia and Joy are just starting out because I've begged for more help. I'm always terrified that I won't get there soon enough. I'll make a single mistake and people will die. It's hard to live your life knowing that if you stumble once, people could die."

"You're not invulnerable, August. You can only do so much."

"Yet people treat me like I'm a god or something. Like I have all the answers. All I can do is freeze time and have superior strength. Of course I can fight, and I'm really good at it, but how will that help if I'm a minute too late?"

I squeeze onto him. "Have you talked to them about this?"

"Of course. Many times. They just tell me I'm a symbol or some nonsense. But with all of that, I don't hate it. I love helping people. I love being there for people... I just wish I didn't have to do it alone. It's like even the police just sit back and go, 'Oh August's has it! It'll be fine' and crack open a beer!"

"I'm sorry. It's not fair you have to do this alone. It's not safe either, for you or them. I'm not much for the hero thing, but I *will* help you in any way that I can."

"Thanks. I'm hoping that this will show them that they really need to step up. There really needs to be more help and support."

"I am too."

He gives me a gentle kiss, and I roll back over as he starts the movie. But wrapped up in his arms, I feel like everything might be alright. The end of this story might turn out happy after all. "I can't wait for Christmas at your parents'. Will there be turkey?" I ask.

"Plenty of turkey."

"And board games where you'll cheat so I'll win every time?"

"Every single time."

"That's hot."

And then everything is okay again because I have August by my side.

CHAPTER TWENTY-TWO

"Things have been strangely quiet," Valerie says.

"Not in our bedroom," I inform her.

She clearly ignores me, pretending I have never existed. That she never met me and will never do so. I am like a wall to her—even as everyone else at the table snickers, even KillJoy, Valerie has given up on me.

Like Valerie says, besides my bedroom, everything has been relatively quiet. It's been half a week and the villains have been silent. It's almost worse because we don't know if August took a killing shot on Marauder, or if they're just lying in wait. Maybe even gathering forces.

I've tried contacting Nolan, but his phone has been turned off. Even so, I send him messages every day telling him that I know he's better than this, that he could come back and redeem himself. I do it just in the hope that he'll turn on his phone and know that he's still loved. That I could forgive him. That I just want him back. But I also know that I need to keep looking forward. If this is the decision he has made, then I can't force him to do anything else.

There's a loud knock on the door before Wyatt rushes in.

"Sorry to interrupt, but I have some rumors that might be beneficial," Wyatt says as he walks over to the table we're gathered at.

"Go right ahead," Valerie says.

"So, there's been some talk that Hazel Mallory has been rumored to have used the snow globe. So I looked into her, and I guess she's having her yearly Christmas party this evening. The only thing is that I'm not sure if they actually connect or if it's just speculation."

"Hazel Mallory... why's that name sound familiar?" August asks.

When I look at Valerie, it's clear she recognizes the name and knows it well by the expression she's wearing.

She's staring at her hands as she picks at a pencil. "She's a failed superhero. She was supposed to have the position August does, but she was dismissed before we even released her information to the media," Valerie explains.

"So she must be powerful, then," August says.

Valerie nods but looks thoughtful. "She could manipulate emotions."

"How would that help you guys?" Amelia asks.

"She could calm people down. If someone was angry and shooting out of anger or fear, she could make them feel calm and relaxed and they would instantly stop. She could make someone who was emotionless feel scared and they would back away. She was quite powerful, but she couldn't handle the training. I always had the feeling that it was more of a public image she wanted than to actually help or save anyone. She failed the first round of testing when she got angry at us for not allowing her to announce her presence in Superheroes United to the press," Valerie explains. "Then she used her powers for attention, so when she was asked to save some lives that very day, she was too drained to do it and multiple people wound up injured and two dead. Another super..." She takes a deep breath. "I was very close to another super who I had been training. She was Hazel's teammate that day, and because of Hazel's arrogance, the other super ended up losing her life. After that, we let Hazel go, but she didn't go quietly."

Even though this was years ago, the pain is still apparent, and I begin to understand why Valerie is so strict. She wants everything perfect and doesn't want anyone fucking up and leaving the heroes she has grown close to dead.

I take a moment to think about what this would mean today. "So if she touched the globe, she could basically convince everyone to hate Superheroes United," I say.

Valerie nods. "She throws a *huge* Christmas party every year because she loves the attention. I guess I assumed a lot of festivities weren't going on with the current threat level, but the villains have been quiet. Maybe they're wanting the citizens more comfortable so they can strike again."

"So, we'll just go to this party, snatch up the globe if it's there, and go," I suggest.

"Yeah, and how exactly are *any* of you going to get into this party? You think they won't notice you?" she asks.

"I know a villain who can put illusions on people," I explain. If we could go into the party looking like someone else, there's a high likelihood they wouldn't even notice us.

Valerie leans forward. "I'm listening."

"She does excellent work. She can make you look like someone else and it lasts about an hour or two."

"And can we call this villain here?" she asks.

I shake my head, honestly not sure if she would come here or not, but also not wanting to expose her when I doubt she wants to be. "No, August and I can go to her. I know where she'll be this evening."

"I'd prefer if all of you could go."

"I'm not sure she can use her power on that many of us. Last time, she could only put the illusion on me and my father, so my brother had to go as himself and he got his ass kicked. It was amazing. I mean... it was really sad. Anyway, just two, maybe three. I don't know."

Valerie is clearly hesitant about this. I know she cares about her supers and really does try her best to keep them safe, even if she's a bit overcontrolling. "I just..."

"I actually think it would be best for me to help from the background," Amelia says. "If they wore cameras and microphones, I could help them from a different location. I'm not good in crowds, but I do excel at small details when given the chance."

Joy nods at Amelia. "Yeah, I could hang back with Amelia. If they need us, we'll be a stone's throw away. Although... I have my doubts about how capable the loud one is."

"No one needs your horribly accurate depiction of me, Joyless," I say. "I'm only loud when I'm unsatisfied."

"Is that why you were making so much noise last night, you were unsatisfied?" Lex quips with a smug little grin on his annoyingly handsome face.

"Ha, joke's on you, we didn't even do anything last night besides having a pajama party with the cat," I say.

"Let's stay focused," Valerie basically pleads. "I'm going to get all the information I can on the party while I set someone to work finding you guys clothes that will be acceptable but safe. We're going to hope at least three of you can go in. If they can't, then August and Landon will. Landon, can you contact the villain you think could help you get in? And are you sure this is a... safe villain?"

"Oh, god yes. She's literally like a cotton ball of sugary fluff. She's not going to hurt your precious August unless she hugs him to death. And I'm too easily jealous to allow her to do that."

"Okay... let's hope this works. If we can get this snow globe and stop Hazel from working with them, I think we could have a better chance at this."

I stand up. "Good, because I want to be done by Christmas. Mostly because I'm lazy and just want to read a book and my body hurts from all this activity you guys are forcing me to do. But also because August promised me a real Christmas and I've never had a normal Christmas, and I want one."

She reaches over and squeezes my shoulder. "I'll make sure you get your real Christmas, even if you sadly end up in a jail cell," Valerie assures me as she gives me a pat.

"Why did that start off nice and end evil?" I curiously ask. "And why would I be in jail?"

She shrugs. "I'm too busy to answer such obvious questions."

"I can't believe we got away from them," I say to August. Oh, and Lex, who I couldn't get away from.

"You basically said, look, a puppy! And ran," August says.

I grin at him. "Oldest trick in the villain book," I say as I park the car in front of the building where they have SAVCGEM meetings. While I know the members don't do anything truly bad, I don't want them to have to deal with Valerie and the others. I just hadn't expected

Lex to already be in the vehicle. Tossing him out along the drive sounded slightly more villainous than I'd like.

He seems pretty low-key about stuff, though, having played a video game through the entire ride while simultaneously talking about how we should go shopping after this. Little does he know that the only shopping I can do is book shopping.

Oh, I miss reading and doing nothing important. I want to be lazy and boring.

August looks up from where he's in a heated conversation via text. "Valerie told me that she's going to beat your ass when she sees you because you stole me without permission," August informs me.

"Tell her that I like it when it hurts, and especially love it when I get to call her Mommy."

August texts away. "She said she's going to take away my glasses."

I look over at August in horror. "What the hell? She truly *is* evil!"

"And why would she take away *my* glasses? Why do I get punished?" August asks, even though he's, sadly, not wearing his glasses. I've tried flushing his contacts, destroying them, but every morning, he has a new pair.

"You did pick him," Lex unhelpfully inputs.

I put the car in park and look back at him. "No one invited you, Lex."

"I don't even know where we're at."

"Supervillain meeting," August says.

I feel the need to correct that statement. "A *fake* supervillain meeting."

Lex suddenly looks excited. "Ooh, I've always wanted a bad boy to show me his candy cane," he says as he promptly gets out and waits on *us*.

We're dressed in our superhero attire, mine a new suit that Valerie handed me in disgust. It's a deep, dark purple that almost looks blue in certain lights, and while it's not black, I'm digging it. I promptly asked August to tear it off my body, but he thought that since the suit has been specially designed to keep me safe, it wouldn't be very smart, even if it would make my balls explode.

Sometimes he's so unbelievably smart.

We get out of the vehicle and head inside. The moment I push open the door to the meeting room, everyone turns to look at me. It's the first time I've seen, or even talked to, my parents since the whole Nolan thing began.

I was planning on avoiding them for eternity and enslaving a new family to call my own, but I suppose I'll have to settle for this.

My father, who's up at the podium, stops what he's doing and stares at me. I'm not sure what they're going to say or do, and I realize I'm kind of nervous. I mean... they did devote much of their lives to being villains and making me a villain. And now I'm dating the city's main hero *and* working against the villains.

Everyone turns to look at us and whispers ignite amongst them.

"Landon!" Dad says.

Mom jumps up and runs at me. "What the hell do you think you're doing not answering your phone? I oughta bend you over my knee in front of everyone for such stupid behavior."

"I'm sorry... I just didn't know what to say and thought you guys would be disappointed in me," I admit.

She grabs me and instead of bending me over her knee, she puts me in a headlock and continues to threaten me. "I used to think you were my smart child, but now Brandon's starting to look smarter than you."

"I'm smart?" Brandon asks, then smiles warmly. "I did save Landon. I'm so smart."

"I'm sorry! Can you let me go?" I ask, but she just chokes me a little more. It makes me cough and August doesn't even bother to save me. "Mom! You're killing me!"

"Do you know how worried I've been? And then Brandon told me you were going up against the Rebellion! You could have *died*."

"That's enough, Patricia!" Dad says as he rushes for me. I can't believe he's planning on going against Mom and rescuing me. "I want to scald him." He holds out his hands so he can use his powers to burn me, I guess.

"Dammit, guys!" I say as I try to pull back.

"Well, you shouldn't be so stupid," Mom decides.

"I'm not being stupid. Do you guys really not see my side on this?" I ask.

"You were always such a difficult child," Mom settles on.

"Enough about that, we need to stop Nolan before he hurts someone. He's already tried killing people. He tried killing August and other innocent people."

Mom shakes her head. "Nolan wouldn't do that. Are you sure it was Nolan? I bet it wasn't him."

"I'm positive it was. I've tried talking to him and getting him to stop, but he won't. Mom… I don't want Nolan to die over this."

She turns the chokehold into a hug which is just as constricting. "You and Nolan have been closer to each other than anyone in this family. If anyone can pull Nolan out if it, it'll be you."

"You're not… happy for him and mad at me?" I ask. I didn't realize how concerned I've been about this until I say it out loud.

"Sweetheart, we have always been accepting of whatever you chose to do with your life. Of course we want you to join us in our villainous ways, but if this is the path you've chosen to travel, we're not going to stop you. If you told me today that you wanted to become a cow and roam the fields, I would buy you a little cowbell for that scrawny neck of yours."

"And we don't want any of you to kill anyone. Being a villain doesn't mean you have to kill or should kill," Dad adds. "It's all about the money! I mean, we should… only… yeah. I give up. I just don't want you guys to hurt others physically. It's okay to hurt them emotionally when you steal from them, though, especially if they're on our We Hate Your Face list. But we don't want Nolan to become a murderer."

"I'll try to stop him, I promise."

"I know you will," Mom says. "Now, do you need our help?"

That is the most horrifying thing I've heard in a while and just this morning Valerie told me that she tried the penis once. "Absolutely not. My god. Do you guys not recall when SAVCGEM tried breaking into a *candy* store? We couldn't even coordinate that right!"

Mom's eyes narrow. "Maybe if you'd been on the lookout like you promised instead of reading a book, we wouldn't have been caught." She still seems to have some hurt feelings over that.

"I had to wash dishes there for a *week*," Brandon whines.

Mom looks past me to August and Lex. "I see you expanded your harem. Inferno, huh? He's quite cute." She pats my back like she's proud of me. "That's my boy, finding all the big-name ones and stomping and squishing them into submission."

225

"I like it when he puts the collar on me and tells me I'm a good boy," Lex says. "It's even better when he chokes me a little."

"That's my son!" Dad says as he pats my back as well, so now both of my parents are patting my back about something that isn't even remotely true.

I glare at Lex, who is also getting the same treatment from August. "None of that has or ever will happen."

"In my dreams it did," Lex says with a smug little grin.

I snort, August scoffs, and Baker shouts, "Threesome!"

"Baker, stay out of this!" I growl. "I don't have the energy for a threesome!"

"I'll give you one of my pills and you'll be able to go all night, kiddo."

"Ew, gross. That sounded so gross and creepy," I say as I shudder. "Anyway! We're here for Evaline."

"Me?" a petite young woman who rarely talks, if ever, asks. Most of the time I forget she's even around.

"Yeah, we need you to put an illusion on us so we can infiltrate a secret party," I say.

"Ooh, we're going to a party!" Baker shouts.

I'm horrified by this idea because I *know* it'll spell disaster. Nothing would be more disastrous than taking this crew. "NO! Just us three. No one else."

"Party crashing time!" Baker shouts.

"Baker, I think we should respect my son's decision to go to the orgy with just his two boys," Mom says.

"Holy hell, it's not an orgy!" I say.

"I met your mother at an orgy," Dad informs me.

"Yes, I arrived late, and he was the only one left to pick from if that tells you anything," Mom adds.

"I love your parents," Lex unhelpfully inputs.

"Good. You can have them."

"Aw! Thanks, but no thanks. Is this what they call don't look a gift horse in the mouth? Why would you look it in the mouth?"

"That's how you tell how old a horse is," August explains, and his weird knowledge is undeniably hot.

"You're so hot," I say.

August beams at me. "Thanks, babe."

"Ew, no." Lex shudders.

"Evaline, please, can we get away from this hell and you help us?" I ask.

She quietly stands up, gathers her bag, and hurries after me.

"Have fun at the orgy!" Baker shouts.

Her face gets unbelievably red as she slows down.

I feel the need to clarify the misunderstanding before she runs off. "It's a party. Not an orgy. I'm not sure what type of parties Baker goes to, but those aren't the one we're going to. And you just need to work your magic on us," I say.

She nods and hurries after us into the hallway. "It only lasts about an hour or two," she explains.

"Hopefully, that'll be fine. Do you want to go to the location with us and touch us right before we go in?" I ask.

"I usually don't let women touch me, but some days, I'm up for anything," Lex says.

Evaline's eyes get wide as she tries to ignore Lex. "I can... sure."

She follows us out to the car only to find Valerie waiting outside it with her arms folded and her eyes narrowed.

"Stranger danger!" I shout.

"Do you really think I don't have tracking devices on you guys?" she asks.

I give her a look of horror. "Oh my god, did you stick a tracker up my butt?" I ask. "August, she violated me!"

"When was I even remotely *near* your asshole?" she asks.

I shrug. "We found the lady who will help us. She's going to go with us so she can work her magic right before the event since it only lasts an hour or two."

Valerie walks up to her and introduces herself, then forces us all into an SUV, leaving the car behind.

CHAPTER TWENTY-THREE

We drive near the location of the party and park. Then Valerie has us pull on suits over the top of our supersuits because of the added protection. Even with the supersuits underneath, they're not too bulky. I turn and look at August who is unbelievably sexy in his gray pinstriped suit and question why I haven't been forcing him to wear this attire for every date we've had.

Valerie found a rich blue suit for me that hugs me just right and isn't uncomfortable, even with the stupid suit and cape underneath it.

"You look so nice," August says to me.

I smile at him. "Thank you. You look very handsome as well."

"Gross," Lex interrupts, like the little attention-deprived asshole he is.

I give him a look of pity. "Aw, did you look at yourself in the mirror?"

"Actually, I did, and I look amazing, but your displays of affection ruined it."

"Focus, please," Amelia says as she draws us over to her.

She hooks us up with cameras and microphones before explaining how to use them.

Valerie comes back and assesses us before straightening Lex's tie. He'd fiddled with it during Amelia's instructions, clearly unsure of how to tie it. I could have helped, but I was too busy admiring August. "Okay, people are starting to go in. There are guards at the door, but they're not taking tickets. The party has been all over social media inviting anyone and everyone, so you shouldn't have issues getting in as long as you don't look like your real selves. Evaline, are you ready?" Valerie asks.

Evaline nervously makes her way over to us. I can tell she's concerned about Valerie, but Valerie has been uncharacteristically nice to her. Or maybe she's just mean to us... which makes sense. My goal in life is to make her life hell.

Evaline nods as she steps up and holds her hands out. The three of us who will be going inside each put a hand in the middle, and she takes all three. She closes her eyes and concentrates for a moment before opening them again. "There. All that's changed is how people perceive you."

I turn to look at August, who is on my left, and let out a squeal that I am not proud of. Instead of the handsome man by my side, there's a woman standing next to me with wavy blond hair that reaches down to her melon-sized knockers.

"Your boobs are *huge!*" I exclaim as I instantly reach out and grab them. It even *feels* like I'm grabbing them when I know they're not there.

"Boobs? I have boobs?" he says. "I just feel you squeezing my chest."

"They're *massive*."

"You look very... old," Lex says to me.

"I'm old?" I ask August.

"You look like you're in your sixties."

"Ah, so I'm like a rich man with my sinfully hot lady," I say before assessing Lex. Sadly, there's nothing funny about him. He looks less attractive than normal. Just very average in every way. "Ew, at least I'm not boring. Ooh. Wanna tell me how droopy my balls look?"

"Get out of here," Valerie barks.

"It was a simple question," I grumble. "Maybe you want to touch August's boobs. I'll allow that."

"*Out.*"

"Fine, I'll fondle them for you," I say as I give the left one a pat.

"Thanks, babe, that makes me feel better," he says with a huge smile.

"I gotchu, babe."

"There is something wrong with you guys and I just can't quite put my finger on it," Lex says.

"You're jealous of our level of love?" I guess.

He looks shocked. "Yes! That's what it is! Not."

We get out of the vehicle and head toward the front door. August takes the lead, moving toward the door as we follow after him.

"Landon, I'm just saying that you kind of look like a pimp daddy," Lex says.

"Does that mean you're both my bitches?" I ask as I take August's hand. "How do I look now?"

"Like a creep who has more money than he knows what to do with."

"So basically, it's like real life," I say. "Lex, give me your hand. I want two bitches."

August thoughtfully looks over at me. "How *did* you get all of your money?"

"I just can't stop staring at your boobs. They're so huge. I wish you could see how pretty you are."

"Landon?" August asks, weirdly still fixated on this whole "Where'd ya get the money from" thing that is really of no concern.

"He must be a stripper," Lex concludes.

"He'd have to be one damn good stripper. He lives in a mansion."

I wave him off like it's really no big deal. "Not a *mansion*."

"I'm sorry, a three-story house where one entire floor is devoted to books and the other to his cat."

"What about the third?" Lex asks.

"You're such a liar, the whole house is Zacia's. I bet she misses me. I miss her. I should have brought her."

Lex snorts. "Yes, you really would have blended in, toting a double D on your right side and a hairless cat that acts like a dog on your left."

I narrow my eyes at Lex before turning my attention to August. "I feel like you should beat Lex up for talking about you that way. Oh but... you'd be beating him up as a woman and now I'm wondering if that would even be hot. Ooh. Let's find a bathroom. I want to look down there and see what it looks like," I decide.

"I... do too," Lex helpfully adds.

August looks surprised? Horrified? Who knows. "No, I'm not showing either of you anything because to me, it still looks like a penis."

"You're so selfish. I'll show you my balls," I say as I head up to the front door where the guard waits.

August steps up to the door as the guard or bouncer, or whatever he's supposed to be, assesses us. So far, I've noticed that he stops everyone and eyes them from head to toe, telling me that he must have some type of power to allow him to judge whether someone's carrying a weapon, or something else. Hell, maybe he just assess whether they're cool enough to join. And if I look anything like what August and Lex are telling me, I'm going to be the coolest one here.

The man stops Lex, looks him over, then waves him in. Then he gives August a smile. "Good evening," he purrs.

August gives him a huge smile, as August is known to do. Clearly, he's oblivious that he's being hit on.

"Evening," August says, and that's when it dawns on me that his voice is the exact same as normal. While he looks like a beauty, he talks like handsome August.

The man does a double take, looks confused, and sends him inside. He barely looks at me. Clearly, I'm not of concern. Unbeknownst to him, I'm the evilest one of them all.

I walk through and meet up with the others. "So, I just realized that August still sounds like a man."

"Don't think *any* of this makes me forget what we were originally talking about," August says.

"Zacia's cuteness?"

"Where'd you get the money?"

I sigh. "My parents used to be a little more... villainous when I was growing up because they had me to help them. When I was like five, they started taking me with them to do little things at first. Shoplift candy, steal an apple, rob the neighbor's house. Those kinds of things. Keep in mind some of the money *did* come from my grandpa who passed away. His name was Tomashock. Get it... because his name was Tom and he could shock people."

They both look surprised, but I know it's not because of the horrible name, but because of the things my grandfather had done.

"You're joking."

"No. My family used to be worse than it is now. While my grandpa was rarely around, my mom grew up doing bad shit whenever he decided to stop on by and take her out for 'family night.' My mom eventually met my dad who was much more low-key than her and together, they began to calm down. So when he died, my mother, as his only child, received all of his money and assets. I also contributed some to it as a child when I might have broken into a bank or two. Nothing of concern, really. But I haven't for years now... I mean besides me trying to flirt with you at the bank. Anyway. Let's look at August's knockers!"

"That is *not* how you change a subject," August says.

"News to me," I say as I look around at the *real* mansion. My house is a doll house compared to this place. The entranceway is a large open space, allowing people to frolic and socialize. There are Christmas decorations hanging from everywhere and people are dressed formally with little dashes of Christmas thrown onto their clothes. Santa hat, garland, holiday ties.

"Everyone's wearing masks besides us," Lex says. "We stick out like sore thumbs."

"Let's steal someone else's mask. We'll jump them in the bathroom," I suggest.

"Or, we could make our own?" August is so naive, but if he wants to play nice, he can do as he pleases because he's adorable and I'd let him get away with anything. So before anyone can get a decent look at our faces, we pull back into the hallway.

"Look for a weak one. They'll be the easiest to steal from. That lady looks like she has a limp, let's go for her," I suggest as I nod to an elderly woman making her way toward the bathroom.

Lex and August stare at me with wide eyes.

They're so dramatic. "I was joking! Gosh!" I wasn't joking.

"Are you sure?" August asks.

"Definitely." Not. "How about we make our own?" That seems to sate them, although they still seem apprehensive. I reach over to August, who is still wearing his suit that looks close to bursting from his now feminine body. I pull his tie free, hold it up to Lex and say, "Burn two eye holes in this."

"Now I *really* know you're joking," Lex says.

"You can do it."

He looks apprehensive as he bites his lip. "Do you remember me telling you how I can't control my powers that well?"

"Just try it," August says, so Lex takes it and holds it up to August's face.

"I feel like I need to burn them while it's on you or it won't end up right," Lex says thoughtfully.

"Then burn it while it's on your own face because you're not disfiguring my man," I say, pulling the tie away from August's eyes and wrapping it around Lex's throat.

Lex grabs for it. "What are you doing?"

"Choking you for even dreaming of touching August's face. August, beat him up."

"Looks like you're doing a splendid job yourself, babe," August says, giving me a supportive thumbs up, like I should continue doing what I'm doing.

I consider it, but I also kind of like Lex, so I let him pull the tie away and stare at it. Within seconds there are two holes burned into it almost perfectly. I set it against August's face and they match with amazing precision. Lex then takes my tie from me and looks me right in the eyes as he burns holes into it. One is huge, nearly melting through the entire tie, and the other is the size of a dime.

"Perfect," he says as he reaches out and wraps it painfully tight around my face. Of course the eye holes are too far apart for it to be of any use.

"I didn't want a glory hole," I say as I lower the huge hole down to my mouth since it's big enough for that.

Lex snorts as he pulls his tie off and starts burning a tiny little hole in it. I catch the burning fabric with my mind, intending to spread the fire a little so his mask is as bad as mine. Instead, I seem to encourage the fire, making the tie combust as Lex throws it in surprise. It lands on top of a wooden flower arrangement that instantly catches on fire.

All three of us watch as it burns.

"I don't suppose you can put out fires?" August asks Lex.

"No... I can't."

I whistle as I stare at the floor and kick at the edge of a rug. "My! What a pretty rug they have! I wonder if it's authentic!" Authentically what, I'll never know.

"Landon."

I look up. "Huh? What? What's going on? Oh no, Lex, what happened to your mask? You can wear mine. I'm just going to wear August's underwear on my head," I say as I hand over my tie.

"Someone tried incinerating it," Lex says.

"Who would do that? I'll kick their ass for you," I say as August picks up the vase of burning wooden flowers and looks around for a place to put it.

"I can't figure it out," Lex says sarcastically.

"Well, when we find them, I'll take care of them for you," I say as I pat Lex's back. "I got your back. That's what best buddies are there for." Then I tie my tie around his face, making it so only his nose sticks out of the open hole.

He just sighs loudly. "August, you have to be a saint to put up with this."

"I think it's cute," August says as the fire finally goes out and he's left with a vase of ashes. He sets it back down and turns to me. "You need a mask."

"Nah, my face is my mask. Let's go snatch us a bad guy."

We head back out while looking like idiots. I am one hundred percent confident that we now stick out even more than we did before. Although, August is pulling the tie mask off like a supermodel. We step into the main room and Lex heads for the drinks. He grabs one for each of us as we observe the room.

People are mostly chatting, drinking, and waiting for something more exciting to happen.

"Do you see anyone you know?" Lex asks me.

"I've never seen the villains without their attire, so they could be standing next to us and I would be oblivious."

"Isn't that your brother?" August asks as he points.

I turn quickly and see Nolan standing in the corner all alone, scanning the crowd. I take a step toward him, but August holds a hand up.

"What are you doing?"

"I want to talk to him," I say. I haven't seen Nolan since the day he met me under the city square's Christmas tree. "He won't realize it's me."

"Sweetheart, your brother reads minds," August says.

"There are too many people, he'll probably keep a block up or it'd drive him crazy," I say, hoping it to be true because I need to reach him.

"It's too risky."

"What if I entertain him?" Lex suggests. "I'll keep him preoccupied and you guys see if you can find the others."

I hesitate because I'm nervous about leaving Lex and my brother alone. I want to be the only one dealing with him, but I know I can't because Nolan has become completely shut off from me. "Okay... just be careful. I really don't think Nolan would hurt you, but I guess I really don't know what he'd do... I almost feel like I don't know him anymore," I say.

August squeezes my hand and I give him a soft smile. "We'll figure everything out. I promise."

"Thank you."

Lex slips between the throngs of people and disappears into the crowd. After a moment, I see him get close to Nolan.

"Come on," August gently urges as he draws me away from the spot where I'm watching Nolan and Lex. "They're going to be okay. Lex is good at this stuff, I promise."

"What all do you know about Lex?" I ask curiously.

August's strong hand on my back gives me some encouragement to walk away from my brother. "Honestly... not much. He's nice, but he throws up a wall whenever you start to get too close. I know it has something to do with his power, but honestly, I don't know much about it. We've just worked together every once in a while," he says as he guides me deeper into the crowd. There are too many people to even figure out where Hazel is. She could be right in the middle of a large crowd and I might not even notice.

"Let's try to fit in..." I say as I look around to see what the others might be doing. "I've actually never gone to a real party. I only go to fake supervillain parties where the main goal is being an idiot."

"Is that *their* main goal? Or is that just what they automatically do?"

"I think they personally think they're cool. Just like I'm cool with my hot girlfriend when I'm pushing seventy."

"You're not pushing seventy!"

"At least let me be sixty-nine. Oh my god, I just realized that you need a name," I say as I pull August to a stop in the middle of the crowd. I eye him as I try to think of a name that has nothing to do with his new... assets. "I don't know. I'm trying to get an overall visual, but your boobs are huge. Like all I'm getting is E*rack*a or something."

"That was the lamest joke I've ever heard."

I grin at him. "Thank you. Ooh. Try to kill someone with your boobs. I want to know if it'll work."

"My 'boobs' aren't actually real, remember?"

"Oh right. Flash me."

"In front of everyone?"

"Yes."

"Right now?"

"Yes."

"No."

I grumble. "You're no fun. I don't think she's down here. Why don't we go upstairs and see if she's up there? I did see a guard manning the stairs, so we need to be careful or distract him. Either I can show him my new saggy balls or you can show him your boobs, and we'll see if he lets us in. Does he look like a ball man or a boob man?"

"It's clear why you never became a supervillain," August jokes as he freezes time, then grabs my hand and tugs me past the man frozen in time and up the stairs.

"It's ridiculous how unfun you just made the penetration of the second floor," I inform him.

"My main goal in life *is* making penetration unfun."

I snicker as I smack his ass. "Aw... don't get down on yourself."

As he steps onto the second floor, he turns to me and yanks up his shirt, showing me his chest. "Did that make it more fun?"

And now I'm giggling like a fifteen-year-old boy who saw his first *Playboy* magazine. "It did. This is why you're my favorite."

He grins as time starts up again and he hurries me down the hallway. "I thought you'd like it."

"You're too good for me. That's all there is to it," I decide.

"I like to think we're perfect for each other," he says, and then gives me a smile that makes my stone-cold heart explode. The massacre of my heart is filled with glitter and sparkles and it's disgusting, but that is what August does to me and I *let* him. That's how much I like him.

I feel like I should express this to him. "You fill me with glitter, and it's disgusting but I love it."

"I understood none of that, but I'll take it. You fill me with... evil thoughts."

I dramatically grab my heart. "That's the sweetest thing anyone's ever said to me."

He beams at me, and that's when I hear talking. I hold up a finger to shush him and point at the door. I press myself against the door and listen.

I can *barely* hear a woman talking. "Yes, he just brought it. I have it sitting right here... I know how to use it! I don't need directions!"

"She has the snow globe," I say as I jab a finger at the door.

"I'll freeze time and we can go in and grab it," August says.

I can't tell when he does it since we're alone in the hallway, but when he pulls open the door a woman in her thirties remains unmoving, phone in hand. What I also notice is a box on a small table in the middle of the room. I creep over to it and pick it up.

"Is that it?" August asks.

"Dunno," I say as I pull the lid off the box and reach inside. What I pull out isn't a snow globe but a strange oval object. "What is this?"

August looks a little concerned. "Uhhh... an egg..."

I turn it in confusion. "An egg? What? This isn't an egg."

"Like... one that goes up the... you know... vagina."

"Ew! Gross!" I cry as I fling it. It smacks August in the face and he jerks back, snapping time back into place as I'm standing there holding a box of... toys while Hazel stares at us. She leaps back in surprise, dropping her phone.

"Who the fuck are you?" she screams.

"Tell me where the snow globe is, or we'll skin you alive, woman," I growl in my most menacing bad guy voice.

"You're so old you'd break your hip if you just tried," Hazel says, and I realize that the world would be a better place without her.

She holds her hand out, clearly planning on working her voodoo on us, but August throws the egg thing at her, smashing it right into her hand. She cries out and jerks her hand back as I rush for her.

I am not at all against beating up a girl. My mom taught me that protecting women and not fighting them was sexist and that villains don't discriminate between age, sex, or gender. They're assholes to all. So I grab the woman, knock my knees into the back of hers, and drive her to the ground. She cries out as I flip her onto her back and stare down at her as I pin her hands down.

"Where's the snow globe?"

"Up your old saggy asshole," she growls.

"How does that even... what?"

She spits at me, but clearly doesn't understand gravity because the glob of spit comes back down and splatters in her face, delighting me so much.

I look at August. "Search the room."

August rushes over to the closet and yanks the door open before looking in at a man who is bound, gagged, and naked. The man looks confused more than anything before rubbing the gag off with his shoulder.

"You didn't tell me you were bringing friends," the man says. "When I asked to bring my friends, you threw a fit!"

Hazel looks confused. "They're not fucking friends!"

"They're not friends or they're not fucking friends as in they're not here for the fucking?"

"Oh my god, just kill them!"

He wiggles around a bit. "I can't!"

"Murder them, dammit!"

He wiggles around some more, rolling and struggling as August and I stare at him flailing about.

"Is this a bad time to say that your tying skills have gotten phenomenally good?" the man asks.

She smiles at him. "Aw, thank you, babe. But I still need you to kill these fuckers."

He flips onto his stomach and starts inchworming his way toward August. August scurries back but there really is no rush, the man's not getting anywhere fast.

"Tell me where the snow globe is," I growl.

"Up your asshole," she growls.

"Joke's on you, I already had August check," I say.

She looks confused, but it's for the better because that was the lamest joke I've ever made and would be really, *really* happy to pretend I never made it.

"I'm... going... to... get... you..." the man growls with every inch he wiggles toward August.

August nonchalantly steps out of reach.

The door opens and Racer stands there with globe in hand, a very confused look on his face.

"What's going on?"

"Kinky foreplay, clearly," August says in a sexy feminine voice as he struts toward Racer. "Want to join?"

"Don't let her—"

I clamp a hand over Hazel's mouth. "She was trying to say, don't let her suckle your dingleberries too hard," I add.

"Ooh," Racer says as August struts up and reaches for him.

That's when my brother steps around the corner and goes, "Landon?"

Racer jerks his hand back the moment August reaches for him and slips out of the way. Because I'm so distracted, Hazel knees me right in the stomach, sending the air snapping out of my body and leaving me falling off her.

"They're trying to steal the globe!" she shouts as she runs for the door. August grabs for her, but Racer throws him to the ground, globe gone from his hand.

I gasp for breath on the ground, wondering if air will ever return to my lungs. Nolan stands there, expression blank as he sets a hand on Hazel's back and guides her from the room without another word.

August throws Racer off him as the bound man starts crawling toward me. He worms his way up, slamming his weight onto my legs. I flip my hand through the air and the man *flies* off my body and rams into the wall as I stare in horror.

"Are you still alive?" I ask in worry. It really wasn't my plan to murder a man while he was just trying to get his rocks off.

He groans as he rolls onto his back, so I deem him good. I scramble up to my feet as Racer throws August to the ground.

"August, freeze time!"

"I don't want to waste it on this," he says as he pulls back, but Racer is already gone. Just as I step toward him, I feel an arm slip around my throat as I'm dragged back. Suddenly, I'm standing in the hallway and given a shove. My back makes contact with the stairway railing as I fall back, tip over it and begin to fall. That's when I realize Racer threw me over the second-floor railing and I'm going to hit the first floor.

I flail, struggling to grab onto something to keep me from crashing my head into the hardwood floor as the partygoers celebrate the holidays down below.

I close my eyes, prepared for the impact, but arms slide around me. I feel drawn into them and look up as August grabs onto me just before I would have hit the ground.

"Holy shitsticks," I breathe.

"I got you," he says as he squeezes me to him. "Thank god I can freeze time. I couldn't handle it if I got you hurt again."

I grab onto him and take a deep breath. I must have been holding it from the moment I fell. When I look over his shoulder, I see Hazel standing before her partygoers.

"Your families, your children, your parents, your loved ones are all unsafe because of Superheroes United! The police have given up on you! They rely on only one person to protect you and he could barely protect his own when the villains struck the bridge!" she shouts.

The crowd goes wild with blind rage. Their noise is almost deafening as they scream and shout. Their noise escalates until I can't even hear what Hazel is saying over the swelling noise.

"We need to get the snow globe," I say.

And that's when Amelia comes over the earpiece. "What is happening? There are people *streaming* out of the house."

August sets me on my feet as we rush into the main room, only to find Hazel gone. It's hard to see anything over the pushing and shoving crowd.

Someone grabs me and I spin to shove them only to find Lex standing there. "I turned away when she was talking and it didn't seem to affect me. Maybe she needs visual attention? Or maybe it doesn't affect supers? But she just... everyone got pissed about the superheroes and then she was just gone. I don't know where Nolan went either."

"Fuck. I bet Racer pulled them back," August says.

When I turn to look at him, I realize that his illusion has worn off, telling me mine probably has as well. It also means that if the mob sees us, they might begin targeting us instead.

The earpiece crackles a moment before Valerie begins speaking. "Wyatt said there are mobs heading toward the Superheroes United base. I think they're planning on targeting it and bringing it down."

"We're headed out now, or at least trying to. It's hard to get anywhere when everyone is pushing and shoving, but we'll stop them before they reach it," August says as he rushes for the door when Sparx, the female villain from the Rebellion meeting, steps in front of it. She raises her hand up and the lights in the room flicker as the people who'd been enjoying the party begin to rush past her, for the door.

"Guys, they're heading toward the van. Hurry up, we need to move before they realize we're inside," Valerie says through the device in my ear.

That's when Sparx waves her arm through the air as August rushes forward.

"Don't touch her!" I yell as I realize that she's conducting electricity with her power.

August pulls back, but she moves into him. I wave my arm but instead of her slamming into the wall, everything in the room flings to the right, of course missing her. But the movement is enough for her to draw back, away from August.

"We have to move. What's going on?" Valerie asks as I hear loud noises coming from their end.

"Go without us, we have a bit of a dilemma," August says.

The villain lifts her hands up as August tries to concentrate, but it's hard for him to stop time again so soon after he used it to rush down the stairs and grab me as I fell.

She thrusts her hands forward and electricity sparks as it races toward us. That's when Lex steps between us and draws his hands up, and fire ignites from seemingly nothing. Fire bursts into a roaring flame at his feet as August grabs me and pulls me back.

"I'll deal with her," Lex says as the fire latches onto the electricity and seems to eat it. The fire spikes and then explodes. "Get back." Lex sounds almost pleading, and it makes me want to rush to him to help, but August pulls me back.

"He can't always control his fire, but it won't hurt him. It *will* hurt us," he says, and thoughts of fire eating into my skin at the broadcasting station race through my mind, so I let him pull me away. For some reason, I know that Lex is facing demons of his own, but I'm not going to be able to be the one to help him. Although, I'll be there if he needs me.

August begins to run, pulling me after him. I glance back one last time as fire licks Lex's feet and begins to eat away at everything around him.

I'm pulled through the back door and into the evening as we slip around to the front of the house, looking for the vehicle we'd ridden here in. It's gone, but my attention is drawn to the mobs of people racing toward the middle of town. They're screaming and yelling, pushing and shoving. And that's when the mob of infuriated people set their eyes on us.

CHAPTER TWENTY-FOUR

"It's Leviathan!" one of them yells. I wave my hand through the air and it's like a wind whips through, knocking them down like bowling pins as August stumbles into the lane of an oncoming car. The vehicle slams on their brakes and August rushes for the driver's seat.

"We need to borrow your car," he says as he tears the door open and roughly helps the driver out. My villain side is a little proud of him for taking over a vehicle. And then as he slides in, he smiles at the man. "Thank you so much for your help and have a wonderful evening. I'll buy you a new car if I have to."

"Sheesh, you're too sweet," I grumble, buckling myself in as August slams his foot down on the gas and the tires squeal. He swings the car around and rushes off, knowing that we need to get back to the Superheroes United building before the angry mob reaches it.

"I'm worried Marauder wants to get everyone to the same location for some reason. If he staged it so it looks like the heroes wounded the citizens, then imagine the backlash that would have," August says.

"He could use Nolan to control the supers and hurt them," I realize.

Again this falls back on Nolan and makes it hard to believe that Nolan isn't doing this on purpose. I need to get there quickly. I need to stop my brother before it's too late.

"Can this go any faster?" I plead. "I have to stop Nolan."

August glances at me before quickly looking away. "Landon... what if Nolan can't be stopped? What if it is what it is? What if this is what he *wants*?" August asks.

I look over at him as his hands tighten on the steering wheel. I can tell it upsets him to say this and go against my beliefs, but I don't blame him. Even I question whether Nolan truly wishes to harm these people or not. But I know my brother. I care about him so much and my heart is telling me that he can't possibly do this. It can't be him at the front of this.

"Then I guess I didn't know him as well as I thought I did," I admit.

August reaches over and feels for my hand. I hesitate before sliding my fingers between his and squeezing. "I trust you."

I hope that trust isn't wrongly given. "We should get these suits off," I say as I grudgingly pull my hand free and start unbuttoning my shirt. I work it off my shoulders and slide my pants down since my supersuit is on under it. Then I reach over and start helping August.

He turns the corner and slams on the brakes. I fly forward, but the seat belt grabs onto me as his hand squeezes tightly, like he's going to keep me from smashing into the dashboard. It'd probably be fitting since that's how our third date went and he still decided to like me.

"What's going on?" I ask as I look up and realize that the street is *filled* with mobs of people. Clearly, Hazel's ability can stretch quite far when she uses the snow globe to aid her.

People are rushing the fence surrounding the Superheroes United building, beating on it and screaming.

That's when I see Valerie, Amelia, and Joy step up to the gate.

"What are they doing?" I ask as I reach for the door.

"Be careful getting out, they're going to be targeting us and we can't hurt them. Besides numbers, they have a huge advantage over us because we can't kill them. That's what the villains want. They want to broadcast us in a negative light," August explains. "I'm sure there are cameras watching us right now ready for us to make a mistake."

"Got it," I say as he pulls me over to his side so we get out of the car on the same side.

"I'm going to freeze time and we're going to rush the gate, get on the safe side of it and help the others," August explains, but before he can do that, I notice the gate sliding open.

I pause, confused on why it *would* be opening when Valerie and the others would be safest with a gate between them. "What are they doing?" I ask as Joy steps forward and waves her hand through the air. A barrier slams into place and the people charging the gate smash into it. The people behind them, driving them harder into the invisible force. That's when Amelia steps into them and the ground begins to rumble and crack. People scream as the cement seems to open up, like it's going to devour them.

"What are they doing?" August asks.

"I think Nolan's controlling them," I say as I press my earpiece. "Valerie, stop them!"

Silence.

August freezes time and we rush into the crowd, racing for the front as we try to weave our way through them. Time snaps back into place and someone rams into me, breaking me away from August and making me fall into another.

"It's Chrono!" someone shouts, and attention turns to August.

"Landon!" August shouts as he tries rushing for me, but I'm not sure he can make it to me as people fill in the gaps.

Someone socks me in the side and I wave my hand without thinking, wishing to just push them back, but my power slams them to the ground savagely.

I fear something has happened to them, but I know I can't control it. I can't do anything until I get that fucking globe back.

"They're trying to kill us!" someone shouts, and the roar of the mob becomes deafening. But they're not mindless, they're still people, and they're kind of afraid of me as I step toward them.

When I raise my hand again, they back away and that allows me to see Valerie as she mindlessly stands there while chaos takes over around her.

That's when I finally find Nolan, just beyond her, face emotionless, controlling the supers.

Just as I go to reach for him, August slams into me, the hit knocking me to the ground. At first, I think he's been shoved or he was moving me out of the way, until I realize that he's wearing the same blank expression he wore when he let them beat him and punch him.

He grabs onto me and drives me to my knees as his elbow slams into my side.

"Nolan!" I scream, knowing that I need to stop him before he causes more damage. "Nolan, please!"

August hesitates upon hearing my voice and I slip my arm around him and grab him tightly. I tear him off me and race toward the gate. People still can't get through because of Joy's barrier, so I know I need to move her without hurting her. I lift my hand and gently push her, but instead of moving, the gate is torn from its hinges and flies through the air. The movement seems to distract Joy, and I slip past the barrier and race up to Nolan. Before anyone can stop me, I grab onto him, desperate to fix this.

"Nolan, please stop!"

"I can't!" he says, voice cracking as his eyes drop to mine. The emotions on his face devastate me and I want to save him. Help him. Do something.

"You're better than this."

He shakes his head. "The voices... the voices are driving me crazy. I can't stop. I can't get away. Voices, so many voices. Marauder makes them stop."

"Nolan, but at what cost? Is it worth killing others?" I ask as I grab his face in my hands and force him to look at me.

"Landon... I don't... I don't know what's happening," he says, voice cracking, hands shaking. "Landon... it's like I can't even hear myself anymore. I don't even know what my own thoughts are like. I can't—"

It feels like a force is slammed into me as I'm thrown off Nolan and hit the ground on my back. It takes me a moment to realize that fucking Racer slammed into me *again*. But when I look up, I realize that I'm lying at Marauder's feet. He's holding the snow globe in one hand while smiling sweetly down at me.

"Oh, Landon. We could have had so much fun together. We could have gone far," Marauder says, voice almost melodious.

"Fuck you," I growl as I struggle to my feet, but the moment I do, I'm lifted into the air. I can't move my arms or legs as I levitate before him as he uses *my* power to control me.

"Landon!" August yells as Racer turns and rushes toward him. Out of my peripheral vision, I see August drive Racer back as they begin to fight.

Marauder clears his throat, clearly annoyed that my attention has strayed off him. "Landon... we could have ruled the world side by side."

I try to use my power to push him back, move something, do anything, but it's like I'm stuck here, three feet in the air, incapable of doing anything. "I don't want anything you're offering."

"I can make you want it like I did to Nolan," he says. "I could weaken your thoughts and your actions until you feel like the only way to survive is to do my bidding. Or should I just kill you?"

"If I can't stop you, someone else will."

Marauder gives me a huge smile, and I realize what's about to happen.

"Oh no, don't start monologuing," I say.

"Shh... you're so cute but I hate everything about you," Marauder informs me.

"Aw, thanks! You're ugly *and* I hate you. Now let me go."

"Let me speak," he says. "This city needs a new leader. It needs someone to realize what it's doing to itself. How it's ruining itself—" Marauder's attention shifts to August and Racer who are still fighting. "For fuck's sake, I'm trying to make a speech, will you two fight *quieter*?"

They don't even try to listen, and I see Marauder's lip twitch.

"As I was *saying* before I was *rudely* interrupted," he starts like he doesn't realize that he's being the rudest one of all. "These people need a new leader. Someone to protect them. Someone to guide them. We have become so dependent on superheroes that the police just sit back and *wait* for a super to come save the citizens. They don't even respond when things are happening anymore because *August* will get it. Well, a new time has risen—For fuck's sake, will you stop wiggling around?"

"Me?" I ask in disbelief. "You want me to stop trying to get free? You ain't that interesting."

"I'm going to start again if you don't settle the fuck down," he growls.

"What's your plan? To bore us to death? Because it's working."

247

I try to get away, but that's when I feel constriction around my body. It's almost like he's crushing my body, squeezing it shut, destroying it. I cry out as my body aches and I realize that I can't do anything to stop him. Maybe... just maybe, I shouldn't have antagonized the man who has my life in his hands.

Marauder clears his throat. "Now, allow me to continue. I am here to—"

And that's when Nolan punches him right in the face and I drop to the ground.

"You will not touch my brother," Nolan growls.

Marauder's eyes shoot up as they lock onto Nolan who is standing directly in front of me, blocking me from Marauder.

"Nolan, move before I kill you," Marauder says, voice calm and quiet.

Nolan rushes forward as I pant, body aching and chest heaving, like all the air has been dragged from me. Marauder's power slams into Nolan, driving him to his knees, but he pushes up to his feet. That's when Marauder grabs for his own head as he cries out, telling me that Nolan is doing something to his mind.

Suddenly, I hear a gunshot crack and the snow globe is torn from Marauder's hand. I watch as it drops to the ground and shatters at Marauder's feet, leaving the man to reel back in surprise.

For some reason, I expect smoke to shoot out, or some visual form to leave it, but nothing happens as the globe rolls and liquid oozes out at Marauder's feet. He roars out as Nolan staggers, hand against his chest, pain filling his face. That's when I feel my power rushing back into me. It's such a comfortable feeling to have it envelop me and wrap around me.

I look back as Valerie aims the gun for Marauder, but Racer pushes Marauder out of the way, disappearing into the crowd.

"Nolan!" I shout as August rushes after Racer.

Nolan looks back at me as he takes a staggering step forward and lands on his knees.

"We have to stop them," August shouts. "Landon, *now*."

I turn to Valerie. "Please help my brother... and if I don't make it... I want you to know that I was the one who TP'd your house."

"You little asshole," she growls. "You'd better make it back alive so I can hurt you myself."

"I will," I say as I turn to the crowd, hopeful that my power is fully back. Hell, maybe the power isn't back at all and I'd just been feeling happiness about Nolan fighting for me. I lift my hand up and the crowd of people scream and cry out as they rise up. I push my hand to the side and they're sent out of my path, revealing Racer and Marauder. And just like that, I know that my power will not let them escape.

I set the people down as I fixate on them, knowing that there's nowhere for them to run. I hold a hand out and draw them to me, pulling them in as they both struggle to flee. August grabs onto Marauder, pushing him to the ground and leaving him with no way out.

Racer, in one last attempt to free them both, breaks free and slams into August. August must freeze time because in the next moment, Racer is on the ground, unconscious.

"Are you okay?" I ask as blood drips from August's nose, but overall, he looks alright.

"I'm fine. Can you help me keep them held here until help comes?"

"Of course," I say, even though I want to rush back to Nolan and make sure he's alright.

Together, we keep both of them from moving, instead forcing them to stay with our powers. When the Superheroes United guards arrive, they lock them down with heavy-duty handcuffs so they can place them in vehicles where their powers won't work. As soon as I'm free from guard duty, I turn away to rush to Nolan.

When I find him kneeling on the ground, I drop down in front of him. "Hey, are you okay?" I ask as Valerie stands guard over him.

"I'm sorry," he says. "My head... I'm sorry I wasn't strong enough. I'm sorry I risked your life and everyone else's." The quiver in his voice makes me want to forgive every wrong he's ever done.

I sink down and wrap him in my arms. "Why didn't you come to me? I would have helped you."

"I'm not sure there is help for me, Landon," he says as he hugs me. "My power has consumed me... I can't explain it..."

Suddenly, Nolan is pulled from me and I look up as Wyatt yanks his hands back.

"What are you doing?" I growl, ready to toss Wyatt into next year if he plans on doing something with my brother.

"Landon, your brother was involved," Valerie says calmly as she sets a hand on my shoulder like she's there to comfort me.

I stare at her in disbelief. "He didn't have a choice. Marauder was doing something to him."

"I know... but he still has to go to court. Everything needs to be done legally."

Nolan looks over at me and gives me a soft smile. "It's fine, Landon. I understand what I've done and what I could have done. I honestly... don't trust myself. I need something... I need to make the voices stop. Maybe Marauder did it to me. Or maybe it would always have happened to me. But my mind is a mess and I just want it to end. He promised me he could end it and whatever he did to me made me believe all of it."

He leans forward and sets his forehead against mine. "It'll be okay. You have August."

My stomach aches as I reach forward and hold on to his cheeks. "But you're my brother."

"Thank you for not giving up on me. Thank you for believing me to be better than I am."

It hurts me, knowing they're going to take him away, and who knows what they're going to do with him. Who knows where he'll end up or for how long. My only hope is that they find proof that Marauder was manipulating him. "I would never give up on you. You're my brother. I'll always love you and believe in you."

He's pulled back and I have to look away. I can't watch them put him into the vehicle without wanting to push them back and pull him to safety. I know I could stop them all, but I shouldn't.

"It's okay," August gently says as he reaches out and wraps me up in his arms. I sink into them, wanting him to make everything better, but I know that I can't think like a villain anymore. I have to do as they ask.

"I don't want him to go to prison. He's not a bad person," I mumble against him.

August squeezes me tightly. "I'll do everything I can, but for right now, this is what we have to do."

I nod, knowing he's right. "Are you okay?"

"I am. I was so scared something would happen to you," he says as he tilts my chin up and kisses me. "I love you."

I catch his eyes, surprise no doubt clearly showing on my face. "You do?"

"Of course."

I tuck my head against his neck as emotions swirl around me. With everything that has happened, it's hard to understand it all. But through all of it, August was always there for me. I also know that he has always truly cared for me and it makes me ache for him. "I love you too."

His grip tightens on me in response. I close my eyes, trying to sink into this moment to keep myself from focusing on anything else that's happening. But I need August and I have him here to protect me and support me.

"And thank you... for saving me from myself. I started to hate this job I was given, but you've filled me with so much happiness," he says, voice soft. "You've made me see everything that is good and fun in this world when all I could see was the pain people were inflicting on others."

"I'm glad I've been able to be here for you," I say as I straighten up so I can kiss him.

CHAPTER TWENTY-FIVE

"This is absolutely horrible and the worst idea I've ever come up with, and it's your fault," I say.

August looks over at me as he fusses with the Christmas tree. "*My* fault? You literally just said 'the worst idea I've come up with.' Emphasis on the *I*."

"Yes, I as in *you*."

He snorts as he plucks a bulb off the tree and relocates it to another spot on the tree that is literally inches from the last spot.

"What are you doing?" I ask in alarm.

His eyes get wide. "I don't know! You're all panicked so it's making me panic. It'll be fine, right? Yeah, it'll be fine."

I rush over to him and grab on, like he'll save me from this hell. "Why did we decide to have Christmas here?" I ask.

"Because we want *both* of our families together."

I squeeze him tighter. "That's right." I jerk back so I can look him in the eyes. "I have an idea. What if we just leave? We run off and leave them to it."

"And make them interact with each other without us?" August asks. "I like that idea."

"Me too!"

That's when there's a gentle knock on the door, telling me that it's definitely not *my* family. With everything going on with the villains, we weren't sure if we were even going to be able to have a Christmas party. When things ended, August and I thought it could be a good opportunity for our families to meet and bond if we had it at my house. I didn't realize how much work a Christmas party was or I sure as hell would not have offered up my house. Even forcing August's team to clean, cook, and put up decorations while I read was exhausting.

I helped them by directing where the Christmas tree should go. Then as soon as I turned my back, Zacia scaled the tree and set to work on destroying all of it. Only once she'd knocked the entire tree over did I realize what was happening. I thought that we should be unique and just leave it on its side, but August, the overachiever he is, put it back up and tried blockading my precious cat from it.

If only he knew that she was currently sharpening her claws on it as we speak.

"What if we trade families?" I decide. "We'll do that. I get to try my hand at a normal family and you get to try out a... um... a not normal family."

I rush to the door, prepared to claim them first. When I open the door, I come face-to-face with August's perfect little family. They're holding food and presents, dressed in fancy clothes and wearing huge smiles. His father, Arthur, is wearing a Santa hat and his little sister, Victoria, is wearing elf ears.

They're so cute and precious and my family is going to ruin them. They're going to *feast* on their innocence.

"Hey, new family. You're mine now even if I have to Stockholm y'all," I decide.

August's mom beams at me. "Aw, you don't have to do anything like that to get us to welcome you to the family," Catherine says as she steps into the foyer and wraps me up in her arms.

"Oh my god, you're my soul mate," I decide as I grab onto her. "If like soul mates were mothers or something. I don't know. Now it sounds creepy. I don't want to bone you or anything, just to get that out there. Holy balls, I need to stop talking. Just to warn you, my family is... unique. They mean well... maybe. I really don't know, but I do know that I'm normal... ish compared to them."

She pats my arm. "It'll be alright."

And that's when I hear them. Instinctively, I use my powers to push the table in front of the door before remembering that I actually invited them over. I'm not sure I've ever invited them over, but I have this time.

August nonchalantly slides the decorative table away from the door and pulls it open, revealing Mom, Dad, and Brandon. There's a small pang of disappointment when Nolan isn't there, even though I knew he wouldn't be.

"Merry Christmas!" Mom says.

I assess them for faults. They're wearing nice clothes… strange. Carrying presents… even stranger. "Merry Christmas?"

"Why'd that sound like a question?" Brandon asks. "Is it not? Did we come on the wrong day? My girlfriend got me a watch, but it has these weird lines on it. I told her it must be from a foreign country, but she just laughed it off."

I turn to August's family. "This is my mom Patricia, my dad Mark, and my brother Brandon. People who may or may not be related to me, this is Catherine, Arthur, and August's sister Victoria."

"It is such a pleasure to meet you," Mom says to them as I stare at her suspiciously. Someone must have replaced my mother, but oh well! Seems like the newer version is highly superior.

I lead them into the kitchen so they can put the food down. Mom hands me a plate and I immediately hold it over the trash can. "Who made this?" I ask, prepared to just save us all from food poisoning if my mom did.

"I did," Dad says.

"Oh, thank heavens," I say as I set the plate down next to Catherine's plate of food.

I step back next to August as the two families introduce themselves and talk. "What is happening?"

"I… I don't know," he whispers. "Do you think this is a dream?"

"Has to be. My family is… trying, and it's so strange."

"Maybe they're planning something wicked," he says. "Like building up to it."

"Ah, shit. I bet you're right."

I keep my eyes peeled, waiting for something, but nothing seems to be happening. That's when my mom grabs a knife. "Mom, don't!" I cry.

She turns to me, looking confused. "Did you want to cut it yourself?"

"Oh, I thought you were going to stab someone. Like that time you stabbed Brandon—" August's family looks horrified. "He's invincible. She did it... don't ask."

I retreat back to August. "August..."

"I think they're just being good," he says as he gives me a smile before reaching over and sticking a Santa hat on my head. "Why do you even look sexy in that?"

"Aw, thanks, babe. It's my ruggedly good looks."

"Rugged...ly? Yeah! Sure!"

I narrow my eyes. "What's that mean?"

"Nothing! It wasn't a jab at your lack of ruggedness, but maybe that's the way I like you."

"Weak, scrawny, can't run for long periods of time. It kind of sounds like you just want someone to bully. Everyone, August is bullying me!" I say.

They turn to me and when Catherine narrows her eyes, I nearly beam at her. "August, you know that's not very nice. You finally managed to find someone who can tolerate you. You don't want him running away now, do you?"

I grin maniacally at August who is glaring at his mom.

"You're right that I don't want him to run away, but I'm not hard to tolerate!" August exclaims.

She just smiles, which makes him shake his head.

The timer goes off and I head over to the oven and pull the turkey out. As we prepare the turkey, everyone talks and helps set the table and prepare the food. When everything is ready, we get our food and all of us squeeze in around the table.

I always knew I was part of a family, there was no escaping that, but as I sit around the table surrounded by people I care about, I truly feel like I belong with them. Especially when I have August by my side.

I look over at him and give him a gentle smile as he reaches over and squeezes my leg. Besides having Nolan here, the day couldn't get much better than this.

After we eat, we head to the Christmas tree where Zacia is at the top, gnawing on the head of the angel. Brandon helps August hand out presents as I reach up to the top of the tree and pull Zacia down, but she refuses to come down without knocking the angel off first. The angel's head falls off, so I discreetly kick it under the tree. Then I carry her over to the spot next to August as he finishes passing out presents.

"Before we begin, I wanted to say a little something," I say.

Brandon, who'd already begun, pats the paper back down on his present like no one would notice.

"I just... things have been a little rough with everything going on, but somehow... this has been the best month or so of my life because I got to learn more about August, I got to meet his family, and I was able to get closer to my own family and reach an understanding with them. So thank you to my family who is clearly trying *very* hard. I know there's no way you'd be acting this normal if you weren't trying. And thank you to August's family for accepting me, even though you know that I might not have the cleanest of pasts, and most of all, thank you August for believing in me even after I lied to you about who I was."

August shrugs. "When we were in middle school, I heard you liked animals, so I was the one who let all the animals loose from the FFA room in the hopes of getting your attention," August says. "What I'm trying to say is that I've spent a long time trying to get you to look at me. I'm so glad I don't have to fight for your attention anymore."

I smile as his words warm me up. "Why did you do everything but talk to me?" I ask.

He starts laughing. "I don't know! The thought of talking to you made my stomach flutter and my heart pound wildly. Sometimes, it still does."

"Oh my god, you're so cute." I lean in so only he can hear the last part. "If your family wasn't here, I'd let you do very naughty things to me right now. Ooh, you could freeze time. I bet you could get the job done before time starts up again."

"I can freeze it for like a minute."

"Plenty of time."

He grabs me and yanks me toward him. "I take back everything nice I've ever said to you."

Brandon must have been eavesdropping because he says, "My girlfriend said that one minute is a very long time. She was very proud of me the other day."

Everyone stares at Brandon.

"Did I tell you guys about the orgy I met your mother at?" Dad asks.

"Oh no. It's starting," I groan. "That's all we need to know from both of you, and moving on! Present time!"

Everyone decides that presents are much more interesting than my parents' orgy story that no one has, or ever will, ask for.

"I have another present I'll give you later," August whispers into my ear.

"Is it the penis?" I whisper back.

He snorts. "I mean, it can be. But that means I have *two* presents for you."

"Ooh."

I grab a present in front of me and tear it open before wondering if I should have waited on opening my parents' present until last in case I need to destroy it. It takes me a moment to realize that it's a life-sized poster of August that they bought from the city's superhero merch line.

"Oh my god," August says in horror as I *beam* at it.

"I *love* it!" I say as I stand up so I can unroll the whole thing. "This is literally the greatest thing you guys have ever gotten me."

"Burn it," August pleads.

I would never do such a thing. "It's so cute!"

"Please! Please burn it!" He sounds so desperate, making my love for the poster grow.

"No, sweetheart. This is mine now," I say as I hurry into the kitchen and return with a hammer and nail. August tries grabbing it from me but I poke him with the nail which makes him retreat. And then I tack it onto the wall.

"This is horrible," August groans, but I'm not sure there's anything better than a life-sized picture of August in his superhero outfit with one of his superhero mottos in bubble letters next to his face.

"I got you the washable one so if you... you know, on it, you can wipe it right off!" Mom says.

Mortified, I turn to face her. "Leave my house."

August starts laughing. "That's what you *get*."

"Shush, sweet angel, this is between me and my mother. Mom... those words should have never been spoken."

She shrugs as she tears open a box, not at all caring that she has scarred me for life. After we open presents, we play board games where my family decides that they'll demolish August's family, but they honestly try their hardest and dial down the crazy... a little.

And somehow, it ends up being one of the best days of my life.

While August deals with the family, I go into a quiet room alone and shut the door. I stare at the phone before taking a deep breath and dialing the number. It takes me about ten minutes to jump through hoops to reach the prison and another ten while I wait before I hear someone on the other end.

"Hello?" Nolan asks.

"Hey... Merry Christmas."

"Merry Christmas... I'm surprised you called. I thought... I thought that after you had time to think about what I did, you'd realize that I'm really not worth worrying about," he says. "You do realize how much I did, right?"

"I know. But I want you to explain yourself. From the beginning, tell me everything. And I swear to God, if you're not being truthful, I'm going to break in just to slap you."

He chuckles. "Alright... so... the voices in my head have gotten awful. It went from being able to read minds when I wanted, to me having to hear everyone's inner thoughts constantly. Every moment of the day, voices just pounded in my head, deafeningly loud. And it starts driving you a little crazy after a while. I could sometimes pinpoint one voice, if I focused really hard, but it would make me feel sick for days after. Marauder... Marauder told me he could help me if I joined him.

"I... I mean I knew he was part of the Rebellion, but at that time, he wasn't doing anything horrible and I was desperate. You don't understand that when your mind is in constant chaos, things start bothering you that never did before. You feel like you're always on edge. And he was promising me an out. But when I got there... I quickly realized he was only wanting me to get to you. Everyone always wants you and... like I said, when I was surrounded by those voices even the littlest of things bothered me. I felt jealous of you. I was jealous of your ability. I was jealous that you could control your power or shut it off when you wanted. I used Mom and Dad to try and get you to join and when you wanted nothing to do with it, Marauder was fine with it. It was strange, but I was happy to have you away from his plans... until he told me what he was going to do. He'd decided that if he couldn't have you join him, he would take your power from you.

"I fought against him. Told him that he couldn't take your power, but he promised to take mine as well. He promised that I wouldn't have to live with these voices anymore and then there you were *wishing* you didn't have your power. So I gave him both. It was like... bliss... in some ways. The voices were gone, but my head was clouded. Like I couldn't comprehend what we were doing, but he made the voices go away! I'm not sure if it was an effect from him taking my power, or if it was something he did to me that made me feel that way. But when he asked me to do things, I knew it was right to do them! It's hard to explain. I almost felt mindless. It was fine... until the voices started coming back. Slowly, very slowly they came back. Whispers. But I could handle whispers when I was used to screams. But with it, came an understanding that what was going on was wrong. But I guess... I guess I didn't fully understand until he was going to kill you. And that's when everything snapped back into place. I'm sorry... I'm sorry my selfishness led to this."

My chest aches for him because I can't stand seeing someone I care about being in so much pain. "I'm sorry you were going through all of that. Why didn't you tell me?"

"I don't know. It's hard talking to people when you hear their thoughts constantly."

"Do you hear them now?"

"I do... they're trying to find a drug to help calm them. Something they give me quiets them for about an hour after I take it, but then they're back, just as loud as ever. Maybe they'll find something to help me."

"I really hope they do."

"Thank you... for everything. For not giving up on me when I'd already given up on myself."

"You're my brother. We might have had our differences growing up, but you were ultimately the one who was always there for me. I want to be there for you, but I don't know what to do."

"Just not giving up on me is enough."

"I'm trying to talk them into letting me see you. It'll take some time, but I think I will be able to, and hopefully, August has enough power to get you transferred or put somewhere else."

"I understand what I did and the lives I put in danger, Landon. It is what it is. They're telling me to finish up. Thank you for calling me. I hope you have a wonderful Christmas."

"You too. I love you."

"I love you too."

I hang up and sink down onto the bed as I curl up around the phone. A few minutes later, August walks in and quietly lies down on the bed next to me. He pulls me into his arms and we lie like that until I'm prepared to put a happy face back on and face our families.

CHAPTER TWENTY-SIX

"Was it as bad as you thought?" August asks.

I smile at him as I sit down on the foot of the bed. "I actually had a wonderful time today," I admit. After we had lunch with the families, they left sometime before supper and August and I spent the rest of the evening together. It was relaxing and wonderful and I loved every moment of it, especially because August was by my side.

"I'm glad."

"My favorite part is my new jizz poster."

He grimaces. "Please no."

"I'm sorry, babe, if you're not here, I'm going to be jerking off to it every chance I get."

"Then maybe I just need to be here all the time."

I quickly look over at him as my chest stutters. "Are you inviting yourself to move in with me?"

He looks alarmed. "No! I'm sorry! I wasn't."

"What if I *want* you to?"

"Then... yes? I'd love to. On one condition."

This sounds exciting. "Ooh, I have to be tied to the bed at least once a week? You get to spank me when I'm bad? You're not allowed to cook?"

"We burn the poster of me."

I cringe back. "What?" I ask, horrified. "I'd rather you cook. I *love* that poster. It's my favorite thing ever and you can't come between me and that poster."

"I thought your cat was your favorite thing ever."

"Favorite nonliving thing, *duh*. I can't believe you'd ask such a stupid thing of me because it's not gonna happen. Wait a minute... you said I had another Christmas present. Is it your penis?"

"Yes, my penis."

"Yay!"

"Alright, I'm going to go get it. Stay right here."

"You're going to go get your penis?"

"Yes, I left it right outside the door."

"Okay! Should I strip?"

He snickers. "If you'd like."

"Ooh. I'll be ready."

He slips out the door and shuts it behind him. I strip in record time and make sure I'm ready for when he comes in. There is no ounce of fabric that will slow me down.

"Are you ready?" August asks through the door.

"Yes."

"I'm going to just freeze time and appear in front of you when you're ready, but only when you're ready."

"Oh, I'm ready. I'm readier than I've ever been in my entire life."

Suddenly, he's in front of me and I just gasp as I take it all in. He's naked but for a... sling that wraps over his cock, the red straps sliding up and over both shoulders, creating a V. The cloth around his cock is red with fluff and frills made to look like Santa.

"Oh heaven save me, my balls are going to explode! Turn around! Turn around!"

He turns, revealing the strap going right up his ass crack, and I start howling with laughter. He loses his straight face and starts laughing as he turns back to face me. "Do you like it?" he asks as if he can't tell by the way I'm melting onto the bed.

"Is this your new supersuit? Please tell me this is how you'll be saving people from now on."

"Only for you, my love," he says, which is definitely good enough. Although I would sell my house to see him save some people wearing that outfit. "What? You're just wearing this evil look on your face."

"I want to see you save people wearing that."

"*Hell* no. Can you imagine? I already have creeps stalking me."

I narrow my eyes. "Stalking you, you say? Where are these... creeps? I will fuck them up."

"I know you will, and I'm kind of worried about them."

"About *them?*"

"Someone looked at me funny yesterday at the grocery store and you threatened to punch his head through the roof. He just wanted an autograph."

"No, he wanted your butthole and your butthole is mine. He was being obscene with the way he was staring at you. People know to back off when I'm coming around because I'll protect you with my life."

"You have way too much power and for some reason, it turns me on," he says.

"Ooh," I purr as I jump up and hold my hand out. I lift him off his feet with just a thought and drop him onto the bed. Then I use my gift to pin his arms and legs down before crawling up his body so I'm leaning over him. I run a finger from the middle of his chest, right down the V of the outfit—is it an outfit?—that he has on.

I lean down until our lips are nearly touching and he fights against my power to push up and meet them, but he can't overpower my ability. I reach the part where the cloth cups his cock and drag my fingers over the Santa face on them. "I wonder if Santa would mind me jingling his bells."

"I bet he wouldn't," August says, which makes me snicker and him automatically smile.

I run my tongue over his lips, teasing his inability to move in order to touch me. Then I nip his bottom lip and pull it as my hand cups and rubs his cock.

"Let me touch you."

"Nah, why would I do that?" I tease as I move my mouth to his throat and run soft kisses down to his collarbone. I suck his neck before running my tongue over the reddened skin as he groans. I can't tell if it's out of frustration of being unable to move or pleasure, but the sound excites me. I draw my hand down, letting the pads of my

263

fingers slide over his skin. He shivers as I kiss a line down his body and I slide my hands up. I push the straps off his shoulders, sliding them off his stilled arms. I pull it down his legs, revealing his hard cock.

"Someone's excited... I think. I can't tell since you're being so inactive... it's like you expect me to do everything by myself," I tease as I slide a finger from the base of his cock to the tip. "It's almost like... I can't tell if you even want to fuck me."

"You're evil."

"Thank you," I say as I lean down so my breath is against his cock before looking up and catching his eyes. "Give me a thumbs up if you want me to suck your cock."

He fights against the hold as I blow on him just to tease him even more. I draw a finger in a circle around the base as he stares at me in disbelief.

"How can you do this to me?"

"Do what, sweetpea? You're the one refusing to give me the go ahead."

He narrows his eyes. "I am?"

"It's really, really sad. I suppose I'll just play with myself by myself," I say as I wrap my hand around my own cock. "Hmm... yes... that just feels so amazing."

"I even dressed up for you."

I start laughing as I lean over and kiss his lips. I love the feel of his cock digging into my lower stomach as I do so. "I suppose you did, so I'll forgive you just this once," I say as I slide down his body and take his cock in my hand. I wrap my hand around the base and I lean down as I slide my tongue over the tip. Then I wrap my mouth around the head of his cock and sink down. I suck as I swirl my tongue. His groans encourage me to take more of him deeper into my mouth, hollowing my cheeks as my fingers slide around the base. I'm not exactly into showing him my gagging skills, so I take as much of him as I can, allowing my free hand to stroke the rest. And then I let the fingers of my other hand trail over to his balls. I cup them and fondle them gently as he groans.

It's fun but hard to keep my mind split on two different things: my power of keeping him held down and pleasuring him. It makes it a challenge, but the way he squirms and groans beneath my touch makes it worth it. I pull my hand away and pat around on the bed until I find the lubricant, which I pop open. I pull off his cock long enough squirt some lubricant onto my fingers which I press against my hole.

"I want to see you touch yourself," he says.

"You're so greedy," I taunt, swinging my right leg over him so my ass is facing him as I press a finger against myself and slowly push inside.

"Are you sure you don't want me to help?" he asks.

"Not allowed to, sorry," I say as I spread my focus between stretching myself, pleasuring him with my hand, and keeping him nice and snug against the bed.

When I can't take any more, I pull my fingers free and press a condom against his cock before rolling it down. Then I coat him in lubricant before sitting on his lower stomach, cock pressed against my ass.

"Ready?"

"More than ready. Are you sure you don't need my help?"

"Not yet," I say as I lift myself up and press his cock against my hole. I slowly press down until I feel myself *just* opening up and even though I'm dying to fill myself with his thick cock, I love the look on his face too much. "Do you like that?" I ask as I press down just a bit more.

"I do, but your hold on me lessened when I entered you. There's no way you're going to stay focused enough to take my cock and hold me still."

"Oh? I will," I assure him. "Don't get sassy with me."

He grins at me, and I begin to sink down, but I fear he's right. As he starts to fill me up, my attention drops from everything else and focuses on the cock inside me. But I will fight to keep his sassy ass pinned down.

I even hold his eyes while doing it so he knows how confident I am that I can do this.

I sink down lower and lower until he's deep inside of me. Then I begin to move, rising up just enough to rock my hips. The slower I move, the more it's driving him crazy, but it's also driving me crazy as well. I want him harder and faster, but the look he's giving me is worth it.

"Feel good?" I ask.

"Oh yes," he moans.

I sink down onto him as my cock aches for attention. The moment I slide my hand around it, I feel him thrust up, making me realize that I lost some attention on my power. The moment his cock hits my prostate, I groan and know that I've lost.

He grabs onto me, mouth melding against mine, tongue invading like he's been dying to just eat me up. He takes my breath away as his fingers and hands travel over my body, making my sensitive skin shiver. He takes my cock in one hand as I melt into him, ready to hand myself over as he thrusts up into me. He spins me around, gently laying me on the bed as he begins to fuck me. I dig my fingers into him as I cry out, needing more, needing all of him.

"There, August... fuck..." I groan as I hold him tightly, wanting to feel him touch me from his lips to his chest to his cock. Even my legs are wrapped around him because I can't get enough of him.

As he thrusts inside me, I know I can't take much more. My body is already unable to handle the pleasure of it. He kisses me as he strokes my cock and I feel my balls tighten. I groan as he pulls back and I tuck myself against him as I come. He feels tight inside me as my body squeezes onto him as cum hits his stomach. His thrusts become shallow as he groans and comes inside me. We desperately hold on to each other as I feel his cock pulse inside me.

Instead of pulling out, he keeps me close to him, breath heavy as he kisses and touches me. He draws his fingers and lips gently over my burn scars, kissing and caressing as he holds onto me. He whispers sweet words to me and tells me how much he loves and cares about me.

And I feel like the luckiest person alive.

EPILOGUE

ONE MONTH LATER

I feel weird walking through the hallway, almost like I'm nervous, but I have August by my side, so it makes everything better.

"You alright?" he asks.

"I'm fine."

"Good. I'm glad," he says as we reach a door where a guard stands. The man pulls it open for us and waves us inside. In the small room there's only one table, not much room for anything else, and at the table sits Nolan.

A smile fills his face the moment he sees me and I rush over to him even as the guards glare at me like they're going to keep me from hugging him, but they also know I could kick their asses if needed. Nolan stands up and I wrap him in a hug.

"Do you want me to break you out, I'll break you out," I whisper into his ear.

He chuckles. "No. You're a good guy now, remember?"

"I don't have to be," I say.

"Yes, you have to be," August, my sweet innocent angel, says in my right ear.

Nolan pulls back so he can look at me. "I'm fine," he says, but there's still a sadness to his eyes that makes me question if he really is. "I don't think they're going to keep me in the prison long. We're still waiting on the court, but they might move me to a different facility that will supposedly help me with my power. They said they might be able to help stop the voices. But enough about me. I hear shit about me every day. I want to know what you two are doing," he says as he pulls back from me and sits down.

After the fight, Marauder and his minions were arrested. The mayor and Hazel tried fleeing together but didn't make it out of the city before they were found. While Marauder was at the head of it, Nolan confessed everything that happened, even when the mayor and Hazel tried playing victims. Hazel did it for the attention, but I'm still not quite sure why the mayor did, since he's still playing the victim card. The rest of us believe he did it for more power. He'd tried running for higher positions in the government, but he never made it and was resigned to mayor. With Marauder's help and the mayor's money, the two could have assisted each other and risen up to a higher power.

Nolan was also taken to prison and kept in a unit where they keep supers, but we're still not sure what will happen to him. We are aware that Marauder was manipulating him, but the courts are still not sure how much. They're currently examining Marauder's power, which allowed him to absorb the powers of others, using an inanimate object like the snow globe, and then harness the powers for himself. When the snow globe shattered, it wasn't just my power that returned, but others came forward and said they'd sold their power to him for a chance to live a normal life. Since only a few admitted to it, there is no way of knowing how many powers he'd held inside the globe. Nolan claims that none were powerful enough for Marauder to use, which is why he targeted me.

Researchers are also trying to determine how others could use the snow globe, if anyone could use it, or if only people Marauder opened his power to were allowed. Of course, Marauder is being quiet and refuses to give anything away, so only time will tell.

I sit down at the table with August beside me. "So... Valerie grudgingly offered me a position at Superheroes United. I think she offered it then deeply regretted it when I told her I'd do it if my catchphrase was 'No evil shall penetrate August, only I can!'"

Nolan starts laughing as August sighs.

"She blew up," August says. "Asked if he could be removed. Ripped up the contract. Forced Lex to burn the pieces. But now she's calmed down and printed a new one for him."

"Ah, that's my brother for you," Nolan says. "So are you going to sign?"

"I don't know," I admit. "They're planning on implementing a better safety plan for the city. The police will be the first on scene and the heroes after, unless it's something the police can't handle. Even then, they still must report. They're also creating a larger team to help August, so the weight of it all isn't only on his shoulders. I will always be there to help him, but whether or not I'll become a signed hero... I'll make that decision after I think about it."

"Basically, you'd rather read and run around and threaten anyone who might threaten August?" Nolan asks.

"Exactly. You should *see* them, Nolan! People used to send creepy stuff to August or stalk him and stuff. Now they're all too terrified to! A woman asked August to marry her the other day and the moment I just *glanced* at her, she started crying. It was magical."

"He has strangely gained his own cult following," August says. "The reason women are leaving me alone is that they now like the 'bad boy' routine."

Nolan smiles. "My brother always has been a charmer when he could spare a moment to look up from a book. What about Marauder? I haven't heard much about him."

"He and the other supers who helped him, as well as the mayor, have been arrested. They're still going through court, but they're being held in Trident, the supers prison where they're unable to use their powers. I'm... I'm so glad they didn't send you there. August and I fought tooth and nail to keep them from taking you. It helped that you confessed so much and were able to assist in keeping the others locked up."

Nolan smiles. "Thank you. Thank you for not giving up on me. And I'm so sorry for everything I've done."

"You've apologized every time I've talked to you. You don't need to apologize anymore."

He gives me a sad smile. "Okay. You didn't bring Zacia?"

"They wouldn't let her come in, so she's out in the car with Lex and Valerie. We're headed to something stupid."

"A charity run," August says. "That's the stupid thing."

"Yeah, well, they should have made it a charity book reading and I'd have been all over that shit," I say, which makes them both laugh.

"Time's almost up," the guard says.

"I already miss you," Nolan says as I stand up and go over to him again to hug him. We hug for like three minutes straight.

"I'll get you out of here."

"Thank you, but it is what it is," he says as he squeezes me tighter.

I nod. "But if you ever need me to get your ass out of here, I gotchu. I'll just lift the whole building up and pluck you out."

"Let's try to see if we can do this the legal way and get out sooner," he says.

"Fine. Boo. Boring. But I guess. I love you even if you're an idiot. Almost as much of an idiot as Brandon."

"Oh no!" he says, like he's horrified.

"I know, right?"

He chuckles and kisses my forehead. "Visit me again now that visitations are allowed."

"I will. I'll bring you a shiv next time."

"He will not!" August exclaims, before nervously looking around to see if the guard heard.

I snicker and squeeze Nolan again. When we're forced to part ways, August takes my hand.

"It'll be alright."

"I know. I just want to do something."

"I know you do," he says as he kisses my cheek before pulling me toward the front door. "But for now, we have to worry about moving forward and helping him when we can."

"I'll distract myself by loving you and making Valerie's life a living hell."

He smiles as he bumps his hip into mine. "Now you're talking."

While Marauder obviously was an asshole, he did bring forth the concern that the city was basically relying only on August. It also showed that August couldn't and shouldn't be forced to do it all alone. Because of that, Valerie put her foot down and started forcing the city to open up to more people and create a team. August, who'd told me that he always wanted to be able to teach others, will be put in charge of training some of the newcomers part time. I told Valerie I could train them up real good and she told me I wasn't allowed around anyone but my cat.

August helps me from the building, and we walk out to the SUV where Valerie and Lex wait.

When we get into the back seat, Valerie eyes us, but it's Lex who speaks up. "Why are you grinning? You guys look so happy it makes my skin crawl," Lex jokes.

"Are you just jealous that no one could ever tolerate you?" I ask.

"Pretty much, if I'm being honest. I'm much better than August," he says. "I could keep you *satisfied*."

"I keep hiring normal gay men in the hopes one of you will fall in love with them instead, but no. You guys only like the... crazy ones," Valerie says, clearly referring to me.

"Thanks, babe. I love you too. Lex, did I tell you about the time August and I TP'd Valerie's house?"

He looks delighted. "No, but do tell. Actually, why don't you show me? I'm free tonight, we can TP it again."

Valerie starts yelling at Lex as I turn to August who is seated next to me.

"Ah, like music to my ears."

He grins at me. "I love the enjoyment you get out of the little things," he says as he kisses my cheek and wraps an arm around me as Zacia jumps into my lap.

I sink into his touch and smile at him. "How did everything become so perfect?"

"You're love blind. Literally, nothing is perfect. It smells like tuna in here," Lex says.

"Quiet, Lex, I'm having a moment with August."

August snickers. "I'm not sure Lex will listen to you," he says.

They start play bickering and I just grin and add comments when needed and I love it. I love being part of this crazy group of people who act like they can't get along but secretly really care and love each other. But most of all, I love being with August, who I'm sure I could spend the rest of my life with.

I lean into him and kiss his cheek, and he turns to me and smiles down at me, the look filling me with so much love.

Nah, that's wrong.

I'm *positive* I could spend my life with him.

He holds something out to me, and I look down at the worn paper in confusion.

"What's this?" I ask as I take it from him and start unfolding the college-ruled paper.

"You asked to see it... so here it is," he says, even though I have no idea what he's talking about.

Once the paper is unfolded, I look at the very top.

To Landon
I'm really bad at this stuff. I don't know what to say. I know we haven't talked much but I really like you. Would you go on a date with me? Yes or no?

And I realize that this is the note he wrote me back in school. He'd told me about it back when I realized he remembered me and had told me he didn't know where it was. That means he kept it all these years.

I reach over to his bag and dig around until I find a pen and I do what I would have done then. Once it's folded back up, I hand it to him as he smiles at me.

"The thing is, with you, I have no idea what you picked," he says.

I grin at him. "Good, I like keeping you on your toes."

He unfolds it like it's made of glass and looks down at the circle around the word "yes."

"I will always circle yes when it comes to you," I say, and the smile that unfolds on his face makes me lean into him and love him even more.

AUTHOR'S NOTE

Want to know more about Nolan or Lex? I have a short story about them available just for joining Alice Winters' Wonderland or my newsletter! I frequently put up teasers, short stories, and giveaways!

facebook.com/groups/AliceWinters
alicewintersauthor.com

If you'd like another action/comedy, check out The Hitman's Guide.

Thank you so much for taking the time to read my book! I really hope you enjoyed! And last but not least, if you enjoyed, please consider leaving a review! Reviews help others find books and my books find new readers!

ACKNOWLEDGMENTS

I couldn't have done this without my amazing team who help me every step of the way. A huge thank you to Courtney, who did the beta and proofread. She also helped with so many other parts of the book, I really couldn't do it without her. I also need to thank Savannah, who helped with the alpha and supported me through all of it! I want to thank my mom who's always there for me. I need to thank Lori who did an amazing job with the edit of the book. I want to thank my beta readers Sam, Jenn, Sara, and Mildred who all are fantastic at finding those plot holes I seem to read right over! I also want to thank the other Snow Globe series authors for letting me be a part of your fun holiday series!

I also want to thank my readers for picking this book up! I hope you enjoyed! I really couldn't have done this alone, and I'm so very thankful to have such a supportive and amazing team of people as well as amazing readers who say so many kind things. A huge thank you to all of you!

ABOUT THE AUTHOR

Alice Winters started writing stories as soon as she was old enough to turn her ideas into written words. She loves writing a variety of things from romance and comedy to action. She also enjoys reading, horseback riding, and spending time with her pets.

Connect with Alice
Website & Newsletter signup: alicewintersauthor.com
Facebook reader group: facebook.com/groups/AliceWinters

ALSO BY ALICE WINTERS

Vexing Villains

A Villain for Christmas

A Hero in Hiding

Mischief and Mayhem

Monstrous Intent

Medium Trouble

Ghost of Lies

Ghost of Truth

Ghost of Deceit

Phoenix's Quest

Nixing the End of the World

Winsford Shifters

Of Secrets and Wolves

Of Betrayal and Monsters

Of Redemption and Vengeance

The Hitman's Guide

The Hitman's Guide to Making Friends and Finding Love

The Hitman's Guide to Staying Alive Despite Past Mistakes

The Hitman's Guide to Tying the Knot Without Getting Shot

The Hitman's Guide to Righting Wrongs While Causing Mayhem

The Former Assassin's Guide

The Former Assassin's Guide to Snagging a Reluctant Boyfriend

VRC: Vampire Related Crimes

How to Vex a Vampire

How to Elude a Vampire

How to Lure a Hunter

How to Save a Human

How to Defy a Vampire

In Darkness

Hidden in Darkness

A Light in the Darkness

Deception in Darkness

Dancing in Darkness (short story)

In the Mind

Within the Mind

Lost in the Mind

Demon Magic

Happy Endings

Familiar Beginnings

Malicious Midpoint

Seeking Asylum

The Sinner and the Liar

The Traitor and the Fighter

Standalone Titles

Unraveling the Threads of Fate

The Last Text

Dear Cassius

Just My Luck

Never Have I Ever Ridden a Bike

Other Titles

Rushing In (Ace's Wild Book 3)

Printed in Great Britain
by Amazon